SETH MABRY

The Ritual Murders

OTIS MORPHEW

ISBN: 978-1-4907-5290-7 (sc)
ISBN: 978-1-4907-5289-1 (e)

Trafford rev.   12/18/2014

 www.trafford.com

North America & international
toll-free: 1 888 232 4444 (USA & Canada)
fax: 812 355 4082

INTRODUCTION

Devil worship, deemed Witchcraft in the days of Inquisition during the fifteenth Century, resulted in the famed witch-hunts of that age where hundreds of women were persecuted and burned at stakes as witches. This continued for many years, but did not put an end to what was later named, or called the rites of Satanism. These rituals were performed in secret, from hidden places, and animals were sometimes sacrificed on an altar in reverence to Satan.

Most generally confined to European soil, it is not known for certain when it was introduced to the Americas,…and though it did eventually raise its evil head, it was not a wide-spread religious practice, or Cult, as it was called. Closely associated with Voodoo, which was brought to this country by arriving slaves in the latter eighteenth, and early nineteenth century,… and used what was called Black Magic, hexes, spells or potions that would enhance a person's life, or death, Voodoo became akin to that of Witchcraft, which was also believed to use magic to perform its rituals.

But of course, it was not! Although Voodoo was believed to cause death to those who spoke out against the Cult, it would also bring death to anyone with a voodoo spell attached to him. It did not use a sacrificial altar in its rites, as did the Cult of Satanism. But like all Cults associated with evil, they evolve, and though very rarely heard of in the eighteen hundreds, one such Cult was formed,…and this one defined the reason why some were afraid of the dark! This one used human blood and sacrifices in their efforts to summon Lucifer. The Cult of Satan was evolving, and if allowed to continue unharnessed?

Such was the Cult now showing its evil in the north Texas town of Tyler, and it was taking its victims in the dead of night, and returning their headless bodies by day. No one saw them, nor heard them, nor was able to stop them and to many in Tyler they were thought to be supernatural.

viiiSeth Mabry*

But they had to be stopped, and the job was given to a United States Marshal, And an ex-gunfighter, who would find the job bewildering, and seemingly impossible without a clue of some kind that would tell them where to look!

CHAPTER ONE

Tyler, Texas is the County Seat of Smith County, and is centrally located on nine square miles of fairly high ground. The town site was plotted in 1846 and laid out with five streets running North to South, and four running east to West. Like every other frontier settlement of it's projected size, a public square was laid out designating its center, and with the business district surrounding it. Business lots were staked out and sold and the false-fronted stores and shops erected. A town had been born, and was quickly coming alive.

Smith County was an expanse of rolling, fertile prairie occupied by the Wichita Indians, and remote settlers that were trying to eke out their living and raise families without being molested or killed by warring savages. In 1839, after the forced removal of the Indian from East Texas, the area was officially opened for settlement. The Wichita had already been operating salt mines in the area, but after their removal, a few entrepreneurs moved in to take them over for profit and it was not long, during the last years of the Republic of Texas that settlers began moving in by the droves to claim the fertile farmlands.

This entire portion of East Texas was part of Nacogdoches County, but this was before Smith County was formed, by the new Texas State Legislature of 1846, and was named for General James Smith, a hero of the fight for Texas' independence. The county's inside boundary covered over 939 square miles of rich, prime farmland and grew quickly in population and wealth. As Tyler grew, more and more stores and shops were erected around the square's empty expanse, and these entrepreneurs were largely immigrants having migrated from Alabama.

Tyler was still very much under construction, as was the Courthouse on the square's North side when in August of '46, they held the town's first election to select a County Judge, a Clerk, District Clerk, Sheriff and

Tax Assessor-collector, as well as a Treasurer and a three-member County Commission. By 1850 a city Government was incorporated and a Mayor, and four Aldermen were selected because by then seven private schools were established in the County, and by the following year the first newspaper was published by the Tyler Telegraph, having been established by David Clopton, the business having been erected on a side street very close to the downtown district.

In1852, a Methodist Church was built on Bois d 'arc Street, along with many dozen log and lumber-sided homes, and not only on Bois d 'arc, but along every other newly formed street crisscrossing those coming from the square. New streets were constantly being cut and graded to accommodate the city's rapid growth. With all this new construction, and the growing community of new families, there arose the problem of supplies for these families, and for the stores and trade goods for the many shops.

The farming community supplied much of the foodstuffs, and those raising cattle supplied beef, but in order to grow with posterity, the farmers must ship their goods to other communities for sale. Salt from the mines, and commodities such as cotton, wheat and other goods were moved by either ox-drawn wagons to and from the cities of Jefferson and Shreveport, or by flatboat on the fast moving Sabine River.

By 1855, almost every vacant lot around the square had its false-fronted store, and all were open for business and doing well. But with all wealthy communities, sooner or later there comes the bad element, men and women of low reprieve,…and as soon as a saloon and gambling house opened, even more of this bad element showed up to invariably spawn gunfights, drunken brawls and prostitution in these establishments. These fights would sometimes carry over into the streets and for the next few years, the Sheriff's job became almost unmanageable because by 1860 there were more than a thousand residents and storeowners in Tyler. There being also a few new flour and grist mills, cabinet shops and wagon factories, some to produce spinning wheels, guns, hats, furniture and much more.

This young, busting at the seams community had grown extraordinarily fast and when the war started in '61, over a hundred young and middle aged men rushed to join the conflict, leaving many of the shops and farms unprotected and easy pickings for the county's bad element. By '62, Tyler became the site of the largest Confederate Ordinance Plant in Texas and a year later, Camp Ford was erected just four miles northeast of town. This Confederate Prison Compound held as many as 6000 prisoners at one time and as the war raged on, soon required 1500 guards to contain them all,… and with a county-wide population that now exceeded 12,000, nearly five thousand of which were slaves, citizen security was eminent.

The square's business was now complete, however, and all the stores open for business. Even the large, open square was most always filled with farm wagons and pedestrians, even the boardwalks and stores were a bustle of constant activity. Even with the war's devastation in the North, life was still good in Tyler, Texas. The war had not hampered the city's growth in the least,...and for the next four years continued to flourish, as did the most of Texas.

Texas was spared the complete chaos and ruin that was taking place in major cities to the North and South. Thousands lay dead and wounded on battlefields, entire communities were burned to the ground, crops burned, lives devastated as sons and fathers died in a terrible struggle that most never knew what they were fighting for.

However, Tyler was not devoid of war casualties, it's own sons and husbands were dying, and even though the ravages of war had not yet touched the town its self, it's citizenry suffered their losses. But through it all they continued to work, hope and pray for war's end, and the safe return of loved ones.

CHAPTER TWO

May 1865, word reached Smith County that Lee had surrendered, the war was at last over. But the price of that war had left a destitute populace in it's wake, yet their doors were open to that destitution. Of course, the news brought many riots and looting, and after an explosion destroyed the Ordinance Works, Union Soldiers began arriving to quell the disturbances, thus the beginning of Reconstruction!

Survivors of the Confederate Army began their long journey home, long lines of maimed and dispirited men dotted the roads and country sides making the trip on makeshift crutches, or with the help of others. Soldiers of a lost cause, many of them with amputated legs or arms, each coming home to regain their former lives, or so they believed. All that was on their minds was to heal, to work their fields and raise their families. Not one of them knew, or believed that they were coming back to nothing. Most of them had no home to come home to, or a family, it was all gone, confiscated, either from unpaid taxes, or unpaid liens. Those that were not foreclosed on were taken over by the Carpetbaggers accompanying the Union Soldiers.

Occupational forces had arrived in Tyler to establish control and once there, set up a regional Reconstruction Headquarters. In so doing, duly elected authority was replaced by Northern Authority with their strict laws and new regulations,…and so came the Carpetbaggers with their legal rights of confiscation, and they were there to take what they wanted.

*   *   *

Colonel Spencer Quinlan was one of these Carpetbaggers. Having been a soldier and leader of men in the war, he was held in high regard by the Lincoln Administration, decorated several times for bravery, and his tactical successes in leading his regiment to victory several times over. One of Grant's most trusted in command, he had become very close to the General, close friends in fact and through it all had been successful in hiding his greed and ruthlessness from him. Quinlan knew, and held close the meaning of the term, "Spoils of War", had known for a long while what war's end could bring a man with vision. That inner greed had always lain dormant, just below the surface of his projected character.

Quinlan was not overly tall, only six feet in height, but was a slender, muscular individual with handsomely rugged features. His face was lean, his eyes dark and alert projecting his intelligence, made more prominent by his forehead which always seemed to be in a frown,...but because of his eyes, seemed only natural and added to his handsomeness. His nose was narrow, offset by a full, black mustache that completely covered the upper lip of a full-lipped mouth.

When the war finally ended, he resigned his post and used his influence with General Grant to gain authorization to participate in the South's Reconstruction process as an advisor,...and with his Lincoln Administration credentials, his vision for self-improvement would become reality.

Tyler had not been his destination of choice he was just assigned to that particular occupation force, but once there recognized the area's potential. While the army was busy enforcing Federal control and reconstructing the abandoned Camp Ford installation for it's own purpose, he was busy looking over abandoned farm and ranch acreage and assessing his future..

Being the legal Military advisor for the area, he convinced Captain Lamar to allow him the task of recruiting the town's law enforcement, sending for six men that had served under him during the war. Although the Mayor and other city officials remained in place, their duties were severely restricted having to present all requests for city improvements to Captain Lamar for approval.

Thousands of acres, prime farm and ranchland lay idle and overgrown in the county, and Spencer Quinlan suddenly came into possession of more than two sections, one of which was owned by a rancher and his wife, already distraught at having lost all three of their sons in the war,...and it had been a surprise to most in Tyler to learn the old couple had sold out and quietly left the county. A lot of them believed they had been forced to sell, and half of those believed they had been murdered and their property seized. However, Tyler, as well as many of the larger towns in Texas having been placed under Martial Law during Reconstruction meant that no one dared voice their opinions for fear of consequences.

The new Sheriff Maynard, and his five deputies were always visible to quell any disturbance, and the soldiers patrolled the streets daily on horseback, as well as on foot. The Quinlan appointed lawmen wasted no time in their domination of the town's citizenry, and they took their orders from only one man.

Once his deeds were all in order, Quinlan quickly put a crew to work on his property, of which bordered the town's western-most limits. The old house was torn down, and because it had been nestled in a grove of Pines and only a few dozen yards from the lower end of a large tree-lined lake, the new house was being erected on the same plot of ground. The home would reflect his inflated ego status. While the house was being built, he unofficially raised taxes on Tyler's merchants, appointing Maynard and crew as collectors, doing so without the knowledge of Captain Lamar,...whom he knew would not have agreed.

He hired a large group of out of work cowboys to beat the brush of the neglected countryside for any and all wild, unattended cattle and horses to stock his holdings, and there were literally a couple of thousand for the taking. Other wranglers were hired to build barns and corrals and to rebrand the stock with the rocking SQ. Colonel Spencer Quinlan was creating an empire for himself, and he was not, and would not stop short of murder to get it. But the remarkable part of it all was that no one knew that he was personally behind any of the wrongdoings. Maynard, his deputies, and Captain Lamar were the hated culprits. Little did they know that Tyler, and Smith County had fallen under Quinlan's law.

By the time U.S. Grant was sworn in as President, Quinlan had already become quite wealthy. He had built and opened three more saloons, one of which was a gambling casino,...and all were under an assumed name. With the two existing saloons, his were more elaborate and therefore more prosperous, mostly due to the gambling and the young, half-dressed prostitutes serving the drinks, girls he had recruited from places like New Orleans and Atlanta,...and no one wondered where or how he had found such young and pretty women. They didn't care! Money was being made again,

Farms were being worked again, abundant crops being sown and raised, Cotton was being shipped to markets in the East and North, fruit orchards were replanted of which, the best suited for the area was peaches. Corn crops, potatoes, beans, vegetables of all kinds were harvested and sold out of open wagon beds in the public square, the stores and eateries,...and a good portion of this wealth found its way into Spencer Quinlan's pocket.

By the time the country had worked its way into the great recession of '73, Quinlan had become quite wealthy, uncaring and morally corrupt, and in ways that he had not foreseen. He had become a brutal and lonely man living alone in his six thousand square-foot, two-storied, Plantation-styled Ranch house, with only his several servants and lackeys to talk to. He was awakened to that fact many times, realized he was not a happy man and knew why? It was during these periods of mood that he would almost hate himself for what he was, but like always, the depressing moods would pass. After all, he controlled an empire, his empire, and he knew of no one else that could say that.

He now owned close to four sections of ranch and farmland, and as the recession slowly bankrupted the country, he owned more than ten thousand head of cattle and employed close to one hundred ranch hands, a remarkable feat for a man on the young side of forty years. He controlled the actions of more than a hundred and fifty men and women in the city and county, and only a handful of his trusted enforcers knew his identity for what he was.

To most all who knew him, he was a citizen like everyone else,…a wealthy Carpetbagger was the whispered comments. Though he was not trusted by the majority, he was accepted as part of the Federal establishment,…an entity they were forced to live with. When in town, he was never without the company of Alex Maynard, whom everyone thought they knew to be a gunman, a man who on numerous occasions had used his gun to keep the peace of which to most, was an unnecessary use of force.

Alex Maynard had been a Lieutenant under Quinlan in the war and was a man who had proven himself to be relentlessly brutal and aggressive in battle, a man that Quinlan could depend on to carry out an order. It was this kinship that brought them all to Tyler at his request. With his, and the deputies help, Quinlan had accomplished the most elaborate scam and cover-up in the history of Tyler, Texas, and neither the army, or President Grant suspected a thing. Quinlan had the full support of Federal Authority.

As the recession took its toll, both of Tyler's banking establishments, having invested heavily in the now defunct cross-country railroad found them selves on the verge of bankruptcy. Unable to recoup their losses, both began calling in notes on liens to try and keep afloat, thus putting enormous strain on the general populace when they could not repay their loans. Shops could not sell their goods, nor afford to offer credit and with mills and factories in the East shutting down, could not restock depleted merchandise. Farmers could not sell their crops with eastern markets closing their doors, and it was the same with cattle.

Jobs were being lost all over the country, with none to be had. People were losing their homes, businesses, land, their way of life and in desperation began a migration akin to the gold rush days of forty-nine, spreading to other parts of the country in search of work, only to find none there either. Desperation led to other things, such as robbery, holdups, muggings and even murder to provide for their families.

The dollar had suddenly lost its face value to that of almost half due to gold supplies being depleted to repay foreign loans that were now being recalled. The whole of Europe was now experiencing the same economic recession as that of America, as it had invested heavily in the civil war with loans to the Government.

It had become a common scene in Tyler to see wagons and malnourished teams of horses or mules tethered in the square. Gaunt looking families were living in the beds of wagons, their dirty-faced children roaming the boardwalks with hungry eyes. Alex Maynard and deputies were kept busy as some fathers were being arrested for loitering or making a pest of them selves begging for food or work. The jail was full, while other families were simply escorted out of town by soldiers and told to keep moving. It was a tragic sight, but inevitable as the country went broke. America was in full-blown depression, its supply of gold all but gone, the new Union currency worth almost nothing, and with silver no longer backing the dollar, silver certificates were fast becoming invalid.

The Grant Administration insisted that the recession would be short-lived, that American currency would regain its value in time and because of this, those with money began to hoard it. Spencer Quinlan was one of these, having foreseen what was happening, he withdrew any and all money he had in the banking establishments and placed it in a safe at the ranch. He was one of the very few that could afford to wait out a recession.

In spite of this, Tyler somehow continued to grow in population and prosperity, mostly due to the Military post. Soldiers had to eat, and the army was still able to pay its bills while other establishments were seeing ruin in their immediate futures, and the hardest hit were the banks.

*   *   *

Lucy Raeline Burks, Hunt, was the widow of Monroe Hunt, and sole owner of Hunt's Savings and Loan. Her husband had returned from the war missing an arm, it having been amputated due to gangrene. He had never quite regained his health, or his spirit, and had fought depressing moods and thoughts of suicide for a decade or more before coming down with pneumonia.

He would surely have died much sooner if not for Lucy, whom he loved dearly and because he loved her, wanted the very best for her future. This is why when there came news that the Great Northern Pacific Railroad was in the planning stage and needed investors, he knew that profits would be tremendously great, and did not hesitate to invest heavily in that future.

However, when the Recession struck the country, and the railroad went bust, he was devastated,...his health went down hill from there.

Lucy Hunt was a strikingly beautiful woman, slender of build and quite a head turner in her business attire. She was only five-foot, six inches tall, but seemed taller in her tailored shoes with two inch, elevated heels. They had no children, due to whatever reason and after Monroe's death had dedicated herself to keeping the Savings and Loan open for business,...and between that and her Church activities, had no social life at all. But the business remained open and with her at the helm, provided small loans to those in dire need, even though she knew they may never afford to repay her, but her civic duty required that she help her people survive. This almost drab existence carried on until the election of Rutherford Hayes as President before the recession finally ended in '78 and now, only a year later, the Hunt Savings and Loan was once again a thriving, money making business, and the devastating ruin of a Depression, not forgotten, but pushed far into the background.

*   *   *

Sighing, Lucy Hunt closed the ledger and put it away in her desk drawer, and with a look at the wall clock, thought about the Council Meeting scheduled to begin soon at the Windsor Hotel, of which she wanted to attend. After all, it was always good for her business to know what was going on in Tyler, and after a lingering look around the old, but familiar office, she stood and pushed her cushioned arm chair back under the desk. Sighing once again, she donned her light wrap, leaned to blow out the lamp and left the office to cross the room and go out through the glass encased door. Locking it, she turned for a look up at the clear, quite cool September sky, adjusted the purse strap on her shoulder and started down the boardwalk.

*   *   *

Alex Maynard was a tall, six feet, one inch in height, narrow of hips and broad of shoulders. The Colt Peacemaker on his hip was not entirely for show either, as he had proven on occasion. His six deputies were of the same ilk, all fairly handy with a gun, and all of them loyal to Spencer Quinlan. On this day, they were all standing against the wall of Maynard's office as him and Quinlan talked,...and when Maynard finally nodded and looked at them.

"I want three of you to go help find them!." He said sternly "Jake, take Morg and Walt with ya….Th' Ramrod reported 'em gone from th' corral this mornin'. They're all prime beef, you heard what he said!"

"Just how long they been gone, Colonel?" Asked Jake Hardin as he came forward a step toward them.

Quinlan turned in his chair to look up at him. "Several hours now, Jake, no doubt they're still on my range somewhere, we just can't track 'em."

"If they are, we'll try and find 'em, Colonel." He shrugged then. "Them or th' hides."

"You thinkin' they'll be butchered already, before they're even off my land?"

"Plenty a hungry families in town, Colonel, ten times that in th' county,…and they know you'll be lookin'!"

"Got that right!" He said angrily. "Got twenty men lookin'!…There's cattle all over my range, most of ten thousand head, why not take some a those, be a week before we missed 'em?…That corral weren't more than a hundred feet from my back stoop, and not a man on my payroll seen or heard anything."

"We'll do our best, Colonel." Nodded Jake and started for the door. "Let's go, boys."

Maynard watched them leave then nodded at the other three. "You boys check out th' wagons on th' square for meat or hides, then get your horses and patrol th' streets before supper." He watched them leave before turning to open the iron safe, taking out a tin box of money and placing it on the desk.

"Any problems, Alex?" He asked, reaching to open the heavy box.

"Usual complaints, Colonel. Sayin' Reconstruction is over, and taxes ought a be, too!…All in all, nothin' major. I turned th' regular tax money in at th' tax office….been thinkin', too, Colonel," He reached for tobacco and papers.

"About what?"

"Reconstruction is over, so is Military rule….What if somebody should go to th' Captain about these taxes we're collecting?"

"I wouldn't worry about it, Alex, nobody likes the army anyway, want nothing to do with it!…Although, it has crossed my mind a time or two. Too many start to complain, let me know,…ain't nothin' that's done, can't be undone!" He took the money from the box and counted out the bills, and then the coins, putting most of it in his inside jacket pocked before nodding at Maynard to keep the rest.

"Thank ya, Colonel." He said, putting the rest in his own pocket. "How many cows would you say you lost to now,…you ain't said nothin' before?"

"Any big spread's bound to lose cattle from time to time." He sighed then. "Coyotes, wolves, rustlers, it's got a happen, can't watch 'em all th' time!...But by god, never right under my nose like that!...Pick a th' crop, they was, all purebred heifers. Bought 'em as calves over in Jefferson last year."

"I remember that." Nodded Maynard. "But you know we won't find 'em, don't ya?"

"Hell yeah, but it gripes my ass, some cocksucker carving up my expensive steaks like that!

"They'll bury th' hides, too."

Quinlan got to his feet as Maynard spoke. "Can't cry over spilt milk, I guess....So, guess I'll take a ride out to th' Casino, Alex, time to collect anyway."

"While you do, I'll collect from th' cathouse." Maynard got up as well. "Meet ya back here, Colonel." He came from behind his desk to follow Quinlan out when he saw him collide with Lucy Hunt on the boardwalk, the impact tripping them both.

"Heyyy!" Yelled Quinlan, and amid a startled shriek from Lucy, both fell in an uncontrollable tangle onto the rough, hard planking, him winding up with her across his lap as she fought to pull her flowing dress down to cover bare knees and legs.

Maynard rushed to offer his help, but Quinlan was already lifting her from his lap and trying to regain his own feet to help her up, and once finally accomplished, he stepped back as she straightened her hair and repined her hat.

As their eyes met, he opened his mouth to speak, as did she, but neither uttered a word. He quickly bent to pick up his hat, his eyes still glued to hers, and at that moment, both knew that something had passed between them,...something neither one of them could explain, but both knew it was something profound. They were jerked from their trance then as Maynard touched both their arms.

"You all right, Colonel, you, Ms Hunt?"

"What?" He looked at Maynard as if he didn't know him for a second, then. "Oh, yes, Alex, I'm fine!" He quickly looked back at Lucy's wide-eyed beauty then. "Are you okay, Ms,..."

"Um,...Lucy!" She stammered, and then smiled with embarrassment. "Lucy Hunt,...and yes, I'm fine." She quickly looked down at herself and began brushing at her dress. "I'm terribly sorry, my mind must have been off somewhere else." She continued.

"No, Maam." He grinned. "It was all my fault, Luc,...ah, Ms Hunt... .I'm so used to just barreling out of places, that I never look!"

"Well, neither was I,…I guess I expected the boardwalks to be empty or something,…I,…I'm fine, thank you so much for your help." She cleared her throat and accepted the parasol Maynard had retrieved from the walkway. "Thank you, Sheriff."

"I'm Spencer Quinlan, Ms. Hunt." He muttered as she looked back at him. "Can I assist you in any way?"

"Oh, heavens no, I'm quite all right, I was just on my way to attend the Council meeting, I'll be fine, thank you, Mister Quinlan."

"Well, may I call on you tomorrow,…you know, to check on you, or something?"

"Well,…I don't know, it's really not necessary, Mister Quinlan, I'm fine."

"Call me Spencer, please,…and I really do want to, I could take you to dinner, it would make me feel a lot better about all this?"

She looked him in the eyes for several more seconds before nodding, and with a smile. "All right,…my house is on Maple, number thirty six."

"Six o'clock okay?"

"Six o'clock is just fine." She smiled warmly and quickly walked away, and his eyes were following every movement of her swaying body.

"Colonel?" Said Maynard as he also watched her. "You sure you're okay?"

"That is the most beautiful woman, I have ever seen, Alex." He said, almost breathlessly. "Who is she, anyway?"

"Lucy Hunt. She told you her name, Colonel."

"I know that, Alex, but who is she,…I've never seen her before?"

"She owns Hunt Savings and Loan. Her old man died of pneumonia a couple a years back. She don't get out that much.…But what she is, is the most vocal complainer about our tax system in town, a real pain in th' ass!… you really gonna call on her?"

"Oh, yeah. I'm gonna be seein' a lot a that woman, Alex!…I don't ever remember feelin' this way about any woman before." He looked at Maynard then and squeezed his arm. "Somethin' happened to me, Alex, and I can't explain it!…But it felt damn good.…Come on, let's do our collectin'." He was still grinning as they walked to the hitch rail and mounted, and as he reined the animal onto the street, he nodded at Maynard. "Alex," He said, stopping his horse to look toward the Windsor. "I just might have to marry that woman!"

"Ya' might ought a think about that one, Colonel.…I agree with ya', she is th' prettiest woman in Tyler,…but I ain't never seen a more head-strong woman than she is. She is trouble."

"She's my kind a woman, Alex."

"I can see that, Colonel."

Emmit Garland Castle was the youngest ever appointed Federal Judge, due to his abilities and reputation as a masterful spokesperson, and not discounting being a close, personal friend to then, General U.S. Grant. He had been only eighteen years old when he was appointed advisor in both the Senate, and the House of Representatives in Washington, this was in 1846. He was given a Federal Judgeship in the nation's capitol in '48, and still served in his advisor capacity for several years before the war started, but once it did, Grant insisted that he be put in his command as a tactical advisor, serving in that position until the war ended in '65.

It was after the war, and the start of Reconstruction that he was sent to Dallas, Texas to oversee the process and serve as Federal Judge, and is where he has been ever since,...and after a devastating war, Reconstruction, crime Syndicates and a marriage in his portfolio,...by 1880, he was still a very content Federal Judge, father, husband and citizen of one of the largest and most prosperous cities in Texas.

He was still in his original office in the Federal Court Building, and well accustomed to his simple surroundings.

Today, however, he was seated behind his paper-strewn, oaken desk rereading the rather lengthy letter from his wife's younger sister when the knock sounded at the glass-paneled door, causing him to look up.

"It's open!" He said, and got to his feet as the door was pushed inward. "Do come in, Marshal." He smiled warmly and crossed the room with extended hand.

"Good job bringing in the Cortez brothers!...How are you, Roderick?"

"I'm fine, Judge, thanks.." He removed his hat and hung it on the coat rack by the door. "How's th' wife and little Grant?"

"Never better, Roderick." He cleared his throat and urged Dempsey toward the chair beside his desk. "Do sit down, Roderick, and I thank you for coming so quickly."

"Not a problem, Judge," He grinned. "I'm only three doors down th' hall." He frowned then. "Is there a problem, Judge, Jailer said it was important?"

Also frowning, Emmit sighed and sat down in his chair. "Unfortunately, yes, it is important....To you and I, because we are the law,...and to Gwendolyn, because it involves her sister, Lucy!...Let me give you a little background?...Back in fifty-nine, Lucy met and married a banker from Tyler, Gwendolyn said they were very much in love....Anyway, Monroe Hunt owned Hunt Savings and Loan, and was very successful!...This was back when Tyler was still in the process of becoming a town. He went to war, and came home minus an arm....He never regained his health and in fact, passed away from a bout with pneumonia shortly after the Recession hit."

"None of this has any bearing on the problem at hand, Roderick, it's only something I think you should know."

"I understand, Judge."

"Okay,...almost two years ago, she remarried a rancher by the name of Spencer Quinlan." He cleared his throat again. "As far as I know, they are very happy, too,...or was!" He picked up the letter again. "We got this letter from her three weeks ago." He gave it to the Marshal then waited until he read it.

"What do you think?"

"Lord, Judge." He sighed, giving it back to him. "It's got a be some kind a maniac loose up there is all I can say!...Five murders in a month's time, all decapitated?...Got a be one sick son of a Bitch!"

"And God-awful dangerous, Roderick. The man is a Sadist!"

"They find th' heads, Judge?"

"No, they have not!" He sighed again then. "Three of the victims were women, but without their heads, Sheriff Maynard could not identify them."

"And the other two?"

"Closer to home, Roderick....One was a deputy of Maynard's....The other was a friend of ours, I'm afraid."

"Jonesie?"

"Benny Jones!" He nodded.

"He was one of th' best, Judge." He sighed heavily. "Fun to be around, too,...what happened?"

"Not a clue....He must have gotten too close to someone, and it cost him his life."

"What about, Lucy, and this Spencer Quinlan, are they okay?"

"After I got Maynard's wire about Benny, I wired him back,...and according to him, they are." He picked up another paper then. "I got this wire yesterday....There's now been two more victims!...One was a Quinlan wrangler, the other a soldier."

"Decapitated?" And when the Judge nodded. "Any clues at all?"

"None at all, Roderick,...but in that same wire from Maynard, he said Benny had been real frustrated the day before they found him, said he complained that there was nothing to go on, no blood trail, no footprints.... But he did comment on the decapitation wounds,...told Maynard, they looked almost surgical!...Anyway, Benny told him there was something he wanted to check on, took a deputy with him. They found the bodies in the square the following morning."

Dempsey had been looking blankly at the wall as the Judge talked, and shook his head when he was done. "Whoever th' killer, or killers are, they're not amateurs, Judge!...They're nobody to mess with, neither." He looked at Castle then.

"What do you want me to do, Judge?"

"This has to be stopped, Roderick, innocent people are being murdered in the middle of the night up there,...and there's no sane reason for it!"

"I agree,...when do I leave?"

The Judge looked at him for a moment. "Roderick, you've worked for me for two years now, you've been a town Marshal for several before that. You are going to be the best there is one day,...but you just do not have the experience needed for this one, at least not alone!...I do not want to lose you, too! Maynard had six deputies and Benny made eight able-bodied men looking for this killer, and he still managed to commit gruesome murders, and plant the headless bodies right under their noses! Those bodies were found by women and children, I might add!" He sobered a bit then.

"Roderick,...it is going to take someone with keen investigative skills to find this man and when he does, to take him down,...and even he may not be able to do it alone. Benny had all of this, and look at him now!"

"Then why am I here, Judge?"

"Don't be upset, Roderick....I am not in the least putting you down, my good friend. You happen to be one of the finest lawmen I know. But you have yet to develop that certain,...I guess you would call it, Killer instinct!... But you will!...You are going to Tyler, Roderick, you're just not going alone."

"Then who's goin' with me,...there's not another Marshal in your jurisdiction, Judge?...And I ain't up to puttin' trust in a man I don't know, experienced or not!"

"And neither am I, Roderick, and frankly, I don't know if we can find anyone,...that will be willing to go, anyway."

"You got somebody in mind, don't ya, Judge?"

"Yes, I do,...but unless you can convince him, I doubt he'll go."

"Who, Judge,...there ain't a man in Dallas who fits tha-..." He looked hard at Castle as he suddenly perceived the answer for himself.

"Seth Mabry?"

"He's a bulldog, Roderick." Nodded Castle. "He's got that sixth sense when it comes to finding his man, as you well know....And we both know he has the ability to stop him!...You think he'll go?...If he won't, the only other source I have is Alex Hayward, and you have never worked with the Rangers."

"And I don't think I want to, Judge." He grinned then shook his head. "Seth Mabry!...You're right, Judge, I don't know a better man to side me in this, but will he go?...I don't know, Judge, I ain't seen 'im in a year!"

"Then it's time you did, my boy. This killer has to be stopped. If he is not, he will destroy the entire intra-structure of Tyler, Texas! Maynard said folks were moving out of the city already....They are afraid to go to sleep at night, the two women were taken from their beds!"

"I can see folks leavin' over somethin' like this." Nodded Dempsey. "Can't blame 'em, neither."

"No, you can't!...Do you know where Seth's ranch is, Roderick?"

"He gave me directions once, I think I can find it."

"Good,...Now if he won't go, I'll wire Hayward for a couple of Rangers to go with you, so come on back here!...If he agrees to go, you can leave from there, or ride back her and take the train. Either way, I'd like you there as quick as possible!...Time is of the essence, Roderick,...and you'll need these." He folded the letter from Lucy Quinlan, and picked up another one.

"This second letter is for Mister Mabry from me, Roderick. It explains the situation in Tyler as far as I know it. It also gives him a free hand to use whatever means he deems fit to stop this maniac,...sort of a license to kill, if he has to!...But he will be working for you, and with you. Use your own judgment in this investigation, Roderick,...but I think you'd be wise to trust Mister Mabry!"

CHAPTER THREE

Seth Mabry was not always a Rancher and family man, he was once called a killer, holdup man and gunfighter,…and wanted in several states for these crimes. He was in fact, a killer, he was a gunfighter, and gunfighters kill men. In those days, he was known only as Dancer, and had eluded capture for years,…and had stolen thousands of dollars. A feared gunfighter who enjoyed what he did, until one day in Arkansas!

That day, he had robbed a coach at gunpoint, and as he was relieving the passengers of their valuables, lost his heart to a lady passenger and from that day onward, he was no longer Dancer, the gunfighter, instead, they were married a short time later and he took his mother's maiden name of Mabry, and never used his gun to do wrong again.

That was twenty years ago now, and he had been a rancher ever since. He had his wife, Laura, and until two years ago, two sons, his oldest having been murdered by a Syndicate Crime Boss in Dallas for being too lucky at cards. His youngest son had been charged with the murder at the time. But the criminal element had no idea that they would awaken a vengeful Dancer, because he alone became the force that brought them all to justice, ending their stranglehold on the large city. Once McCleary and O'brien were convicted and executed, he and his family returned home, minus their beloved Tommy.

That was two years ago, and though Tommy is never out of their minds, they are going on with their daily lives. But today, although it was not any different than the day before when they worked cattle until well after dark. Seth decided to quit early, and it was only in the mid-afternoon when he told Greg and Trey they should quit for the day.

"What's wrong, Daddy?" Queried Gregory Mabry as Seth reined his horse back toward home. "You feel bad, or somethin'?"

"What?" He turned in the saddle to look back at him.

"You sick, or somethin',…it's only a little past noon?"

"No, son,…I ain't sick. Just don't feel like workin' any more today,…but don't let that stop you two!"

"Takin' off early is okay with us, daddy. I was just worried about you is all."

He nodded and continued on toward home, with them close behind him, and once they arrived at the barn dismounted and passed his horse's reins to Trey while he bent and slapped the day's dust from his clothing. Once done, he straightened and caught Greg staring at him and studied his face for a minute.

"I ain't sick, son,…why should there be anything wrong, we did a days work already?...We moved th' herd, put out some salt." He thoughtfully stopped then to roll and light his smoke before looking skyward at the low-hanging clouds. "I think it's enough for today, that's all."

"Yes, sir,…but it ain't like you, wasting daylight this way!"

Seth sighed as he exhaled smoke skyward then gazed at the distant tree-shrouded grave by the creek. "I don't know that anything's wrong, son." He looked back at him then and grinned. "Your mother would call it anxiety, I think, maybe expectation."

"Or premonition?"

"Yeah, somethin' like that….Maybe we got company comin', or something. Anyway, I feel like knockin' off early." He drew smoke into his lungs and exhaled as he looked down toward the rambling ranch house, with it's long, covered front porch, and then past it at the mile long stretch of road before it disappeared into the trees. "Right now,…I just want a relax in that rockin' chair yonder, prop my feet on that porch railin' for a while." He grinned at Greg and abruptly walked away toward the house, leaving a confused Greg Mabry watching him go.

"Don't worry none, Greg." Said Trey Mathers as he exited the barn. "That's exactly how Ms. Mabry said he acted when you and Tommy didn't come home that time,…it was like he knowed somethin' was wrong!"

"How do you know all that, you were in town, too?"

"She told me all about your daddy after he went after you, said he always knowed when somethin' was about to happen!"

"Well, I ain't noticed it!...But whatever it is, he's some uneasy about it!"

"Could be he's just tired, too, ya think a that?" Returned Trey. "He ain't so young anymore."

"I know, and that's what worries me sometimes. He's gotten older since Tommy died, really took a lot out of 'im, Mama, too!...She spends too much time at his grave, and that ain't good for her."

"That's for sure," Sighed Trey. "Sure wish I could help 'em."

"That makes two of us....Come on, let's go sit with 'im, might learn somethin'." They walked off down the slightly uneven ground toward the house and were soon climbing up to the porch where Trey settled himself on the top step as Greg sat down in Laura's rocking chair, and that was when she pushed open the door to lean against the jam and peer at them.

"Hi, Mama." He grinned, looking up at her.

"Hello, all,...quitting early today, what's the occasion?"

"No occasion, my dear." Returned Seth also looking up. "Got done early today, is all,...no place like home, ya know!"

"Yes, but it isn't like you,...you all right?"

He looked at Greg and grinned. "A mite edgy is all, I'm fine, sweetheart....Could use some coffee though."

"How did I know that?" She smiled. "I'll put some on." She frowned worriedly for a moment as she studied his face. "I'll start supper, too, you'll feel better once you eat." She closed the door and went back through the house.

When she was gone he looked at Greg and grinned. "You take after your mother, you know that?...I'm fine, I'm not sick, and I don't hurt anywhere." He grunted then as he shifted his weight in the chair. "If you don't count arthritis!...Now, like I said, just because I take off early, sure don't mean you two have to do th' same! You want a finish out th' day, that's fine."

"No, sir!" Grinned Greg. "I'm all for takin' off early!"

"I'm good with it, too, Boss." Returned Trey.

"We just worry about you, Daddy."

Seth sighed then. "I know, son,...we've been through a lot this past couple years,...and you're right, too!...Today just don't feel right for some reason,...I don't know, it's just, different!"

"Maybe it's the weather, a storm brewin', maybe?"

"It's summertime, son, August, we need th' rain. Way th' sky looks, we'll get some tonight, too!...No, it's just a feelin' I get sometimes, usually when something's gonna happen."

"A premonition."

"Yeah,...saved my skin a few times in th' old days." He took tobacco and papers from his shirt and was just rolling his smoke when he felt the urge to look up the road again and got to his feet.

"What is it, Daddy?" Queried Greg urgently, also getting to his feet to stare at the road, and then they saw the distant horse and rider just leaving the trees.

"You was right, Daddy,...who do ya think it is?" He asked, absently reaching down to remove the tie-down loop from his pistol.

"Guess we'll find out,...don't be too hasty with that pistol."

"Want I should get th' shotgun and watch from cover, Boss,...could be one a them gunslingers lookin' for ya?...One a them New York killers'r somethin'?"

"I don't think so, Trey,...looks like a cowboy."

"Gunslingers look like cowboys, too, Boss,...and he ain't one, ain't sittin' his horse like one, you don't mind me sayin'."

"You're right, and I don't mind, Trey....But we'll cross that bridge when he gets here."

They watched the rider's slow approach for another several long minutes before Seth smiled and poured fresh tobacco into the paper he still held in his hand.

"You are right, Trey." He said, licking the cigarette and putting it into his mouth. "He, for sure ain't no cowboy." He struck a match and lit the smoke. "Looks like th' law's come callin'. In fact, that will be United States Marshal Rod Dempsey, I recognize th' horse!"

"That th' Marshal you told us about, Boss?"

"Th' very same one, Trey."

"He knows who you really are, right,...think he's comin' to arrest ya?"

"Nothin' like that, Trey....He's one of just a handful a men, I'd call friend!...A damn good man, too,...he knew my mother!"

"I remember you sayin' that, Boss."

They continued to watch Dempsey's approach and was able to see the wide grin on the lawman's face from fifty yards away.

"Afternoon, Seth?" Nodded a still smiling Dempsey. He stopped his horse and dismounted amid groans from tired saddle leather to vigorously shake Seth's extended hand. "Damn good to see ya!"

"Good to see you as well, Rod. How's things in th' big city?"

"A little too quiet with you gone, Seth." He shrugged then. "But that's a good thing."

"Yes, sir, it is!...How's th' new Marshal, and Mister Hurd?"

"Still on th' job and doin' well, both of 'em!"

"That's good to hear." Nodded Seth with a grin. "So, what brings you out to paradise, Rod,...got business out this way?"

"Yes'ir, I do....Got somethin' to ask of ya',...a favor, ya might say." He looked around at the large house and barn then. "I can see why you call this place, paradise, Seth, I really like it!...Near-bout missed th' cut-off back yonder, though, ya might need to put up a sign along th' main road back there."

"And have people comin' in here all th' time, forget it, couldn't stand that!" He caught movement from a corner of his eye then and turned to place a hand on Trey's shoulder. "Rod, this is Trey Mathers. Trey, meet the U.S. Marshal, Rod Dempsey." And as they shook hands, he continued. "Trey's our wrangler, drover, field hand and all around go-to man. Been with me for ten years now!"

"I'm sure glad to meet ya, Marshal, heard a lot about ya!...Here let me put your horse up for ya."

"Thank's Trey." He took rifle and saddlebags from the horse and watched Trey lead it away.. "Seems like a good man."

"He is,...you said you had something to ask me, Rod."

"Heyyy, Marshal, Dempsey!" Called out Greg as him and Laura descended the porch steps to the yard and came toward them.

"You're lookin' well, Greg, good to see ya." He shook his hand and then Laura's. "Very nice to see you again, Ms. Mabry." He said, removing his hat. "Hope all is well with you?"

"Thank you, Marshal, we are all very well. What brings you out this way?"

"Got a little business with Seth here,...rather, Judge Castle sent me out to talk with 'im, so here I am!"

"Well, you can talk with him over supper, be ready soon!...You'll stay the night, too, sleep in Tommy's old room, he would like that." She turned and hurried back toward the house.

"That settles it!" Grinned Seth. "Come on to th' porch, Rod, rest your haunches."

"Don't mind that a bit!" He grinned as they walked then placed a hand on Greg's shoulder. "You stayin' out a trouble these days?"

"I've had enough a that for a lifetime."

"That you have, son."

             *   *   *

The meal was laced with laughter and ranch talk, and as it drew to a close, discussions turned to the events of two years ago and ultimately, the trial and executions of the two Crime Bosses and finally, Seth pushed his plate away to immediately roll and light his after-meal smoke.

"Have enough to eat, Rod?"

"Too much, I think!" He shook his head and smiled across at Laura. "Don't believe I've had a better steak, Ms. Mabry....Eating in a café every day sure don't replace home cooking."

"Well, you are quite welcome, thank you." She smiled then got up to pour more coffee all around.

"Marshal?' Queried Greg. "Have there been any more killers from New York in town?"

"None that I've heard about, I'm glad to say!...There was another high-dollar Lawyer, though. Thought he could lay claim to McCleary's holdings!"

"What happened?"

"Emmit Castle happened!...Man left town like a cur dog."

Seth listened to the conversation and laughter for a few minutes, but still couldn't understand why the uneasy feeling had not gone away, and he knew that it should have, unless the Marshal's visit was something more than that.

"What was it you wanted to see me about, Rod?" He asked during a pause in their conversation. "Must be important."

Dempsey sighed, and used the table linen to wipe his mouth before nodding. "You could say that, Seth,...to Emmit Castle it is, rather to Ms. Castle! To her, it's personal,...to me and Emmit, it concerns th' law as well."

"My,...that sounds rather mysterious, Marshal." Returned Laura.

"Yes, Maam." He said, taking the letters from his pocket. "Before I tell you anything else, Seth, I'd like you to read this." He gave him Gwendolyn's letter from her sister.

Frowning, Seth unfolded the pages and began reading, and when he was finished, reread it then sighed and frowned at Dempsey. "Is this on th' up and up, Rod?" He asked incredulously. "I've seen a few men butchered by Indians before, and that was enough to turn my stomach!...But I never heard tell of anything like this!...What kind a man would do somethin' like that?"

"A mad man, Seth,...and he's very cunning!"

"What on earth are you talking about?" Queried Laura.

Seth passed the letter to her, and as she read. "What's this got to do with me, Rod, or you?...Ain't there any law in Tyler?"

"Dear God!" Exclaimed Laura as she read. "This is horrible!"

"They've got a Sheriff and six deputies." Nodded Dempsey in response to Seth's question. "You read th' letter. Right after th' Judge received it, he assigned th' most experienced Marshal he's got to go up there!...He was killed, too, along with one of th' Sheriff's deputies assigned to help 'im....Only thing I can figure is, they found th' killer, or was closin' in on 'im!...Whatever th' case, he was better than th' both of 'em."

"Dear God in heaven!" Blurted Laura as she finished the letter, and as Greg took it from her, dabbed at her eyes with the table linen.

"I'm beginnin' not to like why you paid us a visit, Rod." Sighed Seth.

Dempsey unfolded the other letter then and gave that one to him. "This is from Emmit Castle, and I have not read it!" He watched Seth read it, and sipped at his coffee while he waited for his response.

"I ain't no law man, Rod." He said as he passed that one to Laura. "I got th' badge he gave, but that's all!...I don't know th' first thing about Marshallin'!"

"He knows all that, seth, and so do I....But you impressed us all when you brought down that Syndicate....He's right about somethin' else, too,... you are more than able to take this maniac out when we find 'im,...and we will find 'im!"

"You know how to do an investigation, Seth,...I have some experience at investigating crime scenes, but I ain't good enough yet to do this on my own! Benny Jones and me are th' only two Marshals under th' Judge's jurisdiction,...or was!...He don't want to call in th' Rangers on this, they got their hands full already,...so I'm it!"

"You recognize and act on your gut feelings, Seth," He continued. "I don't know how to do that yet!...When you start somethin', you don't let go,...and that's what we need here."

"Two years ago, it was personal, Rod. I was hurt, and I was mad, killin' mad!"

"Sure ya was." Argued Dempsey. "But you didn't kill anybody ya didn't have to! You showed restraint for th' law,...you did it th' right way. You're a rare breed of man, Seth, you proved that!...When Emmit called me in his office yesterday, there had already been two more murders. One was a Lieutenant from Camp Ford, th' other was a wrangler that worked for Emmit's wife's sister and her husband. It was her sister that sent that letter."

"The Army investigatin' this?"

"They have been since it started." He nodded. "But they're nowhere close to a suspect either. Th' Judge thinks they're not doin' all they could do, for whatever reason!"

"Well, I don't want him to go!" Blurted Laura when she realized that Dempsey was there for more than just advice. "He could lose his head, too!"

Seth smiled at her warmly then looked back at Dempsey. "Any clues at all, Rod?"

Dempsey shrugged. "Th' last wire Emmit got from Jonesie, uh, Marshal Jones, He mentioned that th' victim's heads appeared to have been removed too cleanly, almost surgically....anyway, it was something very sharp!" He sighed then. "Jonesie was th' most experienced Marshal this side a Waco, Texas, Seth. He could hold his own with any man,...at least we thought he could. There had to be more than one man to do 'im in, I know that!"

"Or one killer in th' dark." Said Seth. "But it does look like he was on to somethin',...maybe a Doctor, or Surgeon,...have all them been checked out?"

"Don't know, maybe that's what Jonesie was doin' when he died." He sighed heavily then and looked at Seth. "Look, my friend, you don't have to do this, it's my job, not yours!...Me and th' Judge just thought it wouldn't hurt to ask ya."

"That mean you're goin' anyway, if I don't?"

Dempsey shrugged. "It's my job, Judge ain't got nobody else. Besides, he said he'd call in a couple a Texas Rangers to help, if you didn't….But I sure would like to have you there to side me, Seth. You're th' best I ever saw!…You wouldn't need to do anything but watch my back, make sure I done it right,…I ain't th' best when it comes to followin' a trail."

"I think you ought a go, if you want to, Daddy." Said Greg, speaking for the first time, and bringing a gasp from Laura.

"Gregory!" She said harshly. "What are you thinking?"

"Sorry, Mama, but people are dying there, innocent people, and some very bad men are doing it!…You know what went on in Dallas, well, this is worse!…They have to stop it!"

She looked at Seth with tears in her eyes. "You're going, aren't you?"

"Do I have a choice, honey, considerin'?"

"No, of course not!…But I couldn't live without you, I've already lost a son to men like that, I couldn't stand to lose you, too!"

"You won't, sweetheart." He said with a smile. "That's a promise."

"Lord, God, I wish I could believe that!" She sniffed then and wiped her eyes with the linen.

"I sure am sorry, Seth, Ms. Mabry….Believe me, Ma'am, it was not my idea, please don't hold fault with me?"

"I know it's not your fault, Marshal." She sniffed and got to her feet. "I'll make up Tommy's room for you." She looked at Seth then. "When are you leaving?"

"First light, I guess." He said this looking at Dempsey, and when he nodded. "First light."

"I'll fix you some food to carry with you."

"I'm damn sure sorry about all this, Seth!" Said Dempsey as he watched her walk across the sitting room. "I just broke her heart for ya."

"She'll get over it, Rod,…Strongest woman I ever knew, besides Mama. I broke her heart real good, if you'll remember….Broke mine, too, th' day I found her grave!" He cleared his throat then. "Except for Laura, I'd be dead now, Rod. I owe her everything!…She knew I couldn't let you go off into somethin' like that letter described alone." He cocked his head toward the ceiling then.

"Hope you like ridin' in mud."

CHAPTER FOUR

Lucy Quinlan pulled the wrap tighter around her shoulders and shivered, though it was more from dread and fear than anything else, because it was quite hot in the shade of the long porch,...and in spite of the constant breeze blowing off the lake. She watched as Spencer talked with his wranglers at the corrals for a time before walking back toward the house and watched him, thinking worriedly that he looked so down and out.

She knew that these brutal murders were taking their toll on him and she was terrified, had been since the headless body of one of their cowboys had been found in the town square. It did not help that three more bodies had been found since she wrote that letter to Gwendolyn. If anyone could get to the bottom of all this, she had thought that Emmit Castle could, in fact, she had been so relieved when the United States Marshal appeared on the scene,...but when he had been found dead also, had almost lost hope.

She still believed that it would take a real lawman to solve the murders, because it was plain that Alex Maynard and his so-called deputies would never do it! Emmit would have to send someone else, and going by how Gwendolyn talked about him, she was sure he would send someone else. She also knew that it would have to be soon,...before any more innocent people fell victim to these mad men.

Sighing, she watched the slow, deliberate approach of her husband, with head bowed and shoulders slumped, he looked so helpless,...and her heart went out to him.

"Are you all right, Spencer?" She asked as he climbed to the porch and walked toward her. "You're going to make yourself sick worrying so much."

He smiled warmly and came on to kiss her on the mouth and sit down. "Lost some more cows last night." He sighed then reached for, and lit his thin cigar. "I'm beginning to think that whoever is doing those killings, is the same person, or persons stealing my cattle!...It almost has to be. Miles was out watching that herd we were driving to the stockyards the next morning, along with three more wranglers, course they weren't together!... But I'm thinking now that Miles must have caught them in the act of rustling that night, and they took him with 'em."

"You really think so?"

"He was found in town, sweetheart." He sighed again then. "Only way we could identify the poor man, was by his boots!...That has to be what happened, he hardly ever went to town, he didn't even drink, that I know of!"

"Lord, God, Spencer,...why is this happening?"

"I wish I knew." He sighed then gave her the paper. "Walt just brought this from town. Looks like your brother in law is sending two more Marshals, hope they don't wind up like the last one."

"God, I hope not, Spencer....But something has to be done!"

"I agree, honey." Breathing deeply, he clamped the cigar in his teeth and gazed off across his holdings. "Alex don't think it's anybody in town doin' it, most of 'em have been here for years....Neither do I, there's good people in Tyler, people that would come forward if they knew anything!...It has to be somebody not from around here, that's all I can figure. But who?...Alex has searched every house and the barns of every farm and ranch in the county!"

"And they are probably all as frightened as we are about it!"

"That's what Alex said." He blew smoke at the roof of the porch before looking at her. "Walt said he saw Bill and Sara Parsons leaving town this morning."

"Wonder where they were going?"

"They were leaving Tyler, honey, had a wagonload of their belongings,... Told Walt, George Simmons bought 'em out!...That makes five closures in the last three weeks. Won't be long, Tyler will be a ghost town if these murders ain't stopped!" He got up then to look down at her. "If I just knew where to look, I'd take every hand I got and take th' bastards down myself!... Just one solid clue is all I need!"

"If you don't calm down, you'll give yourself a heart attack, Darling." Soothed Lucy. "Besides,...that Marshal Jones had some sort of a clue, didn't he,...what happened with that?"

"I don't know, honey,...Alex was under that impression, but he never said what th' clue was, said he wanted to check somethin' out first, to be sure!...Whatever it was, it got him and Alex's deputy killed!" He looked toward the door then as the neatly dressed black man came out with a tray of lemonade balanced in his hand, and sat down again.

"Ah thought you and th' Missus Quinlan might like some refreshment, suh."

"Thank you, Ezra." Nodded Quinlan. "Set it down between us here."

"This is very thoughtful of you, Ezra, thank you so much."

"You is most welcome, Missus Quinlan, you, to, suh,...most welcome." He grinned widely and started back.

"Ezra?" Said Lucy, stopping him. "Could you have our carriage brought to the house, I'm going to town this morning?"

"Yes'um, I shoah can!"

"Have Walt do that, Ezra." Said Spencer. "Tell 'im I want six armed men, too, they'll be goin' in with us."

"Yes suh, right away!" He scampered down the steps toward the corrals.

"I do wish you would sell th' Savings and Loan, honey,...it's a bit much, you havin' to go to town twice a week to do the books, keeps you worn out all the time."

"You know I can't do that, Spencer." She sighed. "There are people depending on my bank, you know that!...And we've also had this discussion before."

"Yes, I know, honey, and I'm sorry....But from now on, you'll be escorted to and from town,...and today I'm goin' in with you, I want to talk with Alex, find out what's goin' on?"

"Your company is always required, my Darling." She smiled and sipped at the fresh lemonade before getting up. "I have to change, I won't be long." She kissed him and quickly went inside.

*   *   *

Alex Maynard reread the Coroner's report again then sighing heavily, dropped the paper on his desk and picked up his cup, looked at it for a moment and then in disgust, got up and went to the pot-bellied stove and was pouring his coffee when the door was suddenly opened,...causing him to slosh hot brew onto his hand and arm. Yelping, he replaced the pot on the stove and glared at the Deputy.

"Just what is your hurry, Mister Gibbs?"

"Jesus, Lieutenant, sorry about that,...but you'd better come take a look."

"Take a look,...where, at what?"

"We got us another body in th' square, Lieutenant,...and it's a hairy sight!"

Without another word, Maynard grabbed his hat and followed the deputy back down the boardwalk. "Where'd ya find it?" He asked as they passed the still darkened storefronts.

"Didn't!"…Westly Wheatfield and his family found it. They was crossin' th' square when th' team got a whiff a th' blood or somethin'. Anyway, when they shied away from it, th' kids seen it, and th' little girl screamed. I heard it and came runnin'!"

"Th' head gone?" He asked as they stepped off the boardwalk into the spacious square.

"Yes sir!…She was also naked, and slit up th' middle, Lieutenant,…never seen nothin' like it!"

"She,…it was a woman?"

"Yes sir, slit from puss to tits, too!…It ain't pretty."

The Wheatfield's wagon had been moved away from the gruesome corpse and both of them were still trying to console the hysterical girl in the wagon's sagging bed as they approached.

"Dear God," Grated Maynard when he saw the sprawled, blood stained body. "God all mighty!" He gasped then and almost gagged as he looked up at the bloodless faces of the several horrified onlookers.

"Gibbs, I want a know if any a these people heard, or saw anything this mornin', or last night!…Write down everything they say. If they did, take em to th' office, if not, get 'em off this square….Where's Jeter and th' others anyway, you seen 'em this mornin'?"

"Walt and Garner ain't on duty yet, Lieutenant, they're at home. I ain't seen Cliff or Jeter since I went on patrol last night."

"Okay, get them statements, then go for th' undertaker….Better get Doc Welch, too."

"Why, he can't help her now?"

"Never mind that, just go!"

"I'm gone!"

"See if anybody has a blanket to cover th' body with!" He saw Gibbs nod and leave, then stared down at the body for a moment before looking at her bare, darkly bruised arms and hands, it evident that she had been bound by the wrists and ankles,…and it was then that he saw the overly large ring on her finger.

"Darlene Suggs!" he thought aloud, recognizing the colored glass setting,…and then remembered the pleasure she had given him only two nights ago. He had liked her as a person, not just that she was a whore.

Sighing, he stood and walked over to the wheatfield wagon to lean on the large wheel.

"It okay we leave now, Sheriff?" Asked Wheatfield gruffly. "My missus and baby girl are some upset over this….I need to get 'em home."

"Just a while longer, Westly, wait on Doc Welch,…I'd like 'im to to check out th' kids, okay?…Now, tell me what happened."

"Nothin' to tell, Sheriff!...We was comin' in for supplies is all, we do it ever month." He looked toward the North end of the square and jerked a thumb in that direction. "Came in back yonder and was crossin' th' square when th' mules shied, that's all."

"Okay, I heard that already. Now think real hard, Westly,...did you see, or maybe hear anything unusual as you came into th' square?"

"Heard what sounded like another wagin', I know, cause th' wheels needed greasin'. Dry as a gourd, one of 'em was!...Too dark to see it."

"Where was Deputy Gibbs when you found th' body?"

"Well, I guess somewhere on th' boardwalk off yonder, he came runnin' when my young'un screamed."

"Okay, Westly, thanks....Doc'll be here in a minute or so, Gibbs'll fetch 'im after he talks with some a these other folks."

"Won't get nothin' from them, Sheriff, weren't a soul out here till th' deputy left to get you."

"Okay, Westly,...look here man." He said nodding at the opposite boardwalk. "Norma just opened her café over there, why don't you take th' family over there, find a table and relax, have some coffee, get th' kids somethin' to drink?...Tell Norma it's on me, okay, I'll be over in a bit."

"Got a be better than this!" He grumbled then clucked the mules on across the wide square.

"Nobody seen a thing, Lieutenant." Said Gibbs, coming to stand beside him. "I'm goin for th' Doc and Undertaker now."

"After you do that, go on to th' office and wait on th' men. Keep 'em there, we're gonna search this town again!"

"I'm gone!"

He watched him leave then looked to see Wheatfield stop his wagon at the café's hitch rail and thought about what he had said about the other wagon he'd heard. If Darlene's body was brought to the square in a wagon, then she had to have been killed elsewhere, he thought,...maybe even somewhere away from town, but where, he wondered? He had checked out every farm and ranch in the county. If any of them had been killed at one of those places, there would have been blood traces, something! But there was nothing, not the slightest hint that anyone might be hiding something,... none of the people gave the slightest hint they might be hiding something,... and something as bizarre as this was bound to make a man edgy,...even the killer. No man could be this evil and still keep a straight face when questioned about it.

'Oh, well', he thought sadly. Something, or someone was beyond evil, and he was preying on the citizens of Tyler,...and he could not do a thing about it! Sighing, he looked at the wide expanse of square for a minute, then went back to the girls body and began walking in circles around her, staring hard at the packed ground for a possible clue,...and expanding the circle as he walked. He knew, and did not expect to find anything, even the wagon's actual ruts were lost, because the square was literally covered with them.

He had only covered a short distance when the Doctor and Undertaker arrived, and hurried back to remove the blanket Gibbs had covered her with for the Doctor's observation,...and as Doctor Welch knelt to examine her, knelt himself.

"Mister Maynard." Began Doc, with a sigh.. "In all my years of practice, even during that bloody war,...I have never been witness to anything as horrific as this! Whoever did this has no humanity at all, he's the Devil himself, straight out of hell!...May God take this poor girl's soul in his fold, and make her whole again. He looked up at Maynard then.

"Have you called her preacher?"

Maynard cleared his throat. "I ya,...I don't think she attended any Church, Doc."

"Doesn't matter, anyone will do, every dead soul needs to be prayed over."

"I'll see to it, Doc,...but tell me,...what kind of knife made those cuts?"

Sighing again, Welch bent to study the protruding flesh again. "Something very sharp, Mister Maynard. A Razor maybe, or a surgeon's scalpel....It's the same cut as all the other victims, except none of the others were gutted this way!"

"Could a hunting knife make a cut that clean, or a cleaver?"

"Sure, it could, but it would take some hacking to cut through bone like that, it would still have to be honed just right!...Even an axe would take more than once to do it, I think."

"Then what did do it?"

"I'm thinking more along the lines of a Cutlass. It's heavy enough,...and if it's honed just right, this wouldn't be a problem for it."

"A Cutlass,...you talkin' about a sword, a saber?"

"No, not exactly....A Cutlass has a much wider blade, and much heavier. It would take a man several strokes with a saber to cut off a person's head. These folks lost theirs with only one very swift, and very clean stroke....Even a keen axe wouldn't do that!"

"Damn it, Doc!" He sighed heavily. "I don't know where to go from here. Whoever's doin' this leaves no clues at all!...Th' Son of a Bitch can't be a ghost!"

"No,...but he can be the Devil!...No human being could be this heartless!"

"Well, this one is!...And he has to be found!"

"You need help, Mister Maynard, that's all.....Don't go blaming yourself too much. The Army can't find him either, and they have more men than you."

"It's hard to believe they're even lookin'!...Well, I got more help comin', it seems. Th' Colonel's brother in law is sendin' a couple more Marshals, but," He sighed as he got to his feet. "They'll likely wind up like th' last one did."

"Maybe not, too." Welch pulled the cover back over the body again. "How many does this make now, nine, ten bodies, I've lost count?"

"Eleven, Doc,...and we identified only three of 'em."

"I thought only two?"

"This girl here worked at th' Dove's nest, name's Darlene Suggs."

"Prostitute?"

"Yes sir, a real likeable person, too!"

"May God rest her soul....Well, anything else I can do?"

"As a matter a fact,...Westly Wheatfield and his family found th' body this mornin' and well, th' little girl's some hysterical about it....They're at Norma's."

"I'll take a look....I'll have miss Suggs certificate of death whenever you're ready,...she have kin here?"

"She was from Atlanta, Georgia." He said, shaking his head.

He watched the Doctor leave then nodded for the Undertaker to remove the body before continuing his walk around the square.

*   *   *

Seth Mabry stopped his dappled gray horse in the pre-dawn grayness of the muddy road, as did Dempsey, and both turned around to wave at Seth's family, who were all three still in the yard and only faintly visible as they waved back.

"You can still change your mind, Seth, nobody will blame ya'?"

"I would, Rod,...but a man's word is his bond....How far away is this, Tyler?"

"A hundred miles, maybe more. We'll be there in three or four days, you ever been there?"

"I think, maybe I was, once, durin' th' war. Had a large prisoner of war camp there." He clucked his horse into motion as he talked. "Town was still under construction in places, some empty lots around th' square."

"Don't think I ever been there, myself. I extradited a prisoner from th' town of Longview last year, took me most of two weeks by horseback."

"That's why they have Stage coaches and trains, Rod."

"I hate 'em, Seth, give me a good horse any day!...Anyway, that Longview is a big place, must be a dozen saloons in town."

"A real sin city."

"You could say so....Have you formed any kind of opinion who we might be lookin' for in Tyler yet?"

"Ain't thought much on it, but it's obviously a real bad man, or men!...I don't believe any one man is responsible.....Truth is, I'm thinkin' more along the lines of a clan, a whole family a folks, maybe.....It's just somethin' to think about, but whoever it is, from what that letter said, they're a murderous bunch!"

"Well, if it is, like you say, a clan,...I wouldn't think they'd live in Smith County. If they did, somebody would a found 'em, or at least be curious enough to report their doings....Wouldn't ya think?"

"What was that other Marshal's theory, you spoke about?"

"He said the cuts were too smooth, said they looked more like th' work of a Surgeon than anything else....Anyway, he was followin' up on that assumption when he was killed, killed th' Deputy with 'im, too!"

"That's where we'll start lookin' then....Anything else?"

"That's about it!" He sighed then. "You ever hear of a murder bein' committed with no clues left behind, I haven't!...But that seems to be th' case here!...Nobody sees or hears a thing, yet th' bodies are all left in th' town square to be found by anybody!...It don't make any sense, Seth."

"No, it don't....But I'd think they'd have to know th' goings on in town all th' time, to be able to leave th' bodies without bein' seen."

"Somebody in town is involved, that what you're thinkin'?"

"Damn if I know at this point, Rod,...can't rule it out though!...And till we can, we have to suspect everybody!...It's obvious to me, th' killings are all bein' done at night, and whoever it is, knows their way around in th' dark!...That bein' th' case, my friend,...when we get there, keep your wits about you, don't get sidetracked. Look twice at everything you see, till you know what it is!...I've never even heard of anything like this, let alone, goin' up against it!...And you ain't neither!...We'll have to eat, sleep and do our investigating together. These killers are damn good at it,...and we just might not find 'em at all."

"We have to find 'em, Seth!...Somethin' like this just can't go unpunished, we have to stop it!"

"I agree with ya, Rod,...but I don't plan on makin' Laura a widow neither. I'll face any man in a fair fight,...but there ain't nothin' fair about what's goin' on in Tyler!"

"Well," Sighed Dempsey. "Can't argue with ya about that..... I trust your instincts, Seth, you lead th' way, I'll follow."

"That could get ya killed, Rod. I've been known to take a few risks!"

"Yeah, well I've been a lawman for a long time, Seth, and I still don't have th' instincts of a gunman, you do!...I'll take my chances."

"Then let's hope you're right!...Well, our road's about to play out,...any more goin' from here to Tyler?"

"Dozens of 'em,...but the only direct route, I know of, is out a Dallas, that bein' th' Stage route!...We'll connect with it some twenty miles due East."

"Looks like we rough it for a spell." Said Seth, stopping his horse to look up and down the wide, muddy thoroughfare. "Nobody been out since th' rain, appears like." They sat their horses on the Texas Road for several minutes before finally crossing it and urging the animals down the embankment and into the tall, wet grass and trees on the other side.

* * *

Alex Maynard was on the boardwalk in front of his office and leaning back in the straight-backed chair against the wall, when he saw the carriage enter the south side of the square. He quickly settled the chair back on all fours to watch Mister and Ms. Quinlan come across to pass in front of him and stop at the Savings and Loan where Quinlan helped Laura out, and when she went inside, looked his way before walking up the boardwalk toward him.

"That all you have to do, Alex?" He said as he approached to shake the lawman's hand.

"In truth, Colonel, yes, sir!" He said, grunting to his feet. "I don't know what to do anymore....Come on, let's go inside." He held the door for Quinlan then followed him in.

"We found another body this mornin', Colonel."

"What?" Spencer turned around, his face showing both shock and bewilderment as he watched Maynard go on behind his desk and sit down.

"A farmer and his family found her at dawn today."

"Good, God, Alex!" He exclaimed with a shake of his head. "What is this, nine, ten now?"

"This one makes eleven, Colonel, and we ain't no closer to findin' th' killers than we was two month's ago!"

"What's being done?"

"Th' men are searchin' th' town again." He sighed dejectedly and reached to roll and light a cigarette. "They won't find anything, Colonel.... What brings you in today, anyway?"

"Mostly to see how things were developing, and you just told me!...The Army still doin' patrolls?"

"Well, yeah,...but you know the Army, everything has to be regulation....It ain't hard to predict when th' patrolls are made, they do it at th' same time, every time, day and night!"...All our killer has to do is check th' time, and he knows when it's safe. He seems to know what we're doin', too, and I can't figure that one out!...I do have a new piece of information though."

"You find a clue,...what?"

"No, sir....Westly Wheatfield and his brood found th' body today, said as they came into th' square, he heard a wagon leavin', said he didn't see it, but it had a dry wheel, said he knew th' sound for what it was!...Anyway, that's th' purpose of our search today. If we can find out which way that wagon left town, we'll know more about where to start lookin' for these Bastards!"

Quinlan fished a cigar from his vest and lit it as he walked to the window to stare out the empty street. "Our killer is not one of the locals then, is he?"

"No, sir. He, or they are outside th' city somewhere, but where?...We've searched every farm and ranch in th' county, Colonel. Hell, I've known all of 'em for years!...We ain't found a thing,...it's like we are chasin' a ghost, or somethin'."

"Any word on when the Marshals will be here?"

"Got a wire from Judge Castle two days ago, said a Marshal Dempsey would be here soon to take over, bringing another marshal with 'im....Way things are goin', they'll both be just another headless corpse like th' last one."

"Maybe not, Alex....Marshal Jones was on to something, that's why he was killed....I think he either identified the killer, or had gotten too close for the killer's comfort."

"I don't know, Colonel, that's what I thought, too!...But we followed up on his Surgeon theory, talked with every Doctor at the Hospital, every practitioner in town, and there ain't but two,...and they can't all be lyin' to us!...Anyway, there ain't but one actual Surgeon in town, he's at Camp Ford, been here as long as you have, too."

"Where were they going that late at night?"

"I don't know exactly, somethin' about talking with the preachers at all three churches. We followed up on that, too, they never made it to any of 'em!"

"Well, he was certainly on to something, Alex, didn't he tell you anything?"

"Colonel, we been over all this before, a couple a times!...If he knew somethin', he didn't confide in me....Said he wanted to be sure first!"

"I'm sorry, Alex, I know we have....Any idea who this latest victim was?"

"One a your employees at th' Dove's nest." He nodded. "Had that fake Ruby on her hand."

"Doreen?"

"Darlene, Colonel, Darlene Suggs,...nice girl."

"You been to her place yet?"

"Did that personally, a while ago. Nothin' there."

"That poor girl." He sighed then. "Was it the same as the others?"

"No head, yes, sir!...Only she had a little extra."Sighing heavily, He got up and went to stand beside Quinlan at the window. "She was sliced open from crotch to tits, Colonel, never seen anything like it!"

"My God, man!" He stared at the floor for a moment before shaking his head. "She the only one cut up that way?"

"She was th' first, so far!"

"Could it be because of who she was, you think?"

"Shit, Colonel,...I don't know what to think anymore. I've had men on patrol every night on horseback, up and down every street, even put a man on th' square!...They still managed to dump her body without bein' seen."

"Then the Deputy should have seen it!"

"Would have if he'd been there. Said he heard a woman callin' for help and went to find 'er,...th Wheatfields got there before he got back!"

"Let me guess,...there was no woman in need, right!"

"That's right, it was a ruse to get 'im out a th' way."

"Then they do know what goes on in town, Alex....Somebody's watching every move you make!" He dropped the cigar and mashed it out beneath his boot.

"I lost a few more steers last night." He said, staring at the street again. "Don't know when they were taken, but had th' same results,...no trail to follow!...Alex, I think I believe I'm feeding this bunch of killers. They are butchering my cattle for food! What do you think?"

"I'd say it's quite possible, Colonel....But if there's more than one of these Bastards, where the hell are they?"

"I wish to God I knew, Alex!...I don't know, maybe they're not even in Smith County, you think of that?...Maybe you're looking in all the wrong places. Wouldn't hurt to make a few inquiries,...in Jefferson, Maybe, see if they've had any unusual murders they couldn't solve."

"I've already thought a that, Colonel, and they ain't!"

"Try Longview then, maybe Pittsburg !...Because I find it hard to believe that something like this was born and bred in Tyler, Texas....It must have happened somewhere else, too, by God!"

"You're right, Colonel, it did!" Returned Maynard. "Five years ago in Lake Charles, Louisiana."

"Lake Charles, where?"

"Louisiana, Colonel, a few miles Northwest of New Orleans. Same thing went on, never caught 'em!"

"Same bunch, you think?"

"After five years, I doubt it!...Couldn't get any more information on it, Sheriff died last year in a fire, burned his records. If he kept any?"

"I don't mind telling you, Alex,...this has got me mad as hell, and I know you are, too. Got Lucy afraid to go to sleep at night, and I can imagine what it's done to folks in town here!" He went to the door then and opened it.

"I'll leave you to it, Alex, keep my informed, will ya?"

"You know I will, Colonel." He watched him close the door behind him then went back to his desk and sat down before taking out bottle and glass. He was trying hard not to be angry with Quinlan, and it was not working. Angrily, he poured a shot glass full and drank it, then waited for the fire to hit his stomach. Get right down to it, he thought, Spencer Quinlan had no more control over him or his deputies. He was the duly elected Sheriff now, three times over!...So why did he stand by and let him raise his voice to him that way?...But he knew why,...Quinlan was as frustrated as he was,...and angry!

He was right, too, he thought. Maybe he should send wires to Longview and Pittsburg, ya never know. He pulled the bandana from around his neck then and wiped his face and brow. It's too damn hot to be mad, he thought. Too damn hot to be drinking, too! He re-corked the bottle and put it away again as he went over his conversation with Quinlan.

CHAPTER FIVE

Laura, Greg and Trey silently watched the two riders until they disappeared into the stand of trees before she broke out in tears and rushed back into the house.

"She sure is hurt over this, Greg." Remarked Trey as he watched her. "I sure hate to see her like that."

"Me, too, Trey." He sighed. "But she's strong, and she knows he's doing th' right thing!" He turned to look at the Wrangler then. "Marshal Dempsey knows who Daddy really is, and he kept his secret. I don't think Judge Castle even knows!...Daddy couldn't turn 'im down, Trey, none of us could."

"You're right about that, I guess....'cept it ain't no gunfighter he's goin' after this time,...he don't know what it is!"

"Whatever it is, it's still a man doin' it, Trey, it's got a be!!...Daddy knows what he's doing, so does th' Marshal. He'll be okay."

       *   *   *

"Didn't know th' country was so rough out here!" Said Dempsey as they stopped their horses in a treeline overlooking the wide and well-traveled road below them. "Feels like we been rained on all day, too,...couldn't be any wetter, that's for sure!"

"Country's th' same all over, Rod,...you're just spoiled to takin' a road to get where you're goin'!...Tell ya what we better do though, we better park ourselves in th' shade somewhere and dry out. We don't that sun's gonna cook us with these wet shirts on."

"Well that's th' Shreveport road down there, we can take it th' rest a th' way!"

"I can remember when there weren't no roads hardly anywhere."

37

"I can too." Breathed Dempsey, leaning his arms across the saddle horn to stare down at it. "And you're right, I like th' roads,...and that one there ought a take us within twenty miles of Tyler."

"Just a minute ago, you said it would take us all th' way to Tyler."

"It will,...with a small detour!"

"And how far might that be?"

"To th' detour,...not more'n seventy, eighty miles. We'll be in Tyler in three days, four at th' most!"

"In that case," Sighed Seth. "It's gonna be dark before long, may as well find us a place for a fire and hold up for tonight."

"I see a clearing just off th' road down there, how about that,...ain't much traffic after dark anyway, except, maybe a coach or two."

"If it suits you,...I could use somethin' to eat anyway."

Dempsey led off down through the tangle of dripping grass and thickets, and they were soon dismounting in a cluster of wild Pecan trees, and only a stone's throw from the muddy, slightly rutted and wide road to Tyler.

Dempsey unsaddled the horses while Seth gathered what dry wood he could find from deeper in the forest of trees, and had a small fire going by the time the Marshal had placed saddles, bedrolls and food on the ground,... and as Seth filled the pot with water, he produced the sack of ground coffee and opened it for him.

"Where do you get your supplies, livin' off th' beaten path like that?"

"We're not that far off, Rod,...got a little store and tradin' post about ten miles South of us." He grinned and poured the grounds into the water then placed it in the fire to boil. "Got his own coffee grinder, salt, sugar and th' like. We get by real well off that beaten path!"

"I could tell." He replied and placed the sack of cold biscuits and ham between them, and as he ate, watched Seth's profile as he stared at the fire. "What are ya thinkin'?" He queried as the older man shifted his weight on the bedroll. "Saddle sore already?"

"Laura calls it arthritis." He grunted. "I call it over th' hill!" He grinned and continued to eat for another minute or so. "My joints hurt some at times, I'm gettin' old is all."

"I ain't far behind ya, Seth, I turned fifty a week ago."

Seth turned to stare at him then shook his head. "Fifty?...Ain't a gray hair on your head, Rod!...But that bein' th' case, we're a fine pair to be goin' on a ghost hunt."

"I was seventeen th' day I chased after you in Nacogdoches."

"That was a long time ago!" Said Seth. "I already felt like an old man, them days."

"Well,...you know what they say, my friend,...no rest for the wicked!"

"Ain't it th' truth?" Grinning, he pulled the bandana from his neck and reached the pot of boiling coffee from the fire and sat it aside to settle the grounds.

"What did you mean by Ghost hunt, Seth?"

"Got a be,...seven headless bodies and nothin' to go on!...I think there's more than one killer doin' this, too,...and that's gonna be dangerous!...No clues, no trail to follow, no blood in th' bodies....Got a be ghosts!" He grinned and reached for the pot again, pouring Dempsey's cup full and then his own.

"That, or a very well trained bunch a men....Whoever they are, they're a blood-thirsty bunch a devils....But why are they doin' it, Seth,...and why decapitation? What are they doin' with these people's heads?"

"Been thinkin' on that, too." He said as he leaned back against the saddle. "During th' war, I was in Louisiana a time or two....One a those times, I had to dodge rebel troops by usin' th' swamps, and it was a dark stretch of th' worst stuff I've ever seen! Dark, steaming hot, polluted water, and stunk like shit!...Any way, I came across a stretch of water and seen at least a dozen poles stickin' out of it with human skulls on 'em!...A damn scary sight, Rod, sent a chill up my spine."

"Voodoo?"

"Don't know, but it didn't do my nerves any good!"

"You think that's what's happening in Tyler,...some sort of voodoo ritual?"

"Damned if I know, Rod, but from readin' them letters, and what you've been sayin', there's no sensible reasoning behind any a these killings,...no other reason to be taking their heads!"

"A voodoo cult would make a lot a sense, all right!"

"We can't reject th' possibility." Agreed Seth. "But still,...I'd think that by now, th' law in Tyler would a already looked th' town and county over pretty good,...so where would a cult hide out?"

"Beats hell out a me, Seth!...There's still the idea it was done by a Doctor, or a Surgeon."

"Yeah,...and it puts us right back to where we started!" He reached to roll and light a brown-paper cigarette, blowing the smoke up through the low hanging branches. "We'll see what th' good Sheriff has to say,...he ought a know a lot more than we do!"

"He wouldn't have to know much!"

"Yeah." Agreed Seth as he reached to pour them more coffee. "We still have a few days to come up with a plan." With that, he picked up a burning stick, leaned forward and scattered the burning wood to allow it to burn out then leaned back again.

Dempsey then scooped up a few handfuls of loose mud and dry dirt, and tossed that on the blaze to help speed the process then he, too, lay back with his own thoughts.

Seth smoked as he looked up through the branches at the brilliant night sky and thought how hurt and upset his wife had been with his decision to do this. He could understand it, too, because he didn't know why himself? He also knew what it would do to her and Greg should he get himself killed. He regretted the decision at that moment, but also knew it was not in him to go back on a word once given.

He was stuck, and he had to see it through, he thought,...because he was fearful that Dempsey would not survive without someone to watch his back, someone who cared about his safety. But they would both have to be alert, and very smart in what they did....Because in all his roaming, all the fights as a wanted gunman, he had never encountered something like what was happening in Tyler, Texas....And he was worried.

It seemed too far-fetched that the murders were the acts of some voodoo ritual, in fact, he had never heard a name put to what he had seen in the swamps that day until tonight,...and there had to be a reason for that!...Most all cults, he knew, had something to do with religion, a belief in something. This, however, could have something to do with sacrifice, he thought, remembering stories his mother had read him from her bible, stories that spoke of sacrificing animals to some Pagan God in a ritual. He tossed the spent butt away and wished he had paid more attention to those stories.

"You seem a little disgusted about somethin', Seth." Commented Dempsey from the darkness.

"What makes ya think that?"

"Heard ya sigh a time or two. Havin' second thoughts?...I wouldn't blame ya none."

"I guess I am, Rod....But I'm here."

"What made you come anyway, Seth,...I could tell you really didn't want to?"

"Th' letter mostly,...and what you told me!...Rod, I don't want you takin' this th' wrong way,...but you're my friend, and I had a gut-feelin' you'd be walkin' into somethin' you couldn't handle alone!...I know you said if I didn't come, a couple a Rangers would go with ya, and that's all good!... Except they'd be lookin' out for them and not so much, you! I ain't so sure both of us can handle it!" He chuckled then. "Ain't sure anybody can....Hell, we could lose our heads over somethin' like this!" They both laughed over that for a minute.

"That really ain't no laughin' matter, Seth."

"No, sir, it ain't!...Tell me what you know about this voodoo stuff, Rod,...what is it?"

"You never heard a voodoo before?"

"Sure I have, thirty minutes ago!...What's it have to do with heads on poles?"

"It's black magic, Seth,...folks say it originated in Africa somewhere, and it's now practiced in places all over th' world, specially in th' swamps a Louisiana!...Some say it's th' real thing, too....It's a religion, I guess, because each cult has it's own voodoo Priestess that performs th' magic....The skulls on posts are to warn nosy people away."

"You believe in it, Rod?"

"Well,...if that's what's goin' on in Tyler, I don't know....I know I don't believe in magic!...But it still gives me th' shivers when folks talk about it!...Must be, I ain't really convinced."

"If that's what is goin' on, th' belief is powerful enough to commit murder! Do you believe that?"

"I believe that anything is possible, Seth!"

"Yeah,...I guess so. Good night, Rod."

                    *   *   *

Doctor Welch grunted to his feet and stared sadly down at Maynard. "I'm truly sorry, Sheriff,...I liked that young man. You absolutely sure, it's him?"

"Yeah," Nodded Maynard. "Those are his snakeskin boots."

"That's sad,...well, the Coroner is here, now," Said Welch. "Come on, Sheriff, let the man get him out of the square."

Maynard nodded and got to his feet. "He's been with me since th' war started, Doc....He was a good Deputy, too."

"What was his name, son?...I'll need it for my report."

"Name was Garner Sanders." He sighed heavily then. "Least they left 'im his pants and boots....Gun and holster's gone though, could be they're armin' themselves now."

"Are you going to be all right, man?"

"Hell no,...not till I catch these murderin' Bastards!" They moved back then while the body was loaded in the Hearse and hauled away. "That man was in my command in th' war, Doc, they all were,...and now, I've lost two of 'em!"

"Wish I knew what to tell ya, my boy, but I don't,...so I'll leave you with your dilemma....Send for me if you need me." He turned and moved through the onlookers then disappeared.

Maynard sighed and looked around at the distraught faces of the thirty or so onlookers, and could see the fear in their eyes as they all watched the black hearse leave. "I'm sorry, folks," He said loudly, to get their attention. "That's all there is to see here, please go on about your business,...okay?" He watched them slowly disperse in the early morning light then sighing again, went about checking the square again,...and that's when his remaining four deputies, all entering the square from different directions, galloped their horses to a sliding halt and dismounted,...and by the look of disgust and disappointment on their faces, he knew they'd had the same luck as he was having.

"Find anything? He asked as Gibbs faced him and shook his head.

"Nobody seen or heard anything like a squeaking wagon wheel, Lieutenant, that, or they're afraid to say anything. How about you?"

"Same!..." He said, looking back at the spot where Garner Sander's body had lain. "They knew he was watchin' th' square, God Damn it,... and they had to know where he was hidin'!" He breathed a disgusted sigh and watched the dregs of the dispersing crowd as they trickled onto the boardwalks.

"How about th' rest of ya, any Luck?" And when they shook their heads he walked away a few yards, cursed, and then came back to breathe deeply.

"He never knew they were there!" He said angrily. "likely clubbed 'im and took 'im away! Poor Bastard didn't know what hit 'im!"

"Weren't no blood on th' ground over there!" Said Walt. "What happened to it?"

"They didn't kill 'im here, Walt!" He breathed roughly then. "They took 'im somewhere else to murder 'im!...He didn't have any blood when they dumped him here!...Who knows what they're doin' with it?...When was th' last time any of you saw 'im?"

"Just after dark." Nodded Gibbs. "I watched 'im hide in th' wagon."

Cliff, Jeter, Walt, what about you?"

"I didn't see 'im atoll since we left th' office, Lieutenant." Returned Jeter.

"Me, neither, Lieutenant." Voiced Cliff. "I went south, remember?"

"I went west." Said Walt. "I seen 'im walk toward th' wagons over there, but that's th' last I seen of 'im!"

"Yeah, I know!" Maynard rolled and lit a cigarette then as he scanned the buildings around the square to at last come to rest on the still darkened windows of the Courthouse, and studied them for a minute.

"Okay," He said, looking at them again. "Starting right now, whatever you four do, you do it in twos. No more one man patrols, or stakeouts!" He nodded at the Courthouse then. "See that window right yonder?...That's Judge Gurney's Office!...And what I'd like you to do right now is check out that whole building, Gibbs, you take Walt and rattle each and every door in there, even th' Courtroom, make sure they're secure on all three floors!... Somebody saw Garner get in that wagon last night besides you, Gibbs.... Jeter, you and Cliff do th' same thing in every building on this square, th' Bastard could a hid behind any one of them windows overlookin' this thing!...When Gibbs and Walt get done, they can help ya.!"

"Now,...when Judge Gurney opens his office this mornin', I'm gonna get a key from 'im, because startin' tonight, right behind that window there is where all four of you are gonna be!...I want eight pairs of eyes on this square every minute of th' night. If a rat walks across this fuckin' piece a ground, I want a know it!" He threw the spent butt away and looked at them.

"We been together a long time, men....And I'd just as soon not lose any more of ya, so keep that in mind, all of ya!...We are not dealin' with ghosts here, they'll bleed just like us....What it all boils down to, is that they're smarter than we are, they're trained killers, all of 'em, bloodthirsty murderers, remember that!...That bein' said, you see 'em leavin' another body, don't charge 'em in a mad rush,...I want 'em followed, we need to know where they live, everything about 'em, then we'll take 'em down!... Better get to it, now. You get done, go get some sleep, and ya better sleep at th' jail for a while till we catch this bunch, and stay together!" He watched them lead their mounts toward their assigned task then cursing, continued his fruitless search of the square.

*   *   *

"Are you okay, Mama?" Asked Greg as he watched Laura working at the stove.

"Wha,...oh, honey, you startled me!...Yes, I'm fine, a little worried, but I'll be all right!" She smiled and began setting the table. "Did you sleep well?"

"Don't be mad at Daddy, Mama?"

"Oh, honey, I'm not mad at your father!...I accepted who he was twenty years ago....I'm just afraid for him, that's all. He's going up against something, he knows nothing about, both of them are!" She got silverware from a drawer and began placing them before looking worriedly at him. "When I read that letter, my heart froze in my chest."

"Why, Mama?"

"Because it's the Devil's work being done up there!"

"What?...Mama you can't be serious, it's just one or two killers on the loose!...Two, maybe three crazies who got mad about somethin',...that's all it is!"

She sat down at the table and smiled weakly at him. "When I was eight years old, down the road from us lived an old woman, a witch!...She lived off in the woods in a falling down old shack of a house! You could smell the odor of rotting wood from the road. My father called it the smell of death!... She was an old hag of a woman that everyone believed to be a Witch, and no one dared go there."

"Father said there were people's skulls on posts and trees along the path to her house, and he said there were snakes everywhere!...He went there once, just to see the place for himself,...and she saw him."

"What happened?"

"He ran away, of course!...But for a long time after that, the covers on our beds would mysteriously crawl off onto the floor at night. We even found snakes in the house, and it had never happened before!...That's what I remembered when I read those letters."

"Mama, there's no such thing as a Witch!"

"Don't be so sure, honey, there had been accounts of people going there and never coming back!...I believed it then, and it's what scares me now."

"I don't know what to say, Mama,...I know you believe that sort a thing is real, but I don't, and neither does Daddy, so don't worry, Mama,...whoever is doing these killings is a dead man when he meets Daddy, Witch or not!... That's the only truth I believe in."

"I know, honey." She sighed then. "So do I.....I'm just being an old fool is all. Your father is a very dangerous man, in his own right, I've always known that!...But I still worry about him. Now come on, get washed up, Trey will be in shortly for breakfast."

"I love you, Mama,...Please don't worry about Daddy?"

"I love you, too, Sweetheart, and I'll try, I promise."

*   *   *

They were up and on the road by dawn, urging their horses to a mile-consuming gallop, and only walking them periodically to cool them down before continuing at a run again. It was late afternoon when they slowed the nearly winded animals to flag down the Dallas-bound Stage and once stopped, urged their mounts in beside it to speak with the driver. Their actions caused the guard to stand a level his shotgun at them.

"Don't you yay-hoos know it's ag'in th' law to stop a mail-coach,...less'n you got it in mind to try to rob us!"

"Settle down, man!" Said Dempsey. "I'm a U.S. Marshal, now lower that damn scattergun!"

"We apologize, Marshal." Said the driver. "We surely do!...Put that thing away, Horace, and sit down!...What can we do for ya, Marshal?"

"You make a stop in Tyler, did ya?"

"Yesterd'y afternoon late, sure did,...why ya askin'?"

"Pick up any passengers?"

"Three!" He nodded. "In th' coach there."

Dempsey urged his horse alongside the coach, causing one of the men to lean his arm out through the window.

"Name's Gordon, I got on in Tyler, Marshal."

"You know anything about th' situation there?"

"If you're referring to those weird Murders, I do."

"I am,...has anything changed?"

"Nothin' for several days now,...don't know about this mornin' yet! But it's th' reason I got th' hell away from there,...because it's due to happen!... Got folks leavin' in droves, too!...Place is cursed, you ask me,...and I don't plan on goin' back!"

"That why the rest of you left?" Queried Dempsey, leaning from his saddle to see inside, and when they answered yes, nodded and glanced at Seth before nodding at Gordon. "Much obliged, Mister Gordon!" He nodded and backed his horse up to talk with the driver again.

"You plannin' on goin' to Tyler, Marshal?" Asked the driver. "Cause if ye are, they already had one Marshal beheaded up there!"

"Thanks for th' tip!...You goin' to Dallas?"

"Last stop, yes, sir!" He nodded.

"I'd like you to get word to Federal Judge Emmit Castle at th' Federal Building. Tell 'im that Marshal Dempsey, and Marshal Mabry are a days ride out a Tyler. I'll wire 'im from there....You got that?"

"Dempsey and Mabry, I got it!"

"Much obliged." He waved them on then, and they watched the lumbering coach move on before spurring the horses to a gallop again on the dusty road.

"We're about a days ride from there, Seth!" He yelled to be heard over the sounds of pounding hooves. "I think!" He grinned then. "We can be there by midnight tomorrow!"

"That's what I thought ya meant!" Nodded Seth. "You sure ya want a ride in at night?"

"What do ya mean?"

"Might think we're th' killers and start shootin'!" He yelled back.

"Good thinkin'!" Returned Dempsey, and they fell silent as they once again adjusted the rocking motion of their bodies to that of the horses.

*   *   *

Maynard looked toward the cellblock door as the four bleary-eyed deputies came out into the office. "Four o'clock, good timing, men. Go pour yourselves some coffee, it's fresh made." He watched, and waited until they had their full cups and moved to sit down against the wall. "Here's your key." He said, tossing it to Gibbs.

"You got time to eat your supper yet, but I want all of ya in there by six o'clock….And don't go in all at once, go one at a time, and try not to act like you got a purpose in goin'!...Our spy could be watchin' even now!" He got up and walked to the window to peer out at the almost empty street.

"Don't let your guard down, men. Till this mornin', we ain't had a body in a few days. Might be another few before they hit again, least that's been th' way till now….Killings started more than a month ago, closer to two now, and we got twelve bodies!...That's six murders a month, men, and them Sons a Bitches are laughin' at us!...They are daring us to stop 'em!"

"What else can we do, Lieutenant?" Asked Cliff as he got to his feet. "You just tell us, we'll do it!"

"I'm afraid I ain't smart enough to do that, Cliff!" He turned to look back at them. "I'm just blowin' steam here, ain't none a this your fault, none of ya!...I do know they ain't done yet, and at this point in time, that's all I know!...Just keep your eyes on that square tonight, and every night till they hit again!"

*   *   *

Lucy Quinlan tightened the shawl around her shoulders and stepped out onto the porch, and seeing her husband at the corrals again dispersing the hands for the day, watched him as she went to her rocking chair and sat down. She was glad now that she had turned over some of her book work responsibilities at the Savings and Loan to her long time employee and loan agent because now, she was not needed there so often. Now, she could spend more time at home with her house and husband, and Quinlan would not have to take men away from their work to be with her,…and he would be here to better run the ranch.

She knew he was taking these mysterious murders too personal, knew he was not sleeping well at night, having awakened on several occasions to find him out of bed and pacing the length of the long porch.

She watched two of the wranglers shaking out their ropes as they entered the corral to catch their skittish mounts for the day and as they did, thought of what Spencer had confessed to her about his mostly unlawful part in the growth of Tyler. She had been disappointed hearing about his reason for coming here at all, and how he had been the one responsible for their extreme taxation.

But then again, he had been the one that, when she had complained about the hardship it presented had abolished it. He had not been an honest man, she thought, but most men were not! The difference was, she knew, was the fact that she was in love with this one. He was not the same man that had come to Tyler back then, he had changed,…and they were happy because of it.

She smiled then as he climbed the steps to come and sit down. "Good morning, Darling." She said, leaning to kiss him. "You look so tired,…did you sleep any at all last night?"

"Not much!" He sighed then. "These senseless murders are all I seem to think about when I close my eyes."

"More cattle gone this morning?"

"I don't know, don't think so,…but we wouldn't know anyway without a head-count….It's inevitable that we lose cattle from time to time, all ranchers do,…to rustlers, and th' country's full of 'em!…Then we got wolves, coyotes and th' like. It just galls me that our beef may be feeding this bunch of murderers, keeping them alive and well to kill again!…It's about more than I can take, too!"

"I know, Darling, for me, too!…But another Marshal will be here soon. I know we'll find those responsible before long, you'll see."

"I hope you're right!…But his predecessor didn't last very long, don't forget that,…and he was supposed to be the finest th' Judge had!…Forgive me, sweetheart, but I'm beginning to think there's a curse on our beloved Tyler!" He shook his head then. "I don't know why I said something like that, I don't believe in such things!" He took a cigar from his vest and lit it.

"I went to see Captain Lamar yesterday," He continued, blowing blue, aromatic smoke upward. "Asked him to declare Martial Law in town till this thing was over and done,…he refused, said he would need orders from Washington, and more troops to support it!"

"Couldn't he request more troops?"

"Said he couldn't get reinforcements,…said every Fort in Texas was stretched thin!…I don't understand it, one of his soldiers was murdered, and he won't even increase patrols in town!…It don't make sense to me."

"You could wire the President yourself, they know you there,…maybe if you explained our situation here,…"

"Wouldn't work!" He said, interrupting her. "The Grant Administration knew me, honey,…Mister Hayes wouldn't know me from Adam."

"You don't know anyone that might help?"

"Not anymore, it's been too long.…Appears we'll have to rely on this new Marshal, and pray for the best,…because Alex is not getting anywhere."

"Well, I hate to,…but I could ask my brother in law to send the Texas Rangers, Gwendolyn says he has as much control over them as the Governor?"

"Honey,…I appreciate your concern, believe me, I do, and I love you for it,…but we have cried on the Judge's shoulders enough already, and he's probably stretched a little thin his self.…No, we'll wait, see what this new Marshal can do. Besides, he's bringing another Marshal with 'im. Maybe two heads will be better than one at this point.…If he needs 'em, I'll put my whole crew at his disposal, anything to wipe this bunch of animals out!"

"It's settled then!" She said smiling. "Let's us go have some breakfast, Ezra said it was about ready. We'll spend the day together, put this behind us for a few hours."

"Best offer I've had all day!" He smiled.

*   *   *

"Jake Tulane!" Smiled Emmit Castle as he looked up. "How are you, Marshal, it's been a day or two?" He got up as he spoke and met him to shake his hand.

"Can't complain, Judge."

"Good, that's good!…Come on and sit down." And while Tulane sat down, he went back to take his own seat. "To what, do I own this honor, my boy?"

"Nothin' special, Judge," He grinned. "I went to visit with Marshal Dempsey and his door was locked." He shrugged. "Just thought Id say hello."

"Glad you did, it's good to see you!…Roderick is on special assignment for a week or so. I sent him to Tyler to investigate some murders, shouldn't take that long."

"Tyler,…ain't that where Marshal Jones was killed?"

"I'm afraid it was, Jake, but where did you hear about that?"

"Old Denver Long, Rides shotgun on th' mail coach. He brings me newspapers from there, and Longview when he thinks about it."

"Yes," He nodded. "Henry Jones was a good man, Jake,...a dedicated lawman, and I'll miss him. Anyway," He sighed then, as if he had to suddenly swallow at a lump in his throat. "Anyway, the driver on that mail coach brought me a message from Roderick this morning, saying he should be in Tyler sometime tonight."

"From what I read, Judge, there's been some pretty gruesome killings over there, decapitations and such."

Emmit nodded and then sighed heavily again. "It's all true, Jake,...to date, according to the Sheriff's last wire, they have had nine murders, all decapitated, and not a drop of blood left in them."

"Well, that's what I came to see Rod about, Judge. I also talked with one a th' passengers on th' stage, and he said that all th' bodies were found displayed in th' town square, put there during th' night sometime....And his count was ten bodies, not nine."

"My God, Ten?"" He dropped his head on folded arms atop the desk for a moment in silence.

"Me and Rod talked about a similar case a while back, Judge." He continued. "Five years ago in a place called Lake Charles, in Louisiana." He waited for Emmit to look up at him before going on. "Seems those bodies was found in front a th' Courthouse there, had folks scared to the point a packin' up and leaving!...Weren't no clues to who did it, no blood trails, no nothin'....And they never did find th' killers!"

"What happened?"

"Nothing, th' killings stopped, never happened again....What's important to know, at least I think it might be important, is that there was thirteen bodies in all before it stopped."

"The same killer?" Asked Emmit in dismay. "Can it be, Jake?"

"It very well might be, Judge. If it is, there'll be two more killings before it stops!...And now, I hope number thirteen ain't Rod Dempsey!"

"Amen, Jake!...My God, thirteen?...How long ago was these other murders again, I seem to recall reading about that, or something about it."

"It would be about five years ago now, Judge....Ya know, I'm due some time off, Judge, if you'd let me, I could go to Tyler and help 'im."

"I appreciate that, Jake, and I know Roderick would. But he has about the best help he could get, I think."

"He does, who?"

"Seth Mabry went with him."

"That's a relief then." Nodded Tulane. "From what I know about him, there ain't none better!"

"That was my thinking, too!...And I want to thank you for your concern, and the information. I should have remembered all of that!"

"Yeah, well, you're human, Judge!" He grinned, and with hat in hand, got up. "I better get back to work, Sir....It's funny, though,...I only came over to talk with Rod about th' similarities of these two cases....Small world, ain't it?"

"That it is, Jake."

"Be a seein' ya, Judge."

Emmit got up and walked him to the door, and once he was gone, closed the door behind him and walked down the hall to the telegraph room. He was more worried now than ever, one, for the lives of Dempsey and Mabry and two, that the killers would murder number thirteen and leave before they had a chance to find them. If that be the case, they would only move somewhere else and start all over again. These murderers were not only ruthless and dangerous men, they were also calculating, and very cunning,...and they had to be stopped!

CHAPTER SIX

Dempsey opened his eyes to the smell of strong coffee and yawning, watched as Seth took the smoldering piece of bark from beside the fire to daintily remove the hot biscuit and ham sandwiches from it, placing them on another similar piece of bark before grinning across at him.

"Get it while it's hot, Rod." His grin widened to a smile as he reached to pour their coffee. "Course, if you ain't hungry?"

"Hell, I'm a comin', man, I'm starving!" He threw off the blanket and moved over to the fire. "It's barely dawn, Seth, how long you been up?"

"Early!" He grinned and picked up a biscuit. "I'm a rancher, not a lawman, Rod,...I work for a living."

"Well, some are luckier than others, I guess."

"Eat your breakfast, Marshal!" They had a good chuckle and ate their first hot meal since leaving the ranch, and when they were done, both rolled and lit their smokes before sipping at the hot brew.

"Still think we'll make it by tonight, Rod?"

"We ought to. I figure we been makin' about twenty-five miles a day, another twenty five today, we'll be there sometime around midnight,... before dawn anyway!"

"We've made fairly good time, all right." Agreed Seth.

"I just hope we're in time to catch these bastards."

"Didn't know murder had a time limit."

"I got a feelin' these do....You remember tellin' me about them poles you saw with human skulls on 'em. I didn't remember it at th' time, what with our talk about voodoo and all,...but somethin' like this has happened before, four, maybe five years ago in Louisiana....The victim's heads were cut off and th' bodies left stretched out in front a th' Courthouse front steps.... Never caught th' killers neither!"

"How'd they stop it?"

"Didn't, they just stopped!...If I remember right, there were thirteen murders in all….It never happened again after that!"

"Until now!" Sighed Seth. "Or, that you've heard about." He reached to pour them more coffee. "That man on th' coach yesterday said there was eleven bodies, didn't he?"

"That why I hope we get there in time. If this is th' same bunch, a couple more murders, they'll move on, and we'll never stop 'em!"

"Then we'll track 'em down, they'll pop up again….Don't fret it too much, time is usually always against ya anyway….By th' time you finally get somewhere, you find out you should a been there yesterday!"

"Sound wisdom, Seth, pure and simple. Well, we best get started."

"Not yet!" Said Seth suddenly. "I hear horses on th' road,…let 'em pass first." He got to his feet, as did Dempsey and were watching when the riders drew abreast of them and stopped their horses.

"Hello th' camp!" Called out an older man, closest to them. "Would that be coffee I smell, Pilgrim?"

"It would." Returned Dempsey. "Light down, we're about to dump it out." He looked at Seth, seeing him remove the tie-down loop from his pistol then watched as the three reined their animals in to the fire. The man doing the talking, he noted, was much older than the other two, and grunted as he dismounted. He was well under six feet, gray-headed with a beard of the same color, dressed in dust-covered once-black britches and scuffed boots. His shirt was a faded blue, and sweat-stained.

It was the old man's darting eyes that caught Seth's attention, and he thought it almost funny that eyes so dark, alert, and hard would be trapped in a face that wrinkled. The man's eyes did not reflect the wide, toothy grin he was presenting them. But it was the low-slung gun on his skinny hips that told him what he was. The other two men were much the same, but half the older man's age. One bent to brush away dust from his pants, and when he looked up, gave Seth the impression he was just along for the ride and whatever it produced. The third man, however, he knew to be the dangerous one. He was slight of build, dressed in range garb, but the two guns on his hips were slung just right, tied to his legs and just right for a quick draw.

"Name's Bill Tooley." Said the old man, reaching a weathered hand out to Dempsey. "We sure appreciate th' hospitality, been on th' road all night!"

"We know th' feelin'" Nodded Dempsey, backing away from the fire. "Help yourselves."

"You heard th' man, boys," Said Tooley as he squatted to pour his coffee. "Bring your cups!" He stood then to sip at the cup and nod at Dempsey, his ever moving eyes darting from him to Seth and back again. "I didn't catch your names, Friend?"

"Rod Dempsey, U.S. Marshal, That's Marshal Mabry." He nodded at Seth. "Where you men from?"

"Over Longview way, left there a few days ago....Headin' for Dallas."

Seth watched the other two men intently while Dempsey and the old man talked, watched them pour their coffee and stand back again, his eyes locked with those of the Two-gun man most of the time, and those eyes were dead looking in the fire's reflecting light, and never seemed to waver from his,...while the second man seemed to be disinterested, his eyes were everywhere as he sipped his coffee with his right hand. The third, however, drank his coffee with his left hand, his right hanging loose at his side.

"Seth," Said Dempsey suddenly, breaking the spell. "Meet Bill Tooley,... Bill Tooley, Seth Mabry."

"Real pleasure to meet ya, Marshal." He grinned again and reached to shake Seth's hand, causing Seth's eyes to narrow at the man's limp handshake. Tooley looked back at the other two then. "Boys, these are Marshals, Dempsey, and Mabry." He nodded at the gunman then.

"That lanky old boy there is called Pecos, Marshal, won't tell me his God-given name for some reason....The other one here is Jesse Creel."

"What business you boys in?" Asked Dempsey.

"Business?...Why we ain't in no kind a business, Marshal. No, sir,...we're just cowboys lookin' for a place to light."

"You got reason to be askin'?" Queried the man called Pecos, his eyes still on Seth.

"Badge is all th' reason I need, Mister!" He looked back at Tooley then. "You boys been in Tyler, by chance?"

"Now, Marshal," Chuckled Tooley. "With all due respect to th' law and all,...I told ya where we been, and where we're bound, the rest is our own business!...Not meanin' any disrespect, you understand."

"Mister Tooley," Sighed Dempsey. "We ain't got th' time to waste right now, and it appears you're all done with your coffee....So, I think it's best you be on your way."

Tooley's eyes narrowed. "That ain't very friendly."

"Won't get any better, neither!...Move out, Mister Tooley."

A grin slowly crept across Tooley's mouth then and he stepped back to look down at Dempsey's holstered gun. "You any good with that thing, Marshal?...Cause if you ain't, maybe you both best go ahead and give us your money and guns?"

Dempsey saw Seth relax his arm at his side and slowly did the same. "Mister Tooley, we're Federal lawmen, you better think twice about what you're plannin' to do here, because you ain't gonna make it."

"Why, Marshal, sir,...I ain't plannin' to do nothing." He nodded his head toward the other two men then. "Don't need to,...old Pecos there'll kill th' both of ya, you don't do what I say, and Marshal,...that's as friendly as I can be! Ya see, Pecos don't like lawmen much, never did, since his pa was kilt by one!...Now, me, I respect th' law,...that's why I'm givin' you old boys this chance....Now,...take off them gun-belts!"

The man called Pecos suddenly went for his gun, but the thunderous explosion as Seth drew and fired drowned out his grunt of pain as his slender body was lifted by the slug's impact, and thrown back against his rearing horse only to fall in a crumpled heap beneath the animal's feet.

As the gunfire echoed away, Dempsey drew his own gun and was covering them as their disbelief slowly subsided.

"Who th' hell are you, old man?" Gasped Tooley. "Pecos was th' fastest man with a gun I ever seen!...Who are ya, you're old as I am, fer God sakes!"

"Your fast gun just said hello to Marshal Seth Mabry." Grinned Dempsey. "Now, speaking of guns, Mister Tooley, drop yours,...do it now, you, too, Mister Creel!" And when they dropped their gun-belts at their feet, holstered his own. "I'll ask my question again now, Mister Tooley....You been to Tyler lately?"

"No, sir, we ain't,...not in a couple years."

Nodding, Dempsey looked at the second man. "Mister Creel, get over there and take Mister Pecos's gun-belt and guns off his body,...give 'em to Seth there." They all watched as the man called Creel did Dempsey's bidding, and when Seth had the weapons. "Load th' Bastard across his saddle now, Creel." He looked back at Tooley then.

"Get th' fuck out a here, Mister Tooley, take your dead with ya!"

"You lettin' us go,...just like that?"

"I got no time for ya now, so git!" Without hesitation, They mounted and spurred their horses to a gallop along the dusty road, and towing the dead gunman's horse along behind them.

"Should a took th' saddle guns, Rod." Said Seth as he gave him the dead man's gun-rig.

Dempsey took the guns then leaned to lay them atop the others. "Didn't think of it....Besides, they won't come back!" He squatted, as did Seth and rolled up their bedrolls, and as he tied the strings, chuckled and looked at Seth. "What do ya think,...how long before they turn Mister Pecos's horse loose?"

"I'd say, about now!" Grinned Seth as he picked up his saddle and blanket and walked toward his horse. "Be good and ripe before anybody has it in mind to bury 'im!" He placed the saddle on the gray as he spoke and tightened the cinches.

"I'd say, you're right, too!" Grunted Dempsey as he swung his own saddle across the back of his horse. "Should a made 'em walk to Dallas, the assholes!...Probably wanted in three states for murder!"

"A little late for second thoughts, Rod." Reminded Seth as he tied the bedroll in place and went back to gather utensils and kill the fire.

Dempsey gave him his reins and took the sack from him, tying it behind the cantle, and both mounted to urge the horses back to a steady gallop on the rutted road..

*   *   *

Alex Maynard knocked at the door, and when Gibbs opened it, walked inside to gaze at the faces of the four deputies. "I found no body in the square this morning, so I take it you didn't see anything?"

"Nothin' but a few stray dogs, Lieutenant." Yawned Gibbs.

"Well, that's a good thing, I guess." He sighed then. "Okay, clean up in here a bit, then go get your breakfast, we'll try it again tonight....If we're lucky, th' Bastards have left th' area."

"I wouldn't wish that on another lawman, Lieutenant!"

"Me neither, Jeter, but maybe he'll be smarter than I am....Cause this has got me lookin' like one dumb Son of a Bitch!...Kind a feel like one, too."

"We all do, Sir!" Voiced Walt.

"I know that, too!...I'm just blowin' off steam here!...I'll see you back at th' office." He left them shrugging their shoulders and scratching their heads as they watched him go.

"Never seen 'im that spooked before." Said Cliff. "Me, I'm scared shitless of what's goin' on here,...but I never seen him that way."

"Well, he's a soldier, Cliff, and we ain't in a war no more,...it's a whole nother thing!...We all know that."

"That do make a difference all right!" Returned Cliff. "Man knows what to do when he can see his enemies."

"Do any of us have any new ideas?" Asked Gibbs. "Lieutenant could use a couple about now,...anything?"

"Nothin' we ain't done already, no!" Shrugged Walt.

"And that tells it all, don't it?" Blurted Jeter. "We all been told what to do for so long, that we only do our best when we're told what to do!...Been that way for th' last twenty years!...Lieutenant says do, and we do it, he even tells us how!...Know what we are?...We are Medicine-show puppets, men on a string. We got shit for brains, is what we got!"

"God damn, Jeter!" Said Walt.

"It's th' fuckin' truth, Walt, and you know it!"

"Okay!" Said Gibbs. "Maybe it is,...so lets change it!...We'll finish up here and talk about it over breakfast,...okay?"

"Yeah, okay, Gibbs,...we'll give it a shot!"

*   *   *

Maynard stepped up to the boardwalk, thought about having some breakfast, then cursed under his breath and instead, turned to once again scan the dark windows of the stores and buildings around the square. He knew that someone was watching him, they have to be, he thought,...but from where? One of those dark windows, a rooftop,...where?...But he knew that if anyone had been there, His deputies would have found some trace of it, they checked every second and third story window surrounding the square, and nothing! Cursing again, he walked on to his office and went inside to pour himself some strong coffee before sitting down at his desk.

There has to be something he was missing, some obvious, minute clue he had overlooked, maybe someone of suspicious nature, some thing, anything! He sipped at the coffee and took the report sheets from a drawer to once more read about every street, every interview, every move his deputies had made in the last two months, and all the while hoping he would read something he had missed the last dozen times he had read them. There was just nothing out of the ordinary there, he thought disgustedly and sighing again, put them away to take out the telegrams he had received.

There had been something he had read in the wire from Jefferson that at the time had caught his interest, so he found it and read it again out loud. "No such murders of that nature in County. Only two strangers in town, last three months, both Monks of religious origin! Sorry-hope you good luck!" Signed Sheriff Casey Weems....Dressed like a Monk, he thought. A lot of preachers and elders wore robes like that, with hoods, too!...But he did not remember any doing so in Tyler. There was, however a Jewish Church in Jefferson, and that could explain that!...That left him with nothing again, except for the squeaking wheel of a wagon.

He knew they had already searched the West road out of town for a mile without finding anything. There was just no place there to hide anyway, save a few farms, and those were checked. Wheatfield had sworn he heard the wagon leaving the square on West Bois d 'arc, but there were any number of cross streets they could have turned off on. Bois d 'arc runs West for three miles, and it dead ends at the start of the Colonel's property line, he thought. And there another road crossed it to run North and South, following the Quinlan fence line all the way South where it crossed Houston street, it being the road through Quinlan's front gates, and running all the way to his house,…and the killers would not have gone there.

They must have turned South right after leaving the square, he decided, probably traveled right across the off-streets then turned East to Cedar road. That had to be what they did, he thought, because Cedar road ran all the way South to Bullard and the Smith County line, more than thirty miles away. What if they were hid out somewhere in that swampy wilderness, maybe even in Bullard?…No. he thought, not Bullard, too much traffic on the road for one thing, for another, they come and go much too fast to be going that far! But the wilderness its self posed a problem, too, being nothing but an overgrown swamp, so overgrown with deep woods, and so vast an area that he had not even thought of sending anyone there to look, and in fact, at the time had thought it unnecessary, because man could not survive in there.…And now, it was not possible without the man-power, and time was too short.

What he could do, he thought, would be to talk with Quinlan about that when he came to town again because there, or maybe somewhere around the Colonel's own very large lake were the two most logical places to hide. But the wranglers would have seen them around that lake, it would have been too obvious to hide, so he discarded that idea. That left him with the Wilderness, he thought and now within reason, he believed that if they were not hiding somewhere in that swamp, they were not in Smith County at all! It would take time to search there, he thought sadly, and he might not have the time. But, damn it, he had to, he was getting nowhere like it is.

He would ask Quinlan for a few men to go in there, he decided reluctantly. He'd been reluctant to do so before, but knew it was his own pride that stopped him. He also knew that if he did not solve this thing, and soon, he would likely not be reelected this time around. "Might be th' best thing for me!" He said aloud, and then drained his cup. Fifteen years on a going nowhere job was long enough anyway!

Sighing, he put the wires away, propped his feet on the desk, leaned back in his spring-loaded chair and closed his eyes as he thought about the squeaking wagon wheel. To now, it had been only a loose-fitting clue. But maybe the wagon did leave the square on Bois d 'arc and turn South, in fact, he was sure of it, and that would mean they went into the swamp somewhere close to town and if it did, there had to be wagon tracks where it left the road, or another road in there they didn't know about? But according to Gibbs and Jeter, they searched that roadside for five miles or more without finding any sign at all.

"Damn it!" He cursed aloud, and then opened his eyes to stare at the ceiling. Whoever these people are, they are very smart, and could in fact be hid out somewhere in Tyler, maybe in several different places. They could even be pillars of the community, church going, and evil as hell!

"That's dumb!" He said aloud. They were all in one place somewhere, and that somewhere was close!

*   *   *

"Finally!" Said Dempsey as he read the hand-painted signpost. "Tyler, twenty three miles….Another eight or nine hours, Seth!" They both dismounted there and tightened the saddles' cinch-straps, and as Dempsey dropped the stirrup his hand came to rest on the holstered guns belonging to the dead gunman.

"You ever tote two guns, Seth?" He asked as he removed his own belt and gun and then removed the two-gun rig from the saddle horn. "I've thought about it before, just never could put money aside to have th' holsters made."

"Only takes one to kill a man, Rod." He commented as Dempsey hung his old one on the horn and buckled on the two.

"Well,…that may be true in your case, Seth, but I ain't half as fast as you." He tied the holsters down and grinned widely. "Feels good,…a little strange, but good!...Sort a balances a man out….How do I look?"

"A little over-dressed." He grinned. "You ever shoot left handed?"

"Once or twice,…didn't hit anything. Guess I'll have to practice."

"Ain't one in a hundred men can shoot with both hands, Rod, so if ya can't, ya best not try….All it's good for is a spare gun, save ya some time in a tight!...Come on, let's walk for a while, I ain't been on a horse this long in a while."

"Suits me." Agreed Dempsey, looking both ways along the winding, tree-lined road. "Ya know, this bein' the only direct road to Dallas from here, you'd think there'd be more traffic. We ain't seen more than a half dozen wagons on it all th' way here!"

"Mail Coach." Returned Seth as they led the horses up the well used road.

"Well, that!...You'd think there'd be more."

"Too hot to travel this time a year, if ya don't have to." Seth rolled and lit a smoke as they walked. "Ain't seen this many Pine trees in a while though,…damn pretty country around here!"

"This stretch of road don't see much sun neither….I've been thinkin' about this thing in Tyler, Seth….The average man wouldn't take th' time to think out his murders like that, wouldn't think a nothin' but getting away! That's why they get caught, too!...But not these killers, they think everything out! They take their victims, kill 'em, chop off their heads and leave th' body in th' middle a town. It would take several of 'em to do that!...And they'd all have to more or less think alike. Each man knowing what the other was doin' at any given time, then workin' together to do it!"

"Somethin' like that don't seem possible to me, Seth. It would take years of training!...That's why I'm thinkin' more and more along the lines of that voodoo cult. Nothin' else makes any sense!"

"Except for one thing, Rod, there ain't no such thing as magic, and that's what you're talkin' about here!...I do believe there's people who practice it, and I say this, cause a what I saw in th' swamps....But it ain't magic! Things happen to people because their minds believe it will,...and people can be made to believe anything...People are conned every day for that same reason."

"That's true, but how can these killers do what they do and leave no tracks, no clues, just headless bodies left in a square for folks to see?"

"Scared people hide, Rod,...they don't fight back, or think, they just run!...That's why they leave th' bodies....And you're right, I think,...they been killin' folks for years, getting' better with practice all th' time!...I can't even imagine why they would keep th' heads, or what they'd want with th' blood, other than th' fact there'd be no blood trail to follow. You're right about somethin' else, too. They all hasve to pretty much think alike, and training makes that happen!...They could be usin' th' heads in some kind a religious ceremony, or somethin', that, or to scare folks away from where they're hiding." He dropped the spent butt in the road. "It damn sure kept me from goin' back!"

"Our job's cut out for us, Rod." He looked across at Dempsey then. "We just might not be able to find 'em, you know that, don't ya?"

"Yeah, I know that." Breathed Dempsey. "But I've been a lawman long enough to know that sooner or later criminals make mistakes, and these bloodthirsty Bastards are criminals!...And Seth,...I don't believe in magic, either."

"Then we'll give it our best shot, literally!" Grinned Seth. "And that's what it's liable to take, too, our best shot!"

"And that's what worries me!" Said Dempsey. "We ain't huntin' no Crime Boss here, or a New York Assassin....Fact is, we don't know what we're huntin,...and our best might not be good enough!"

"Well, they're assassins well enough." Said Seth. "And a lot more dangerous than them from New York, they showed themselves,...these use th' dark for cover, and that's one a th' things I want a talk to ya about.... We'll have to know what we're doin, too, all th' time!...We start somethin', we finish it, no stopping to think about th' right or wrong of it, or if it's accordin' to th' law, we finish it!...We have to shoot a man, shoot 'im, don't hesitate, you do, he'll kill you, or me,...or both of us!...And like I said, I don't intend to make Laura a widow."

"I'll do my best, Seth." He sighed. "I like livin', too!"

"I know that, Rod. I'm just preparin' th' both of us!"

"You're worried, too, ain't ya?"

"Anything I don't understand, or can't see worries me, Rod....But, I got a say, this scares me some!...Never had to fight ghosts before....Now, let's ride a while, I'm tired a walking!" They mounted again and had just settled the animals back to a mile eating gallop when they saw the loaded farm wagon lumber its way off a side road onto theirs and start toward them.

They slowed their horses to a walk, and when the family got close, Dempsey raised his hand to stop them.

"Hello folks, how are ya?" He smiled and urged his horse alongside the wagon load of tied down furnishings, giving it the once-over before reaching out to shake Wheatfield's work-hardened hand. "I'm United States Marshal, Rod Dempsey."

"Name's Westly Wheatfield, Marshal." He said nervously, then turned to nod at his family. "My wife, Ethyl here, my little girl, Emily and my sons, Clyde and Amos."

"Pleased to meet you all." He nodded at Seth then, still sitting his horse on the road in front of the wagon. "That's Marshal Seth Mabry over there." He looked back at the load on the wagon. "Looks like you're pullin' up stakes, Mister Wheatfield, your land play out or somethin'?"

"Best farm land, I ever had." He said sadly.

"Then why leave it?"

"cause we're scared to stay anymore, Marshal. Somebody's killin' folks here, choppin' off their heads and such!...I ain't gonna stay and bury none a mine....My little girl done found one a them headless bodies th' other mornin' in th' square!...She ain't been th' same since....We're leavin'!"

"I'm real sorry to hear that, Sir....But that's why we're here, ya know, to find these killers."

"They's already been a Marshal here once, and he's dead now, too!...That's what'll happen to you, you go there."

At that point, Seth urged his horse up on the other side of the wagon where the boys were seated. "I bet you boys know about every crook and cranny on that farm, don't ya,...I know I did at your age?...I must a fished near about every creek and pond in that part a th' county....That what you do?"

"We fish all th' time!" Nodded Jason.

"I'll bet you see just about everything that goes on around ya, too?" And when they both nodded. "You ever remember seein' anybody that didn't belong there, people you never seen before,...anything like that?"

"Seen two men wearin' blankets once." Said Clyde. "Had em pulled up over their heads, looked funny, too."

"You seen 'em, huh?"

"Yeah, we both did." Nodded Jason.

"How long ago was this, do you remember?"

"Near about four months ago, now."

"Where'd you see all this?" Asked Wheatfield. "Ya never told me or your ma about it?"

"WE forgot till just now paw." Returned Jason. "But it was on Hick'ry branch!...But it was two men with blankets over their heads."

"Went all th' way to their feet, too!" Said Clyde excitedly. "They had funny lookin' shoes with strings holdin' 'em on their feet!"

"They see you?" Asked Seth.

"Yeah,...passed right in front of us, waded across th' crik and kept goin'!"

"They say anything?"

"Uh-uh,...we said hi to 'em, but they just looked at us and kept goin."

"You know who they was, Marshal?" Asked Wheatfield. "Think them was th' killers?"

"At this point, Mister Wheatfield, we don't know anything!" Said Dempsey as he glanced at Seth. "Is there a Monastery, or Church around here somewhere,...some Church elders wear smocks like that?" He was watching Wheatfield's worried expression as he asked the question.

"The nearest Church of any kind is in Tyler." Said Ms. Wheatfield, speaking for the first time as she glared at her husband. "We never go to any of them."

He looked at Seth again, seeing him shrug slightly, and then frowning himself, nodded at Wheatfield. "Seems a shame to be leaving good land to waste like this, Mister Wheatfield....You sure you can't wait till we get to th' bottom a this?"

"No, Sir, we won't!...Th' Devil's work is bein' done here now!...We want no part of it!"

"Then I thank you folks for talkin' with us." Sighed Dempsey, touching his hat. "I want a wish you luck somewhere else, to." He Nodded at Ms. Wheatfield and waved at the boys as Wheatfield whipped the team into motion. Once the wagon was past, he urged his horse in next to Seth.

"Guess we know what they look like now,...and what to look for!"

"What,...Monks?" Queried Seth with a sigh. "Monks do God's work, Rod."

"Yeah, you're right." He sighed again and grinned. "Monks wear smocks, it's all I could think of....They just built a new Church in Dallas, a Monastery,...or Mosque, as th' Judge called it. Anyway, it's a big domed building."

"Muslims." Nodded Seth. "Laura told me about 'em....But I don't think it's th' same thing."

"Is that a gut feelin'?"

"I don't know what it is, Rod....I just don't believe Muslims are cuttin' off people's heads."

"Neither do I, but if it ain't,...It's still a religious Cult a some kind!" He watched the distant departing wagon for a second then shrugged. "Don't know about you, but I still ain't discounting voodoo, it's a religion, too, a twisted one, I know....But according to that Louisiana story about th' thirteen murders, there was witnesses who claimed that people into voodoo wore them same robes!...Does that make sense?"

"You're askin' th' wrong man, Rod....Nothin' makes sense about this!"

"Well, I don't think that statement's a gut feeling!...And I'm startin' to understand how these killers can scare a town full a people, too!...It's getting to me, and we're only talkin' about it!"

"Well, don't get too bent out a shape, don't want a prove that farmer right!"

"Yeah." He frowned then. "Somethin' ain't right about it though....If those boys did see our killers that day,...why'd they let 'em live?"

"Soft spot for kids, maybe, who knows?...Maybe they was lookin' th' territory over, huntin' a place to hide?...But them boys was lucky that day, I think!...Could be our killers are so sure a themselves, they think folks would be too scared to say anything....Or,...they could a been Monks!"

"Possible, I guess." Sighed Dempsey. "But I don't think, probable."

"Me neither,...I think it's best we stick with this ritual thing you spoke of....If it is a Cult doin' these murders, it's for somethin' real special,...and I wish I knew what?"

"How th' hell are we gonna find 'em, when th' Sheriff, his Deputies, and th' Army can't?...That's what I want a know!"

"Won't know that till we do,...and we won't, sittin' around here jawin'!"

*   *   *

Alex Maynard had coffee ready by the time the deputies staggered in from the cellblock. "Finally!" He grinned, looking at each of them. "You sure must a slept well, you rattled th' windows out here."

"I could argue that point, Lieutenant!" Yawned Gibbs as he grabbed his cup.

"Same here, Lieutenant." Said Jeter, taking his coffee and sitting down in a chair along the wall. "Ever try and sleep in a sawmill?"

"Didn't bother me none!" Grinned Cliff. "Where'd you sleep, Boss?"

"Me?...What little I got was in this chair, business of law never sleeps, ya know!...Finish your coffee, and whatever else ya need to do, then go get your supper,...I want ya back in that Courthouse by six o'clock."

"Yes, sir, Lieutenant,...but is it okay if we run somethin' by ya, first?"

"Well, yeah,...shoot!"

"Well, Lieutenant," Began Gibbs with a look at the others. "We talked about all this over breakfast this mornin',...and we done come up with an idea."

Maynard got up from his chair and walked around his desk to sit on a corner of it. "Continue, Mister Gibbs, I'll listen to anything!...God knows I can't figure it out."

"Well,...th' way we see it, we done searched most a th' largest houses in Tyler, searched th' Churches, too, where th' preachers would let us!...What I'm sayin' is, we weren't really allowed to search them Churches, any of 'em, and they got a have big cellars in them big-ass buildings. Got other buildings on th' property, too, and we weren't allowed in them atall!"

"I know Gibbs, but we can't force our way onto Church property without probable cause, it just ain't done!...Without th' Pastor's permission, our hands are tied,...you all know that."

"We could with an open, floating bench warrant, one with Judge Gurney's name on it."

"A what?...An open, floating Bench Warrant?...Ain't no such thing, Mister Gibbs. Now, a Bench Warrant is an arrest warrant issued by a Judge, or th' Court, ordering the arrest of an offender. I guess it could be left open for any offender we might find,...it's also for when you don't behave yourself in a Courtroom....But it does not cover searching a Church without permission....How'd you come up with that?"

"I read law books, Lieutenant, not good enough, I guess....But if you could get th' Judge to issue a floating search warrant. And leave it open so you could fill it in as ya need to, well, it would cover every buildin' in town, includin' a Church!...Wouldn't it?"

"It would, and I have thought a that!...You're on th' right track here, all of ya. Good thinkin'!...We do have probable cause, by th' way, but out of respect for Church privacy, I let it go." He looked up at them then. "It's different now, we got nothin' to go on....Two months and twelve unsolved murders, and we know nothing!...I'll see th' Judge while you eat your supper, you can do your search tomorrow."

"I've been doin' some thinkin' today myself,...and there's still one area in this county we ain't searched yet."

"Th' Wilderness?"

"The Wilderness!" He nodded. "There's forty or fifty square miles of thick, overgrown, and damn near impassable swampland between here and Bullard, and all of it's East of th' Colonel's ranch!...We don't know what's in there, could be any number of old houses big enough to hide them Bastards!...I'm thinkin' that as soon as th' Colonel comes in again, I'll borrow a couple dozen cowboys and we'll go have a look!"

"We talked about that, too, Lieutenant." Said Jeter. "It'd take that many men a week to go two miles in there a'foot!"

Maynard go up to go pull on his hat before looking back at them. "That might be far enough, too damn late to do any good, but far enough... because I got a feelin' they're close in out there!...Likely be gone when we get there, but we'll know! You men go get your supper now, and remember,... don't go in that Courthouse in a wad. Somebody's watchin' what we do, when we do it!...There's somethin' th' four of you can do while you're there, too....Come up with a list a places that Son of a Bitch could be watchin' us from, we migh a missed somethin'."

"When do you expect that Marshal, Boss?" Queried Walt.

"Any time now, I guess!...Got a wire two days ago, sayin' he was on his way,...by horseback, I guess! Can't be too worried about all this, or he'd been here two days ago!...We can't expect too much from 'im, he can't do more than we ain't done all ready!" He turned to look out through the afternoon window.

"Man can't fight what he can't find!" He said dejectedly. "He'll learn that, too!...Can't defend his self against somethin' he can't see, neither, and he's gonna learn that th' hard way, I think,...just like the other one did."

"You're gonna explain all a that to 'im, ain't ya...what he's up against?"

"Oh, yeah, He'll know everything we know,...which is nothin'!...And he might have some ideas, we didn't think of, too, and we could sure use 'em. So we'll give 'im th' courtesy he deserves, after all,...he carries a bigger stick than we do!"

Okay, Lieutenant." Said Gibbs as they all got up to place their cups on the desk.

Nodding, Maynard opened the door, and they all followed him out.

CHAPTER SEVEN

It was close to midnight when they began seeing the remote houses, most of which were of milled siding, with a few log structures in the mix. Some sported whitewashed picket fences around the yard, while others only chicken wire stretched between posts. But these dwellings soon became closer together, the closer to town they came, and all of them had their barking dogs and chickens raising hell in the yard.

They slowed their horses to a walk along the wide road into Tyler. The houses were all dark, and still some distance apart that far out, but occupied both sides of the street. A few of the dogs began running into the road to bark and nip at the legs of the tired horses.

"Guess we're here!" Said Dempsey tiredly. "Reminds me of th' streets a Dallas,...got no use for dogs!"

"Dogs let ya know somebody's around th' house." Replied Seth. "Keeps th' crooks away....Ain't got 'em penned up, cause they're afraid! Odds are, somebody's watchin' us ride by from every one a these houses, got a loaded gun in his hand, too!"

"That's why I'm glad th' moon's out!" Said Dempsey. "We look like cowboys."

"What say ya, we still gonna wait till light to go in?"

"I'd think so....Like you said, some trigger-happy Deputy might take us for th' killers! Everything seems to happen at night anyway....Never can tell, though, we ride in now, might catch somebody in the act!...Now, that would be luck!" He shifted his weight in the saddle. "But I think it's best nobody knows we're here yet, if the killers do have somebody watchin' the Sheriff's movements, we might tip 'im off to somethin'!"

"Thinkin' like a lawman now, Rod!"

"I hope that's a compliment."

"It is!...You're a good man, Rod, and my friend, and now that we're here, I'll tell ya what I think!....There's somethin' very strange and evil goin' on here, and we are ridin' blind right into th' middle of it! The only thing we know about these killers is that they're butchers, they kill with very sharp weapons from the cover of darkness....We won't be able to see 'em, so we likely won't even know they're around."

"I realize that, Seth, what's th' point?"

"Getting out of this alive, Rod!...Just remember this,...when we're in th' dark, look hard at it, if somethin' else is there, it'll move and you'll see it. It might be so slight, you'll think you didn't see it at all, but you'll see it!...If you see it, shoot it, don't take time to think, don't wonder if it's real, just shoot! It could mean your life, and Rod,...don't worry that it might be an innocent person there,...innocent people don't lurk in th' dark. You hesitate, yo-..."

"Dead!" Interrupted Dempsey. "I understand all that, Seth!"

"I hope so....You'll have to know the difference in the tricks dark can play, and what might be real. We have to think alike, watch the other's blind side and at the same time, try to think like these killers do!...Whatever it is, whoever they are,...we have to stop them!...They got a be insanely evil to do all this anyway."

"You got that right!" Replied Dempsey, turning to look at another of the darkened houses. "You're right, too!...There's a man against that house there with a gun in his hand, I just saw 'im move."

"I see 'im....I'm beginning to think this is a fair-sized place, too, houses everywhere out there!...Wonder where town is?"

"Can't be far, I can make out what looks like Church steeples off yonder, got a be close."

"One would think!...What you want a do when we get there?"

"I guess, find th' Livery and get some sleep, you up to it?"

"Have been all night. I could use a bath and a shave, too!...I'm used to shavin' every day."

"Hotel's got bath tubs, we'll check in first thing in the mornin',...clean up before callin' on th' Sheriff."

"Makes sense to me." Sighed Seth. "This bein' th' main road in, ought a be a Livery on it!"

*   *   *

"Not a bad lookin' town." Mused Seth as they walked out of the Windsor Hotel onto the boardwalk. "Then again, everything looks better after a good bath and shave."

"I'd say so." Nodded Dempsey as they stared across the square's expanse at the Courthouse and surrounding shops. "Nothin' movin' much,...half th' stores ain't open yet. A little odd, ain't it?"

"Not when you're afraid, I think....And this is one town that's plenty scared."

Dempsey pulled his pocket watch and looked at it. "Eight o'clock,... most towns would be alive already."

"Café's open down there, just saw a man go in. Want a eat before we call on th' good Sheriff,...might be too busy later?"

"Are you serious, I'm starving, come on." They stepped off the boardwalk and started across the square. "I think it's a good idea nobody knows we're lawmen, Seth." He reached and removed the badge, placing it in his shirt pocket. "If somebody is watchin' things around here, a badge might be a hindrance."

"And a target." Grinned Seth. "But I ain't no lawman, Rod, remember that!" He said, still studying the buildings surrounding the large square.

"On this trip, you are....You did bring your badge, didn't ya?"

"In my pocket, yeah."

"Then you're a lawman. You got all the privileges, remember that." They stepped up to the boardwalk again and into Norma's café to stop in the doorway and scan the half-empty room.

"Law's already here." Commented Seth, nodding at the five men across the room from them.

"Looks like,...come on, Seth, let's sit by th' window here." They removed their hats and seated themselves to watch the middle-aged, tired looking woman as she came to take their orders

"Well," She said as she stopped at the table. "New faces in town, that's a change! What'll it be, gents?" She asked, looking from one to the other. "Steak and eggs, you look hungry?"

"And a pot a strong coffee!" Nodded Seth.

"Ain't seen you two around, ya just get here?" She asked as she wrote on the pad. "Don't mind me, I'm just nosey as hell."

"Got in last night." Grinned Dempsey. "Town looks dead out there, what's that all about?"

"Twelve murders, that's what!" She leaned down closer to them then. "Found th' bodies right across the square yonder!...Had their heads cut off and their blood drained out,...most horrible thing I ever saw!" She straightened and turned. "Coffee on th' way, Steak and eggs comin' up!"

"Twelve bodies, Seth, not eleven!...If it's th' same Cult as that in Louisiana, one more and they'll be out a here!...You're right!" He sighed. "We might not find 'em."

"Then we best introduce ourselves to th' Sheriff." Agreed Seth. "See what we can add to th' problem."

"Yeah," Nodded Dempsey as Norma placed the hot pot of coffee and two cups on the table. "Are you, Norma?" He asked as she started to leave.

"Every overweight pound of me, Dearie."

"Well, Norma,...would one a those men over there be Sheriff Maynard?"

"Got his back to ya there!" She nodded, looking toward the table. "Other four's his deputies....Sorry excuses for th' law, to!....Ain't done a thing to find them murderers."

"Would you mind tellin' 'im, we'd like a word with 'im?"

"I guess not." She ambled over to their table and bent to talk with Maynard, who turned in his chair to peer at them, and then said something to his deputies before getting up to come toward them.

"I'm Sheriff Maynard," He said as he studied them. "Do I know you?"

"Not yet!" Replied Dempsey, reaching into his shirt for the badge. "I'm Federal Marshal, Rod Dempsey," He nodded at Seth then. "This is Marshal Seth Mabry. Will you be going to your office when you're done here?"

"Yes, sir, we will." He said, shaking both their hands. "Been expectin' you for a couple a days now, so I don't know how much help you'll be at this point....But I need all I can get!"

"That's what we hear, where's your office?"

"Turn right and down th' boardwalk, it's in th' next block."

"See ya there."

Nodding, Maynard went back to his table just as their own breakfast arrived.

"Enjoy, boys!" Smiled Norma as she placed the plates in front of them. "What do you think of our esteemed Sheriff Maynard?"

"Can't answer that yet,...Thank you, Norma."

"Man looks capable enough." Said Seth as he began cutting the meat. "A mite wary of us, I think."

"No man likes the idea, he needs help doin' his job....But there ain't a lawman alive wouldn't need help on this one."

"Us included!" Nodded Seth as he ate.

"Speaking of which, I'll need to wire th' Judge that we're here....I'll do that later."

*   *   *

Maynard and deputies were in his office whey they walked in, and as Dempsey went to shake his hand again, Seth studied the office and it's furnishings, what little it had, save a gun-rack, six occupied chairs along the wall and his desk, it was fairly bare,...and the distrustful, expressionless faces of the four deputies was what he expected to see.

"Marshal Dempsey," Said Maynard then, meet my deputies, that first man is Gibbs, next to him there is Walt, Jeter and Cliff,...all good men, served under me in th' war."

"Pleasure meetin you all." Said Dempsey, nodding at them. "I'm Marshal Rod Dempsey, my partner there is Marshal, Seth Mabry, and now," He said, looking back at Maynard. "I need to know everything you know about these mysterious murders?"

"That would be nothing, Marshal!...Whoever's doin' this leaves no clues, no tracks, no nothin' to go on!...We've searched every street, every house and alleyway in th' city." He sat down on the desk's corner while he rolled and lit his smoke. "Whoever they are, they're able to take their victims without a sound, nobody sees or hears anything. We don't even know they're gone till we find their headless corpse out there in the square, that, or somebody reports somebody missing. We don't know how they're able to do that without bein' seen by somebody, I've had men on patrol most every night since th' first murder."

"Norma,...waitress at th' café, said there was twelve murders, we only knew of eleven. When was th' last one?"

"Two mornings ago, a young prostitute name of Darlene Suggs, found another one a my Deputies yesterday morning, he was number twelve!... Eight of the victims were women, but Darlene was cut up more than the others. None a th' other women were naked, neither, but she was."

"The others fully dressed?"

"Except for underclothes, yeah, at least they were covered....Darlene was completely naked, her head was gone, and she was laid open from crotch to rib-cage,...ugliest sight I've ever seen." He cleared his throat then. "I never want a see it again."

"You knew her, didn't ya, Sheriff?"

"Several times, yeah....A sweet girl!...A farmer's little girl found her body that mornin', hit 'er pretty hard!"

"We heard about that." Nodded Dempsey.

"Heard about it?"

"We met th' Wheatfields on th' road yesterday, they were loaded up and leaving."

"I thought as much,...they're just one of many that's gone now."

"What are you doin' now with your investigation?"

"My deputies are spending their nights in Judge Gurney's Courthouse office facing the Courtyard, they can see the whole square from there,... and I have a search warrant to search all three Churches, and their holdings today. They refused us access th' first time." He shrugged then. "Now, Marshal,...we don't really believe our killers are hiding out in a Church, but then again, they could be!...There's buildings on those properties that are big enough to hide a couple dozen men."

Dempsey rolled and lit a cigarette as Maynard talked, and when he was done. "Here is what little we know, Sheriff....The two wheatfield boys told us they saw two men dressed like Monks while they were fishing about four months ago, does that mean anything to you?"

Maynard frowned at him for a second. "Nobody we've talked to has mentioned anything like that!...We don't have a Catholic Church in Tyler, and I'd think they'd be the only ones to wear robes like that,...but then again, I don't think they'd be called Monks,...would they?"

"I don't know that, either." Sighed Dempsey. "Do you have any ideas, or theories, because we really need some?"

"Other than ghosts, no, sir!"

"Well, we have rattled that cage ourselves."

"Ain't nobody could do more than we're doin', Marshal." Stated Jeter flatly, and at that moment Seth opened the door and went out onto the boardwalk. "And I don't think no one or two U.S. Marshals is gonna make a Difference, especially an old man like that partner a yours!...You should a brought a more able-bodied man with ya, we're dealin' with more here than just drunks!"

Dempsey frowned at Jeter for a moment, then grinned. "Mister,...Jeter, is it?...First off, we're not here to make any of you men look bad, we were sent for because you needed help!...And that old man out there singlehandedly brought down a Crime Syndicate in Dallas two years ago, when none of th' rest of us could!"

"That's enough, Jeter!" Warned Maynard.

"Oh, no, Sheriff, that's okay. All of you need to know who Seth Mabry is!" He looked at the gun on Jeter's hip then. "You any good with that pistol, Jeter?"

"Good enough,...what's that got a do with anything?"

"How about you,...Gibbs?...Walt, Cliff, you all any good?"

"We can hold our own, Marshal." Said Gibbs. "Let's leave it at that!"

"Can't, you brought it up!...Now, I know you all resent us bein' here, you think we might show you up by solving this case when you couldn't!... You are far from wrong about that!...We have a job to do, same as you, we don't do it for fame and fortune, and we don't do it alone. We work with local law enforcement to help them solve it and once it is, we give credit where it's due!...Now, back to Seth Mabry!...On the very best day the four of you men ever had, if all four of you were to brace that man at the same time,...he would kill all four of you, and walk away whistling!"

"With all due respect, Marshal," Laughed Gibbs. "I don't think so, we're better than that!"

"That's enough, Gibbs, they're here to help us, not kill us!...What's your theory, Marshal, we're runnin' out a time?"

"Quicker than you think, too!" Said Dempsey. "About five years ago this same thing was happening in Louisiana. There were thirteen dead women and men, all with their heads removed, and all of 'em found on th' front steps a th' Courthouse....According to the story, the last victim was a woman with a baby, they took 'em both!...I didn't remember that part till just now....Anyway, they left no clues, no blood trail, no nothing to identify 'em,...the murders just stopped after that. No one was ever caught, and there were never any suspects!"

"Just like here!" Voiced Maynard. "It's got a be th' same bunch then.... Why are they doin' it?"

"Seth and me believe it's a Cult of some kind,...and everything points to voodoo."

"Voodoo?" Grinned Maynard. "Is that stuff for real...Black Magic?"

"To folks in Louisiana and Mississippi, it's all too real....They've been rumored to sacrifice animals, and people in black rituals, and use the heads and skulls on poles stuck in th' swamp to scare people away!...That could be what's goin' on here and if it is, your number thirteen victim will be another woman with a child. We need to find that woman before they do,...so I suggest you check with every Doctor in town for any patients with a child below the age of four,...and hope there's not too many! I don't know the age of the one that was taken!"

Maynard thought about that for a good long moment before nodding his head. "Son of a Bitch!" He said and shook his head. "After what you said, I'm beginning to make some sense out a this thing." He looked at Gibbs then.

"Do that right now, Mister Gibbs, and don't look like you're on a mission!"

"You got it, Lieutenant."

They watched him leave, and he looked back at Dempsey just as Seth came back. "What if it ain't voodoo, we're lookin' at here, Marshal?" He asked, nodding at Seth at the same time.

"Maybe it's not, but it has to be a Cult of some kind, Sheriff, and these murders are for some kind of a ritual, ain't a doubt in my mind about that!...

What I'd like one of your men to do now, is go to all the business places on th' square out there, find out if anybody dressed like a Monk has been seen in, or around their store in th' last four months. I say this, because th' Wheatfield boys saw two of 'em, and they were seen in Louisiana, too."

"Jeter!" Jeter nodded and quickly left the office. "What else, Marshal?"

"Well, since you're not able to see 'em leave th' bodies, Id say somebody in town is tellin' 'em where and when it's safe to do what they do, so...We think you are being watched, Sheriff."

"Hell, Marshal,...we already know that!...We just can't find th' Bastard, or where he might a hid?"

"He's watchin' from somewhere high up, Sheriff." Said Seth. "He'll need to be able to see th' square and most a th' homes and streets around it!"

"I know that, too, and we have searched every building with a top floor that's out there,...so if you have any suggestions, I'd sure like to hear 'em!"

"All right,...what's the highest point in town,...I ain't talkin' about no Church steeple here?"

That would have to be the tower on top a th' Courthouse, but there ain't nothin' up there but a-..."

"Clock." Said Seth, cutting him off. "A man with a long field glass could see just about everything....I noticed last night that the clock is lit up at night, got a lantern of some such behind the numerals and hands, really makes 'em stand out!...Somebody lights them lamps at night, so I'd guess there's plenty a room up there to hide a man."

"Check that out, Walt."

"On my way, Boss!"

"You're an observant man, Marshal, I've been lookin' at that clock for twenty years, and checkin' my watch afterward. That never crossed my mind."

"At what intervals have the bodies been showin' up?" Asked Dempsey.

"I don't know, not more than three or four days, why?"

"Because they are hunting number thirteen right now!...And I think they'll try to take her tonight, or maybe tomorrow night."

"If they do, they'll want a be sure none of us are around, so how will they know that?"

"Only one way they could know." Replied Seth. "They have a signal, and that brings us back to your spy."

"How does he do it?"

Seth looked at the lantern on the wall peg then nodded and went to take it down and light it. "Can I borrow one a your wanted posters?" And when Maynard took one out of the drawer and gave it to him, he went back to the wall and held it where the light was on that wall, then used the poster to block it from the wall a few times.

"Morse code!" Said Maynard quickly. "Billy Gaye's our spy!"

"Who's Billy Gaye?" Queried Dempsey.

"Telegrapher!...He could use that light like a telegraph key. Late at night, no one would notice it!...If they did, they wouldn't think anything about it, they'd think it was wind getting' in or something." He looked at Dempsey then. "It has to be him, he replaced old man Weathers almost three months ago."

"Want me to go get 'im, Lieutenant?" Asked Cliff, pushing to his feet. "I know where he is."

"On what charge?" Asked Dempsey. "Suspicion?...let's wait till your man gets back, if that is where the spy spends his nights, there'll be some evidence of it. Catch him in the act and then arrest 'im, maybe we can find where th' rest of 'em are."

"Yeah, you're right!" Breathed Dempsey. "He'll damn sure tell us, too!... It's settled then, we wait!...What are your plans for th' night, Marshal, nothin's gonna happen till then anyway?"

"What do you think, Seth?"

"I'd like to have a talk with those preachers, one of 'em might have some background on people like these,...if what they're doin' is based on a religion of some kind?"

"Sounds good to me." Nodded Dempsey. He turned back to Maynard then. "What was Marshal Jones working on?"

"He was on his way to do the same thing, that and talk with th' Doctors, or Surgeon at th' Fort. Said it would take one to remove a head that clean!...He took Stan Webb with 'im to watch his back....They were victims four and five."

"They went after dark?"

"Close to eleven." He nodded. "Didn't make sense to me, but he said it would be past th' Pastor's meditation time, and he'd be more willing to talk."

"So, what do you think happened?"

"Accordin' to Reverend Peters at th' Methodist Church, they never got there!...I believe they either stumbled on to a kidnapping in progress, or that fuckin' Billy Gaye warned th' bastards they was there!"

"Henry Jones was a seasoned manhunter!" Said Dempsey angrily. "Don't make sense they could a killed 'im without a shot bein' fired....Didn't you hear one, anything at all?"

"No shots were fired, Marshal,...we would a heard it!...And they was likely too far away to hear a yell. They turned up in the square out there two mornings later, headless, and without their guns." He moved in front of Dempsey then. "And please, sir,...don't stand in my office and talk to me like it's my fault they're dead!...I lost a deputy that was also my friend that night!...Besides," He said, turning away to stare at the wall. "I already blame myself,...I should a sent more men with 'em."

"I ain't blamin' you, Sheriff, Henry was my friend, too, that's all."

Maynard stared at him a moment before looking at the floor. "I'm at a breaking point, Marshal." He went back to his desk and sat down on it. "This thing has got me at the end of my rope, I'm mad as hell!" He sighed then heavily. "I try not to show it in front of the other men,...and Cliff, you keep your mouth shut!...But I'm frustrated....I don't know what to do, that I ain't done already."

"Ain't none of us ever seen anything like this, Sheriff, let alone know how to fight it!...And just so you know, I'm mad, too!...Now shake it off, it's gonna take us all to catch these Bastards!"

"We might not catch 'em at all." Reminded Seth. "Rod there is right, Sheriff, it's gonna take us all."

Maynard looked up, and then nodded. "What ya got in mind, Marshal?"

"First, I think it's best nobody knows me and Seth are lawmen. And second, before any decisions are made about what to do, we ought a wait till that clock tower is checked out. If it is th' hiding place, your job will be to arrange a welcome for our Mister Gaye, or whoever he is?"

"I'll consider that a pleasure!" He nodded. "Okay, we got all day to wait, it seems! Can I offer you some coffee, water, or maybe something stronger?" They all looked up then as Walt rushed back into the office.

"Found this up there, Boss, it's a telescope, found it rolled up in a rag and hid against th' wall!...That's where he's been hidin' all right!...Even found rolled-up blankets there."

Maynard took the long-glass from him and looked it over before giving it to Dempsey. "Anybody see ya go up there, Walt?"

"Don't think so, I was careful."

"How big is the light up there, Walt?" Queried Dempsey.

"Hell, I don't know,...it's just a couple a big, coal-oil lanterns as far as I can tell. Got a curved piece a tin attached behind 'em, I guess to reflect more light on th' clocks."

"Any other piece a tin laying around?" Asked Seth. "Somethin' a man might use to block out th' light if he wanted?"

"Yeah, I seen one." He frowned at them then. "What do you mean, block out th' light If he wanted,...Marshal, I don't-..."

"If he wanted to use the light for a signal, Walt, think about it!" Demanded Maynard.

"You mean, lika a,…Billy Gaye, by God!…You think it's him doin' this?"

"Could be!" Nodded Maynard. "Won't know for sure till we catch th' son of a bitch!…There any place on them stairs a couple a you could hide, we need to catch 'im up there?"

"There's a door about half way up, on a flat part a th' staircase, got a be a store-room!"

"That ought a do it!" He grinned. "You two best get some sleep now, cause that's where you're gonna be tonight!…And don't let th' Bastard get away, and don't kill 'im! He's gonna tell us where the rest of 'em are." They watched the two men shuffle off into the cellblock before Maynard turned to Seth with a nod.

"I have to hand it to you, sir, you solved one a my biggest frustrations in all this!…It never crossed my mind that th' clock tower was his hidin' place. I thank ya."

"No need, Sheriff." Nodded Seth as he rolled and lit a smoke and then went to sit down in one of the deputy's vacated chairs. Leaving Maynard to look at Dempsey with bewilderment.

"He don't cotton much to slaps on th' back,…Alex, is it?…It's just his way."

Maynard moved in closer to him then. "He's a strange man all right, Marshal, but smart as hell, I think."

"Yes he is." Nodded Dempsey, and was about to go sit down himself when Mister Gibbs returned and changed his mind.

"What did you find out?" Asked Maynard as he stopped to face them.

"Well, Lieutenant, accordin' to th' records, both of 'em, Doc Welch, and Doc Richards,…there was nineteen women gave birth in th' last year and a half, ten of 'em was girl babies." He looked at his notes then. "Seven more gave birth between then and two years ago, all boys."

"Ten women with girl babies." Nodded Dempsey.

"That ain't countin' them that deliver their own, Marshal, got no records on them, them delivered by mid-wives neither!…How we gonna find 'em all?"

"That's to be determined….You get names and addresses?"

"Right here!"

"Think you can bring 'em in, or convince 'em to come in on their own?"

"Depends on their old man, I guess, if they're married?…But, yeah, I can do it!"

Nodding, Dempsey looked at Maynard. "Ya got a meetin' hall, or a town hall?"

"Well, yeah,…back room at th' Windsor, City Council meets there."

"That'll do,…take 'em all there, Mister Gibbs, but you better make arrangements first!...When you go for 'em, ask 'em if they know of any woman that gave birth on their own ?"

"Then what?" Asked Gibbs. "How we gonna watch 'em?"

"You see any of th' Colonel's men in town today?" Asked Maynard.

"Couple of 'em at th' café." Returned Gibbs. But that was thirty minutes ago."

"Go see,…If they're still there, send 'em to th' ranch and tell th' Colonel I need a dozen men here by five o'clock today."

"If they ain't?"

"Come back here, I'll send Cliff out there.…At any rate, I want 'em fully armed!...You can start rounding up these women and children after that."

"On my way, Lieutenant." He opened the door to leave. "Here's Jeter, Sir." He let the Deputy in before leaving.

"No Monks have ever been seen around here, Lieutenant." Said Jeter, looking at them both.

"Okay,…catch up with Gibbs and give 'im a hand, he went to Norma's, then to th' Windsor."

"I'm gone!" He quickly left and jogged back down the boardwalk.

"Looks like we wait." Sighed Maynard as he shrugged at Dempsey. "Seems that's all we been doin' lately."

"We got work in progress now, Alex,…we're getting' somewhere." Said Dempsey. "We got no choice but to wait till dark, that's when this bunch works,…besides, we have to give Gibbs time to get these women into custody,…with no spy in that tower to warn 'em tonight, maybe they'll make a mistake!"

"Praise th' Lord!" Breathed Maynard. "Let it be so?"

"You wait here,…me and Seth are going to Church.…You ready, Seth?"

*   *   *

"This ain't gonna be easy, Seth." Said Dempsey as they walked around pedestrians on the boardwalk. "A preacher can be a tight-lipped person at times."

"Only when someone confesses a crime, Rod, that would be in confidence.…And, maybe not, too. Seems to me, he'd be just as scared at what's goin' on here as everybody else in town, some could be in his congregation.…I think, that between th' three of 'em,…we ought a find out somethin' we don't know."

"Like what we're lookin' for?"

"Exactly."

"We're pretty much together on it bein' a Cult a some kind, right?"

"I think it has to be,...voodoo, maybe, maybe somethin' else!...It's the way these folks are killed that worries me, the missing heads would tie in with voodoo, but it could also tie in with other rituals. That's what we got a find out."

"Most of the stores are open, at least. Different look from this morning."

"People need supplies."

They walked the remaining quarter of a mile in the shade of spreading elm and pine trees to finally open, and go through a wrought-iron, walk-in gate that was nestled between two limestone pillars of carefully-placed stones.

"Somebody's quite th' gardener!" Commented Dempsey as they walked up the circle-shaped, stone walkway and up the, also stone steps of the Methodist Church.

"Big place!" Remarked Seth, looking up the sheer face of the building.

Dempsey took the short, cast-iron mallet and gave the hanging bell-shaped gong a hit, and the vibrating sound was loud as it echoed around the building,...and a few minutes later, one of the twelve-foot tall double doors swung inward and they were greeted by a middle-aged man in a white robe that was worn over a pair of black trousers. The robe was tied at the waist with a black sash.

"The Church is always open, Gentlemen, no need to ring for assistance." He stepped back and gestured them inside with an extended arm. "Please, pray at your leisure."

"We are sorry, sir," Said Dempsey as they both removed their hats. "I am United States Marshal, Rod Dempsey, and this is Marshal, Seth Mabry.... We're here to talk with Pastor Peters,...it's important."

"I'm so sorry, but the Reverend is resting in his chambers."

"Wake him up, please....Tell 'im it concerns the murders in town here."

"That is a terrible thing. Yes, do come in while I wake him." And when they were on the polished stone floor of the Cathedral, the elder shuffled off down the long aisle between the many rows of hardwood pews and disappeared through a draped doorway.

"Look at this place!" Said Dempsey, his voice echoing in the large, empty room. "Reminds me of a castle in pictures I've seen." At that moment, they saw the elder returning with an older man in suit-coat and pants and when they got close, the Elder bowed slightly and shuffled back down the aisle, his sandals making small slapping sounds as he walked.

"Gentlemen, I am Reverend Peters, how may I help you?" He shook their hands as he spoke. "This is concerning the tragedies in our city?"

"Yes, Sir, it does....I am Marshal Rod Dempsey, this is Marshal Seth Mabry. We'd like ask you a few questions about it."

"Of course,...it's a horrific thing, so devastating!...Almost my entire congregation is afraid to attend church right now!" He sighed then. "I have been praying for the madness to end."

"We want a end it, too, Reverend, and that's why we're here."

"I don't understand?"

"We have a theory to run by ya....We believe these murders are bein' committed by some sort of religious Cult, specifically voodoo!...Or it could be somethin' totally different. That's why we'd like your thoughts on it."

"I have thought about it!" He sighed then. "I have given it a lot of thought, in fact." He nodded then. "Please, we can be more comfortable in my office." They followed him down the aisle and through the drapes to finally enter a large, uncluttered room, occupied by an oaken desk with a lone figurine depicting Christ's Crucifixion. Behind the desk was a large, spring-loaded, cushioned armchair and in front, a half-dozen straight-backed chairs. The walls were lined with shelves loaded with books and other religious figurines.

"Please, sit, won't you?" He gestured at the chairs, and as they seated themselves, reached to take a book from a shelf behind the desk and sat down.

"Marshal, ah, Dempsey,...I came to this country twenty years ago, and I brought most of these old books with me on the boat, at great expense, I might add....I helped build this Church, with the help from a group of Wichita Indians, and a few good men from town....The Indians, poor souls were starved for the word of God!" He looked around at the bare room then, and sighed.

"They were living with only meager supplies in what we would call, poverty today. Yet they were happy, and very open with their hospitality.... That is what I hope to project here!" He looked intently at them then.

"I do not think, voodoo is happening in Tyler,...In fact, the only country where voodoo is a wide-spread, ah, religion of sorts, is on the Continent of Africa....It was actually introduced in certain parts of this country by African Slaves. But the practice is very territorial, particularly in the state of Louisiana, and I believe, some parts of lower Mississippi. A voodoo sect has never been known to relocate once established....And that makes it is very unlikely they are here."

"Then what are we up against?" Queried Dempsey.

With a look upward, Peters made a sign of the Cross. "May God forgive me?" He looked back at them then, and opened the book to the bookmarked page. "I can almost tell you for certain that it is Satanism." And seeing the frustration on their faces.. "Witchcraft, Marshal,…Devil worship!...Don't tell me you've never heard of it?"

"Well, Reverend,…I'm afraid not!...We've read the Bible, and had it read to us, we know about th' Devil, how he was banished from heaven and such but,…who would worship that son-…,…sorry, Reverend." He said, looking at Seth's grinning face. "No, sir,…we can't picture anybody wanting to go to hell that bad!"

"They don't want to go to hell, Marshal, they want to bring Lucifer back to earth in human form!" He chuckled then. "Let me explain the difference between Satanism and voodoo. Voodoo uses fear and magic spells to gain wealth and power, control over others who believe and practice the religion. The spells, or hexes, as some call them, is performed by a voodoo Priestess who conjures up the magic. She uses dolls made of straw and bound with twine. She then gives them to her followers who in turn use them to enhance their own wealth and even romance."

"Should a Sect be threatened, or a disbeliever is vocally denouncing them, she will have a follower provide her with something personal, like a bit of hair from that person. She'll braid the hair and use it in place of twine to tie dolls with, place a pin through the doll's heart then have the follower place it in the other person's home, usually in the bed….Now here is the intriguing part. If that victim believes in the power of voodoo, even in his subconscious, even if his mind rejects it, the belief alone could cause his death!...Have there been any dolls found here?"

"Nothing like that was mentioned, no, sir." Dempsey cleared his throat then. "Okay, so we might not be looking for a voodoo Cult here, but whoever they are, Devil workers, or somethin' else, there was a case in Louisiana where this exact same thing was happening. They murdered and beheaded thirteen women and men. Number thirteen was a woman with child. Their bodies were never found!...The murders stopped then, and they never found those responsible. Left no clues at all, they just disappeared…. Could this be the same bunch?"

"I would say, it's very possible, yes!...They perform a ritual as they pray for Satan's return to rule the world. There is chanting as they say his name over and over again, and it is culminated with the sacrifice of a girl child on an altar while the male followers rape the mother atop the same altar. Once it is over, the mother's head is removed and her blood drained."

"My God, Reverend!" Blurted Dempsey as he about gagged.

"What's the purpose of takin' the heads, Reverend?" Queried Seth.

"Sometimes the thirteen heads are placed atop posts all around the altar,…supposedly, to give Lucifer a choice as to who he might want to appear as when he arrives. The blood of all the victims is poured from a cauldron into a trench that encircles the altar."

"Getting back to the heads, you said sometimes?"

"Yes, sometimes they don't use the heads at all. Each Cult is different, depending on the whims of the High Priest, I suppose….Anyway, toward the end, the High Priest will sprinkle a powder of some kind on the rivulet of blood, causing it to burst into flames as the chanting reaches fever pitch….Then it's over."

"Why are they doing it all again here?" Asked Dempsey.

"They do it over and over again, who knows?...They know the Devil isn't going to appear! His influence may be present, but no amount of chanting, death or sacrifice will bring Satan from his fiery hell, so they keep trying!... And they will until they're stopped,…it's all in this book right here!"

"What's your opinion of 'em?" Asked Seth.

"They're murdering heathens living off the fear and wealth of their victims, and they are thieves as well."

"How would you suggest we find 'em?"

"I have no idea,…but a Cult like this survives on secrecy, and depending on it's size, would need someplace to live and perform their rituals. That place will usually be an abandoned structure somewhere, one so old that it has been forgotten, or one that is so well hidden in overgrowth that no one can see it."

"Which means that we might not find them before they take victim number thirteen." Sighed Dempsey. "We thank you for your time, Reverend Peters."

"How would you look for 'em, Reverend?" Asked Seth as he got to his feet.

"I'd ask someone that has lived here for generations."

"Indians." Nodded Seth. "Anyone in particular?"

"Joseph Peters….He's a Wichita and twenty years my senior when I arrived here!...He actually took my name as a form of respect….He has a log house in the Flint Basin, some eighteen miles southeast of town. His cabin is close to the railroad there, and he speaks good English, as well."

"Like Rod there said, you have our thanks." Said Seth, reaching across the desk to shake his hand, as did Dempsey, and as they turned to leave.

"One more thing that could help you, Marshal….For some reason, the full moon has something in common with the Satanic rituals….It's mentioned in the book, but gives no meaningful explanation. Perhaps knowing this, it will give you time to find them….May God be with you in your effort to find and destroy these vile advocates of Satan. We shall all pray for you every day."

"Thanks again." Nodded Seth, and they both left, both in deep thought as they opened and closed the tall doors and walked back to the wrought-iron gate.

"Seth,…all I can tell we accomplished here, is a lot more to worry about!"

"Oh, I don't know about that, Rod….We know it ain't voodoo." He closed the gate behind them then stood and looked back at the Church. "Is there a full moon this month?"

"Don't ask me, I never thought about them things much."

"It was three quarters full last night, means we might have another day or two to find these people."

"If he's right about that part of it?"

"He said it was in th' book, what have we got to lose?"

"Just some poor woman and her little girl, that's all….Where to from here?"

"Two more preachers in town, maybe they'll tell us somethin' else."

CHAPTER EIGHT

Maynard was in his office when they got back, and as they hung their hats on the rack, he sat down on the corner of his desk and waited for them to sit down.

"Well, how'd you do?" He asked curiously.

"Th' good Reverend Peters more or less confirmed our suspicions." Said Dempsey. "Knocked our voodoo theory out a th' picture, and replaced it with somethin' worse!...And after he gave us th' facts on it, we both agreed with 'im."

"Well, what is it?"

"Devil worshippers." Said Seth as him and Dempsey both rolled and lit a smoke. "And for what it means, Sheriff, we never heard of it, neither!"

"It's truth though." Stated Dempsey. "He got it right out of an old book on th' subject. Told all about their rituals, beheading their victims, all of it....It seems they're crazy enough to believe they can conjure up old Satan with a ritual. The victim's heads and blood are all part of it, except for the girl baby, they murder it on the altar as th' ritual ends. Guess that's when Satan's supposed to make his entry."

"Supposed to?"

"Seems all their rituals are failures, so they relocate and do it all over again."

"Sons a Bitches!" Voiced Maynard angrily. "Don't guess you asked 'em about th' baptisms?"

"Completely forgot about that."

"I'll send Gibbs when he wakes up."

"They bring in any a th' women?" Queried Dempsey.

"Some,...I told 'em to knock off and get some sleep, they been up since four o'clock yesterday. I'll get 'em back on it before dark."

"You got a calendar, Sheriff?" Asked Seth.

"Yeah, I do." He got off the desk and went to close the cellblock door, revealing the large, almost shredded calendar tacked to it. "Sorry for th' shape it's in, men use it for knife practice. Pretty good, too, especially Gibbs."

Seth walked to the door and tore off two of the pages for a look then turned to nod at Dempsey. "August twentieth."

"What about it?" Asked Maynard also looking at the calendar.

"Seems these Devil rituals are performed on the night of a full moon." Said Dempsey as he watched Seth come back and go to the window to peer out.

"What are ya thinkin', Seth?"

He looked back at them. "About that Clock Tower...Sheriff, who lights them lamps at night?"

"Janitor,...Old Ira Clampett!...He was Judge Gurley's house man till th' Courthouse was built. Judge gave 'im th' job when he moved in....Naw, he ain't th' spy, if that's what you're thinkin', he's seventy years old, black, and can barely get up and down them stairs. Can't read, neither, from what I heard."

"Your Deputies know about 'im?"

"Sure they do,...they know what they're doin', Marshal, they'll get our man."

"Who is this Colonel,...th' one that's gonna send you some men?"

"That'll be Spencer Quinlan, Seth." Replied Dempsey. "I told you about 'im, he's Judge Castle's brother in law."

"They'll be guarding th' women at th' meeting hall." Added Maynard. "Unless you have a better idea?"

"No, sir,...That's good thinkin',...I was just curious....One would a thought th' Army could a helped with that."

"Captain Lamar claims he can't spare th' men and keep up his patrols, like they're doin' any good anyway!...One a th' victims was a soldier, too."

"Figure that!" Sighed Seth. "We should have it covered, since we don't know where th' killers are."

"Then what do we do th' rest a th' day?" Shrugged Maynard.

"Wait!" Replied Dempsey. "One clue at a time, Alex. When it shows it's ugly head, we'll find another until we can put this thing together." He glanced at the calendar then. "And we got three days to do it!"

"Th' first bein' our spy." Nodded Maynard.

"Providin' he talks!" Said Seth. "If he's a strong member a this Cult, he might not talk at all,...he might die first!"

"That's hard to believe,...I never met a man that wanted to die."

"He might not want to,…I'm sayin' he will, if he believes he'll be with his God….A sane man knows th' Devil ain't real, but his influence on some people is very real!…And Sheriff,…There ain't a sane man in this Cult!"

"I believe that!…But I'll tell ya one thing….Billy Gaye, or whoever he is might be insane,…he could even be willing to die for th' Devil,…but just how high is his tolerance for pain?…He'll give us our clue, Marshal, I'll guarantee that!"

"Now I didn't hear that!" said Dempsey. "You do know that human torture is against th' law, don't ya?"

"Yes, sir, I do….But this man ain't human, none of 'em are."

"It's hard to disagree with that, Rod." Said Seth as he mashed out the spent butt beneath his boot.

"I ain't disagreeing with th' man, Seth." He grinned at Maynard then. "I just don't want a know about it!…Whenever this man is caught, the next morning I will accept this information with gratitude, and with no questions asked."

"Understood." Nodded. Maynard

"I didn't hear any of it." Said Seth. "So I think I'll saunter off to this hotel and see how th' women are, you say there's a few over there now?"

"Yeah,…one of th' Colonel's cowboys is watchin' 'em till th' rest get here."

Nodding, Seth left the office with a "Be back in a bit."

"He's a strange man, Rod." Said Maynard, watching him leave. "Maybe different is a better word,…and I don't mean that in a bad way either!…How long's he been a Marshal, two years, that what you said earlier?…Anyway,… he sure don't say much."

"Let me tell you about Seth Mabry, Alex." Grinned Dempsey. "Durin' th' Recession of seventy-three, a New York Crime Syndicate with a boatload a money moved their operation to Dallas and began bailing folks out a hock. People there were so much in need that they agreed to their terms of repayment, a very bad decision!…The Crime bosses began bribing, stealing and even committing legal murder. What I mean by legal, is they had a judge and several lawyers in their hip pockets by then….It was all during the period of Federal control, so they did it all quietly and made it work, nobody complained to the Federal authority because they ruled th' land….In seventy seven, Reconstruction ended, but by then they had a stranglehold on Dallas, and the Government ruled they could take no action in city business unless it was asked for, course it was not! All the bosses had to do was keep their crimes from becoming federal ones."

"I was town Marshal then, under the thumb of th' City Council, who was in hock to them also, and they kept my hands tied….Sheriff owed 'em too, by th' way....Well, two years ago, one a th' bosses made a mistake, he murdered Seth's oldest son, and to cover it up, blamed Seth's youngest son for th' murder, and that became their downfall!"

"Him?" Queried Maynard, nodding at the door.

"Seth Mabry." Nodded Dempsey. "He single handedly brought down the whole operation, took out every killer they sent against 'im....Seth Mabry is the fastest man with a gun I have ever seen, Alex. He has a sixth sense about things when it comes to investigatin' a crime like I never seen, a talent I wish I had! Judge Castle made 'im an honorary Marshal for life, without the duties of one. That's why the Judge wanted him on this case. If any man can bring this bunch down, it's Seth Mabry!"

"With a reputation like that, he must a been an outlaw?"

"Before th' war, yes, one a th' worst!...But twenty years ago, he met his wife and that all ended!...Until his son was killed, he had not worn that gun for eighteen years."

Maynard stared at him for a moment then shook his head. "That's some story!"

"But a true one!" Nodded Dempsey. "I've never known a better man, even if I did try to catch 'im once....He ain't a man to cross either."

"I understand,...I also remember readin' about that big trial two years ago."

"Biggest Dallas ever had!"

"Well,...guess I'd best wake th' boys now, Rod. Still got some women to find and bring in. When I'm done, you can spring for some dinner at Norma's."

Thanks."

*   *   *

Maynard replaced the old pot on the pot-bellied stove after pouring more coffee around then sighing, stared through the window at the few pedestrians on the boardwalk across from his office.

"It goes with th' job, Alex." Said Dempsey. "I feel that way a lot, sometimes."

"I know, Rod." He sighed. "Usually it's just boredom, and I can handle that,...but this waitin',...it's got my nerves shot!...It's all we been doing for two months now, waitin' for somebody else to be murdered!...Then, when they are, I can't do a damn thing about it, or find anything that'll tell us who did it!...We're close to finding somebody now, and can't even do that till sometime tonight!"

"Wish I could help you, but I can't!...Half th' job sometimes is waitin'!...We can't solve every crime that's committed neither....So try and relax, Alex."

"Yeah." Sighed Maynard as he looked at Seth, who appeared to be relaxed while he sipped his coffee. "What about you, Seth,...you ever get frustrated?"

"Never had a job like this, Sheriff, I don't know!...No time for it on a ranch, got too much to do."

"Must be nice." He saw the man pass the window then and got up as Quinlan came in. "Ahhh, good to see you, Colonel." He met Quinlan and shook his hand.

"Good to see you, Alex." He said, as he looked Seth and Dempsey over. "When Steve brought me your request for men, I couldn't stay away....Do you know who we're after?" He asked, looking back at him.

Maynard took his arm and turned him to face Dempsey. "Colonel, this is U.S. Marshals, Dempsey and Seth Mabry." And as they shook hands; "And to answer your question, Yes, sir,...we do know who we're after....We just can't find 'em yet....Are th' men with you?"

"They'll be here before dark, Alex....Now, what do you mean, you know who we are after, but can't find them?"

"You want a tell 'im, Marshal?"

Quinlan listened intently while Dempsey told him what they believed they were up against and when he was done, just stood there with a stunned look on his face for a minute. "Are you sure about this?"

"Everything points to it!" Replied Dempsey. "If it's the same Cult, one more murder will take place before it's done, at least another woman and her child will be kidnapped, and if they succeed, we'll never find her body!...If we can't find 'em before that happens, we might not find 'em at all!"

"That's the damndest thing I ever heard of, Marshal!...Something like that is,...unbelievable.,...They have to be stopped!" He looked at Alex again. "You're bringing in all the women with young children, aren't you?"

"Them with two to four year old girl children, yes, sir." Nodded Dempsey

"That's what your men are for, Colonel, to guard th' Cult's next victim!...If they can't find one, they might make a mistake."

"I don't think I quite understand all this."

"The thirteenth victim will be a woman with a girl child." Said Dempsey. "We think, likely under the age of four. The baby will be murdered on an altar as her mother is being raped and beheaded there beside her....It's all part of a ritual to call the Devil back to earth."

"Dear God in heaven!" He looked at Maynard then. "You gonna be able to find all these women, Alex?"

"White, black, Indian?" He shrugged. "There's no way to know who they all are, Colonel....Gibbs and Jeter are out bringing in all that we can find right now. We just hope that's enough to frustrate th' Cult into makin' a mistake."

"How can these Bastards take somebody without being seen, for God sakes?"

"Th' same way they took your cattle, Colonel, at night!...They know how to use the dark,...they're like shadows."

"They're successful because they're killers, and damn good at it!" Voiced Dempsey. "And they can see you before you can see them."

"Sons of Bitches!...How could a human being-..."

"They ain't human, Mister Quinlan." Said Dempsey frankly. "Not any more, at least!....They're insane murderers possessed with the idea that Lucifer will rule the world someday, if they can bring 'im back!...That's all speculation on our part, but it's the only explanation."

Quinlan stared at them in awe of what he'd heard, but then dropped his head to stare at the floor with obvious emotion. "You do know you won't find all these women, don't you?" He looked back at them. "There's ten thousand people in and around Tyler, most darkies bear their own, so do Indians, and I have to say, most white women, too!"

"We know all a that, Colonel." Said Dempsey. "We just want a make it harder for 'em,...give us a chance to see 'em."

"Do you have any clues yet, anything?"

"With luck." Said Maynard. "We will have by tomorrow. We found where their spy was watching us from....We think he was using the same language a telegrapher uses to tell this bunch when it's safe to do their business."

"How?"

"Th' Courthouse Clock, he uses th' light like Morse Code."

"Billy Gaye, for Christ's sake?"

"We'll know that tonight,...we're setting a trap for 'im."

"That's good." He nodded. "That's very good! What else is planned,... what about th' women you can't find?"

"Me and Seth'll be ridin' th' streets tonight." Said Dempsey. "We could get lucky."

"Well," He said, nodding at both Seth, and Dempsey. "I'm glad you're here....I was gonna wire Judge Castle you weren't here yet, when I left, but-...." He looked at Maynard then. "If Billy Gaye is part of this thing-..."

"We'll take care of it, Colonel."

"Course you will….Well, I best get back to th' ranch, Alex, Lucy is some worried about all this. Use my men where you need 'em, you need more, send me word."

"Thanks, Colonel, I will."

Quinlan nodded at them and left, and as they watched, climbed into his buckboard and whipped the team into motion.

"What position does Mister Quinlan hold here in Tyler, Sheriff?" Queried Seth. "Appears to me, he's a man you're used to takin' orders from."

"You're right!" Nodded Maynard. "We all are!...We were in his command durin' th' war. He was sent here durin' Reconstruction by the Lincoln Administration, and was more or less put in charge a things,… along with that Numb-nuts, Captain Lamar!...But they tended to follow his instructions, too. Anyway,…he sent for us with a job offer, and here we are."

"Seems like a likable fella at that." Grinned Seth., looking at his watch. Don't know about you, Rod, but if we're gonna ride th' streets all night, I'd like an hour's worth of siesta."

"He's right, Alex." Agreed Dempsey. "We'll check with ya before we start our watch….Let's go, Seth."

*   *   *

"It's a quarter of six, Mister Gibbs." Said Maynard. "You get 'em all?"

"Countin' them earlier, twenty two in all, Lieutenant." He said, coming on to sit down against the wall. Three of 'em gave me three more names, got them, too!...all at th' meetin' hall, husbands and all….They was a few more comin' in though, guess Jeter sent 'em in."

"Have any trouble?"

"Some a th' men-folk was reluctant, but agreed when I told 'em why?... They're likely scared, too."

"Stands to reason!" Sighed Maynard, looking toward the window. "Here's Jeter now." They were waiting when the Deputy came in. "Thought you went with Gibbs, where ya been?'"

"I remembered who one a th' midwives was, nigger woman called Samantha!...She gave me six more names of women with girl babies, I brought 'em in."

"That's good,…th' guards all in place?"

"Twelve armed cowboys, yes, sir, got there a few minutes ago. I put 'em all inside with th' women."

"All right,…now, both of you go get your supper, I want one a you behind that window again tonight,…that'll be you, Gibbs. Mister Jeter, along about eight o'clock, I want you in that store room up them stairs, Cliff'll be with ya"

"What about me, Lieutenant,…I could help there, too?"

"Jeter and Cliff'll handle that!...You hear any shooting, give 'em a hand."

"Yes, sir,…let's go Jeter." He went to open the door and stepped back. "Here comes Walt." They allowed the Deputy inside before leaving and closing the door.

"There's been twenty-seven baptisms in th' last two years, Boss, all but one bein' four years and older. Family with th' two year old must a left town, th' house was empty.….Didn't bother with th' rest!...Lieutenant, there could be a hunnert women out there with two year old little girls, no way we're gonna find 'em!"

"I know that, Walt, but like Rod said,…maybe them we did find will make it a bit harder on th' Bastards to find what they want,…and without a spy in that clock tower to guide 'em, maybe the Marshals can spot 'em, they'll patrol th' streets tonight!...We are due some luck, Mister McArthur.…Now go get some supper, Gibbs and Jeter are there. One of ya make arrangements with Norma to send what food she can to th' hall later, she can't supply it all, go to that Mexican joint, a pot a beans and tortillas will go a long way. Gonna be forty-odd mouths to feed over there."

"What time you want me in th' Courthouse?"

"I changed my mind on that,…Jeter and Cliff will handle it."

"Where do ya want me?"

"I want some authority at that town hall, that's where you'll be."

"Where's Cliff at, Boss, I ain't seen 'im?"

"Don't worry about him, he's asleep back there. Get goin' now."

"yes, sir, I'm gone."

*   *   *

Both Dempsey, and Seth were silent as they saddled their horses and once done, stood in the stable's open doorway to smoke while the last vestige of daylight turned into shadows along the wide street.

"Clock in th' tower just lit up." Commented Dempsey. "Wonder when our spy will show?"

""If I was to guess,…I'd say sometime after th' sidewalks fold up, and folks are in bed.….Around ten, maybe eleven." He stepped on the spent butt then. "Hope it all works out!...Anyway,…remember what I told you about them shadows tonight, Rod, not all of 'em are friendly!"

"I remember, Seth." He said, also dropping the spent cigarette and stepping on it. He stooped then to test the leather strings around his horse's feet. "I wouldn't a thought a this."

"I rode through a sleepin' Comanche camp like that once,...dogs didn't even hear me!"

"Alex Hayward said he did th' same exact thing back in seventy-four, took a whole troop a rangers in to surround th' camp."

"They muffle a horse's hoof pretty good,...a scared horse can still give you away though, it'll spook at them same movin' shadows, so be ready!... We're huntin' people who use razor-sharp knives the way we use a gun, and they use the dark th' same way,...That's why nobody sees 'em."

"You sure got a knack for makin' me feel good!"

"Always glad to help." He moved in beside his horse and pulled himself into the saddle with a grunt.

"You got some sort a route in mind?" Asked Dempsey as he mounted.

"A plan wouldn't work on somethin' like this, Rod,...likely wastin' our time as it is, especially this early,...Better chance will be after midnight, I think."

"Not always, they got Henry Jones before midnight."

"that's true,...hard to figure what might a happened there....Whatever it was, your friend had no time to react to it,...might not have seen 'em at all." He shifted his weight in the saddle. "Well,...we can maybe this thing all night, Rod,...you ready?"

"Lead out."

*   *   *

"Shit!" Exclaimed Jeter in a loud whisper. "It's hotter'n hell in here!" He opened the supply room door a crack to look down the narrow, faintly lighted staircase as it spiraled its way into the darkness two floors below them. "Where th' hell is he?...Strike a match, see what time it is."

"No fuckin' way!" Whispered Cliff. "That Son of a Bitch smells th' sulphur, he won't show for sure!...Now relax, it ain't even ten o'clock yet,...he ain't gonna show till he's sure nobody will see 'im."

"Well I feel like a wet pig in these clothes!"

"You smell like one, too, both of us!...Now be quiet and watch th' stairs."

"I still think one of us ought a be in th' tower, catch 'im between us when he shows,...what do ya think?"

"Jeter, stop talkin', he'll he-..."

"I see somethin'!" Whispered Jeter, cutting Cliff off,…and straining his eyes at the slow-moving figure as the man came up the stairwell, pulled the pistol from it's holster and ever so quietly eased the hammer to full cock and closed the door.

"Lock it." Whispered Cliff. "He'll try the door when he comes by."

Jeter managed to quietly lock the door with the key they had used to get in, and several minutes later were rewarded as they heard the sound of the knob being tried.

They could hear the faint groaning of wood as he crossed the level platform and continued his climb toward the clock tower, and after a few seconds, Jeter unlocked the door again and eased it inward until it was open all the way. With a look at Cliff's dark outline, he stepped out onto the solid portion of the staircase.

"Billy Gaye!" He said loudly, the pistol pointed at the cloaked man's back. The man had stopped at the sound of his voice. "You're under arrest, Billy, come on back down here." The killer, still thirty feet above him on the stairs, quickly, and deftly raised an arm toward the back of his head as he spun around on the step and then, without a sound threw himself bodily through the air down toward the surprised Jeter, wielding the long, curved sword in an arcing motion over his still cloaked head,…and Jeter fired a split second before the killer's hurling body struck him, knocking him to the platform on his back as the deafening noise subsided.

Too late, the Cultist realized he had leaped too far and tried to use the sharp sword as he hit the deputy, striking the wall instead of Jeter's head as his momentum threw him headlong onto the downward, spiral of steps to freefall precariously for several plummeting yards before he was able to regain his feet and continue downward toward his possible escape.

As quickly as Jeter had called out, and the shot was fired, Cliff was in the doorway as the Jeter was knocked down and quickly stepped out onto the landing with a cocked pistol.

"Stop right there!" He yelled, and as the killer continued to descend, fired twice, hearing the dull sounds of bullets on flesh, and then the plummeting, rolling thuds of the man as his lifeless body came to a stop on the stairs.

"Shit!" He yelled then quickly holstered his gun to kneel beside Jeter on the landing. "Come on, Jeter, wake up man."

"Get 'im, Cliff!" He yelled, his arms and legs flailing wildly as he tried to get up. "He'll get away!"

"He's dead, Jeter, calm down." He sighed heavily then. "And so are we when th' Lieutenant finds out,…this was th' only lead we had." He helped Jeter to his feet and walked down the stairs to where the crumpled, dark-looking body lay in a twisted heap against the stair's hand-railing. He heard the running footsteps then and looked down as Gibbs ran up the staircase to stop and stare at the corpse.

"Shit, man!" He groaned. "Lieutenant wanted 'im alive!"

"So did we, Gibbs. He almost beheaded Jeter up there....We had no choice!"

Sighing, Gibbs reached to remove the hood from the man's head and struck a match. "You know 'im?"

"It ain't Billy Gaye." Said Cliff as they were joined by a still shook up Jeter.

"Jesus, God!" He blurted. "I never seen a man move that fast before,... Bastard was twenty feet above me on th' stairs when he just turned and jumped right at me!...All I seen was a blur till he hit me."

"You're lucky he overshot you," Said Cliff. "Look at th' wall up yonder."

"What th' hell is that?" He gasped, seeing the weapon protruding from the door facing.

"It's a sword a some kind." Said Cliff, shaking his head. "His aim was better, your head would be layin' here, too!" They all three heard the crash then as the Courthouse front door were thrown open and shortly after, a puffing Alex Maynard stopped at the bottom of the stairs.

"I heard th' shots." He said breathlessly. "Anybody hurt?"

"Only our spy, Lieutenant." Said Gibbs. "He's pretty much dead!"

"Dead?...What th' hell happened?"

"I had my gun on 'im, Lieutenant." Said Jeter. "He was almost to th' tower when I told 'im to stop!...But all he did was turn around and dive down at me. I barely seen 'im jump as dark as it was, fell right on me before I knew what was happening!"

"He was getting away, Lieutenant, I had to stop 'im." Said Cliff with remorse.

"Billy Gaye?"

"No, sir." Said Gibbs, striking a match to hold on the man's face. "We never seen 'im before,...have you?" He spotted the lantern on the wall then and lit it, throwing the stairwell into a much better light.

"I don't know 'im neither." Sighed Maynard, bending for a closer look at the clothing. "Rod was right though, dressed like a Monk!...Looks a little familiar, but I can't place 'im....He say anything?"

"Never made any sound at all!"

"What's this thing?" He asked, moving the leather boot aside with his finger.

"Scabbard for that sword stuck in th' wall up yonder." Said Gibbs, pointing upward. "Accordin' to Cliff, th' man hadn't misjudged his jump, Jeter's head would be down here."

"I'm sure sorry, Lieutenant." Said Jeter. "It just happened too fast."

"Well,...at least he won't be sending any more messages....Better go bring that big knife down, Cliff." He looked at Gibbs then. "Open his robe, check his pockets."

"Ain't no pockets." Replied Gibbs as he opened the robe. "Just a loincloth."

"Appears he was hit twice, one in th' leg, one in the ass!...Hope it hurt like hell!" He grunted to his feet. "Well, th' fall killed 'im, Cliff, not you, likely broke his fuckin' neck!" They all four pulled their guns when they heard the arriving footsteps, but put them away as Dempsey and Seth entered the lantern's light.

"We heard th' shots, Alex, figured somethin' went wrong." Said Dempsey as Seth went to kneel by the body.

"Look at this, Rod." And when Dempsey came to squat down beside him. "Look familiar?"

"I'll be damn!...who would a thought?"

"Who is it, Rod?" Queried Maynard.

"Don't know who he is, but he opened th' door for us at th' Methodist Church today."

"By God, you're right!" said Jeter and Gibbs almost at once. "He's th' Elder, th' one who said we couldn't look around!"

"What's a Church Elder doin' worshippin' th' fuckin' Devil?" Blurted Maynard. "Do ya think th' Reverend knows?"

"I don't know," Said Jeter angrily. "But he's, for damn sure gonna open them doors to us now!"

"Now wait a minute, Sheriff." Said Seth, looking up at them. "I don't think he would a given us all that information if he knew about this!...Damn good place to hide out though, nobody would ever suspect 'im."

"I think we should have another talk with 'im, though." Added Dempsey. "Might be more of 'em hiding out there."

"I'll do that tomorrow, first thing, Rod." Breathed Maynard.

"Be better tonight!" Returned Seth. "Probably a dozen Elders boardin' there,...wait too long, clues disappear."

"Me and Seth'll go, Alex, we got horses out front.

Maynard nodded then looked up as Cliff gave him the sword and looked it over. "So, this is what Doc. Called a cutlass?" He said, turning the wide-bladed weapon over in his hand. "Shit!" He blurted as blood dripped from his thumb. "I barely touched the edge on this thing!"

"Think how easy that thing could lop off your head, Alex." Grinned Dempsey ironically. "That's what Pirates used on th' high seas, and a hell of a weapon in a killer's hands!"

"My strait-razor ain't that sharp!" Said Jeter.

"Well, cut that scabbard off th' asshole's back and put it away!" Said Maynard, giving it to the deputy. "Take it to th' office….Cliff, go fetch Doc Welch, tell 'im to bring the Undertaker."

"Best stop at th' hotel first!" Said Seth. "Your Deputy was standin' in th' square as we rode in with his gun drawn."

"Sure will." Said Cliff and hurried off into the darker part of the building.

"Walt," Sighed Maynard. "See if you can find a pail a water and soap somewhere,…clean th' blood off these stairs, Judge Gurney'll be pissed, he sees it."

"You got it, Boss." He hurried away also.

What's your plan at th' Church, Rod?" Asked Maynard as they got to their feet.

"Direct approach, Alex….He either knew about this, or he didn't!...If he didn't, we'll search th' premises, see if any more of his Elders are a part of it. Either way, we'll get some answers."

"We get anything, we'll come tell you, Sheriff." Added Seth. "We don't, we'll stick to our plan and patrol th' streets. They won't let this stop 'em from takin' their next victim."

"We don't find anything, we'll see you after daybreak, Alex." Said Dempsey. "Let's go, Seth."

"Luck!" Said Maynard as he watched them leave.

"Well, Seth," Sighed Dempsey as they went back toward the street door. "So much for our first break!"

"We still have a couple a days, Rod."

"You really think th' full moon has somethin' to do with it?"

"I believe it does, yeah,…these killers are gonna be blind now with no information from their spy,…maybe they'll make a mistake!...Their time is runnin' out, too!...If they can't do their ritual on th' night of th' twentieth, they'll be forced to wait till th' next one, that or leave!"

"Their leavin' is what worries me, thirteen people are gonna die somewhere else."

"We ain't done yet, Rod." They walked down the Courthouse steps, mounted and urged the horses to a trot across the square toward Bois d 'arc street, passing the hotel just as Jeter was leaving to go for the Doctor.

"Feels like we're losing this one, Seth."

"It ain't over yet, don't get careless!...And don't forget to watch your ass."

"The shadows, I know." He said as they entered the tree-lined darkness of Bois d 'arc and then rode in silence until they came to the wrought-iron gate, and it was at that point that Seth suddenly stopped his horse in the street to twist around in the saddle and stare into the darkness at the silent, pitch black shapes of the houses behind them.

"What's wrong?" Whispered Dempsey.

"Listen!"

"I can't hear a thing." He whispered after straining his ears for a minute. "What do you hear?"

"Nothing!...There's no night sounds. No birds, no singin' june-bugs, nothing." He sighed then and dismounted to lead his horse to the gate, tying it to the iron ring that dangled from the column.

"You think they're here somewhere, don't ya?"

"They could be anywhere, and we wouldn't know it."

"I take that as a yes."

"I'm just a little on edge, Rod." He lifted the latch and opened the heavy gate. "Come on, let's wake up th' good Reverend." He led the way up the rock-paved path and climbed the steps to quickly stop Dempsey as he reached for the bell.

"Doors always open, remember?" He slid the latch back and eased the monstrous door open enough to go inside.

The enormous room was partially lighted with candles along both walls and behind the podium,...that one lighting up the carved figure of Christ on the cross. Seth nodded at Dempsey and they started down the long aisle between the empty pews, their boots making a dull, echoing sound on the polished stones. They were almost to the altar when an Elder, who had been kneeling in prayer, got to his feet in front of the platform supporting the altar,...causing them both to freeze momentarily in surprise. But seeing them, the smock-covered man came toward them.

"Welcome." He smiled then gestured at the altar. "Please, you are in God's house, feel free to talk with him."

"We're sorry," Said Seth. "We didn't come to pray."

"We're here to see Reverend Peters." Said Dempsey.

"I am afraid that's impossible, the Reverend is sleeping at this late hour. Perhaps I can be of help?"

"Afraid not!" Said Dempsey forcefully. "We have to see 'im now,... so, please, go wake 'im, we'll wait in his office." And when the man didn't move. "Right now, man, go wake 'im up!"

Bowing slightly, the Elder hurried off through the row of pews and through the curtains, with them bringing up the rear. He was gone by the time they pushed through the drapes and entered the Reverend's office.

"I sure hope he ain't involved in any a this." Sighed Dempsey as he sat down in one of the armchairs. "You think he is?"

"My gut feelin' says he ain't." Breathed Seth, as he looked around the dimly lit room's many shelves of books and idols. They heard hurrying footsteps then and were both standing when Reverend Peters entered.

"My word, Marshal,...what brings you back so late at night?"

"A man was shot tonight at the Courthouse, Reverend."

"Dear God!" He said, and quickly made the sign of the cross. "Is he asking for last rites?"

"No,...nothing like that." Replied Seth. "He's dead."

"Then I don't-..."

"Reverend," Said Dempsey stopping him. "When we were here earlier, who was the man that let us in?"

"Why, I believe that was Brother Thomas,...why, would you like to speak with him?"

"We would,...but he died tonight at the Courthouse."

"Mother of God!" Gasped the Reverend in disbelief then made the sign of the cross again. "Why,...how?"...I don't understand!"

"He was not who you thought he was, Reverend." Said Seth. "Tonight, like every night, he would dress himself like a Monk and spend his nights in the Courthouse clock-tower."

"Wh,...why?"

"He was the eyes and ears of th' Cult you told us about." Said Dempsey. "Sheriff's deputies found bedding and a telescope up there....they suspected all along there was a spy somewhere tellin' these killers when it was safe to take their victims, then again when it was safe to leave the bodies.....So they set a trap for 'im."

Tears were running down the Pastor's cheeks as he listened, and his face was ashen, as he suddenly had to catch himself against the desk.

"We know this is a shock to you, Reverend, I apologize for being so blunt!...But what did you know about this man?"

"He, um.,...he came here about a year ago from somewhere in Louisiana,...he had impeccable credentials from the Methodist Church of New Orleans. He said he had been told by God to come here!...He seemed so devoted,...I don't think I've ever seen anyone so sincere in his love of God!"

"It appears he was, sir!" Said Seth. "It was just for the wrong God."

"Do you know what he was,...before the Church, I mean?" Queried Dempsey.

"A Telegrapher for the Army, I believe."

"He was usin' that knowledge to send his messages to the Cult."

"May God forgive me,...I didn't know."

"We know that, Reverend," Sighed Dempsey. "But if you don't mind, we'll have to see his living quarters, and those of the other Elders."

"Of course,…I'll take you to his cell." He straightened and led the way out into the hallway where they followed him to the utmost rear of the Church, where Peters opened a door and allowed them inside.

"As you can see,…he had nothing. Only one of two vestments on a rack there, his crucifix there on the bed."

The room was quite small, with only space enough for the bed, a desk and chair, and the few idols hanging on the walls. After walking around the small bed, Dempsey sighed, and was about to come back to join them when his boot-toe caught on the large, round, woven rug covering the floor beneath the cot and looking down, he stopped at sight of what appeared to be the edge of some sort of artwork. "Grab the end of th' bed, Seth, help me move it."

Once the heavy, wooden bed was against the wall, Dempsey knelt and pulled the rug away from the strange drawing. They all three stared down at the large, hand drawn circle with its five-pointed star inside. Each point of the star touched the circle, and each line was a continuation, crossing each other at the star's center.

"What is it?" Queried Seth as both him and Dempsey looked at the Reverend Peters, seeing him wide-eyed and continuously making and remaking the sign of the cross on his chest while his mouth was moving in silent prayer.

"Reverend?" Said Seth again, causing Peters to jerk and stare at him. "What is that?"

"A hexa,…a Hexagram!" He stuttered. "It's a," He cleared his throat. "Some call it a Pentagram."

"What's it mean?"

"It's a symbol used in Witchcraft,…and in the rites of Satanism!…May God have mercy on our souls!" He made the sign of the cross again before he looked at them. "Could it be possible he was choosing their victims from members of my own Congregation?"

"I'd say it was very possible!" Nodded Dempsey. "Do you think it's possible more of your Elders are Cult members?"

"God forgive me, I don't know!"

Seth was still looking at the drawing while they talked, and noticed that the star's center didn't look right and squatting, used a fingernail to pick at it, moving it some as he did. Curious by then, he took the knife from his belt and pried up the cover to reveal a hole with its contents. "Take a look, Rod." He said as he removed the animal's polished, horned skull.

"What is that,…a goat?" Queried Dempsey"

"I'm afraid so," Sighed Peters. "It's used in some of the rites,...there should be other bones there as well."

"There is," Nodded Seth. "Loose bones."

"We need to take a look at the other Elder's quarters now, Reverend."

"Yes, of course....How could I have not known this, Marshal?...Are my eyes so clouded, I could not see,...my heart so blind, I could not feel the evil that surrounded me?"

"Don't blame yourself, Reverend." Sighed Dempsey. "This bunch is good at deception, like the bible said Lucifer was!...Now, let's wake up them Elders."

*   *   *

"I sort a feel sorry for th' Reverend." Sighed Dempsey as they walked to the gate. "Really shook th' old man's faith."

"Cult like this destroys lives, Rod, everything it touches!...Th' Reverend was right, evil is all around us, all th' time, we just don't recognize it."

"Bein' a mite profound, ain't ya?"

"If that means I don't know what I'm talkin' about, you're right!" He reached to push open the gate then, and quickly placed a hand on Dempsey's arm, stopping him.

"You see somethin'?"

"Felt it!...You're right, Rod,...they're out there!...They're gonna try tonight, I can feel it!"

"How,...we got their spy?"

"Prob'ly knew who they wanted weeks ago,...they just don't know where they are now, or where th' law is,...but they likely know where them are that we missed."

"Okay,...where are they, where do we look?"

"All I know is, it don't feel right,...but they're out there somewhere! Where's th' poorest part a town?"

"I wouldn't know that, Seth,...in Dallas, it's th' south side."

"Then let's go south, down that first street there." He loosed the horse's reins and mounted, as did Dempsey and urged them across Bois d 'arc Street onto the side street.

They were silent as they walked the booted animals along the dark lane, and the trees were so thick that hardly any of the moon's lunar light shown through the heavily foliaged branches at all to light the way. Even the houses took on an eerie look, appearing as pitch-black blobs of density against the slighter hue of reflected light. Both kept their eyes glued to those blobs in passing, looking for any flutter of movement that might not belong.

The horses made no sound at all, save an occasional grunt, or snort, but that only brought a soothing pat on the neck for reassurance. Other than that, not a single dog barked, or gave chase, and after the third long block of deserted street, and of seeing nothing, Seth reined his horse onto another side street, this time walking the animals east bound, and only three streets South of the town square still a quarter mile to the east of them.

They had only gone a short distance when Seth stopped his horse again to listen, peering hard at the street's shadows ahead of them. He saw the movement then, a darting blur of two figures as they were crossing the wide street. He could tell by the bulk of one that he was carrying something across his shoulders and because of the load, was not moving as fast as the other figure. He thought of this in the smallest part of a second and as he did, he drew and fired, the explosion was sudden, and very loud in the night's stillness, and he saw the figure stumble and drop the load he was carrying as he fell....As he did, Dempsey fired at the second figure as he was making the safety of the houses across the road.

Seth kicked his horse into a run toward the still struggling man in the road, and as he stopped his horse and dismounted, the man regained his feet and stumbled toward him, wielding the Cutlass in an arcing motion as he came.

"You better stop, man, I'll kill ya!" And when he didn't, fired a second time, the slug stopping the killer in his tracks with its impact, and knocking him to his back in the road as the thunderous concussions died away in the distance. Dempsey was already running toward what appeared to be a body in the road as Seth holstered his gun and went to pry the sword from the man's hand. Laying the weapon aside, he struck a match to peer at the assassin's heavily tattooed face and wide open eyes. This one also wore nothing but a loincloth beneath the robe.

"Damn it." He breathed, and at that moment, he knew that these killers would all have to be killed, to be stopped! Their training had been too extensive, he thought then sighing, stood and went to remove the rope from his saddle before coming back to work the loop over the man's head and shoulders. Straightening again, he sighed and continued along the dark road to where a kneeling Dempsey was still trying to wake the young woman. "How is she, Rod?" He asked as he knelt to strike another match.

"She's breathin', I think, but real shallow!...I can't wake 'er up."

"Black girl," Said Seth as the match flared. "Pretty, too!...Appears they settled for second choice."

"Her eyes are open, Seth, but she don't see nothing, must a used a drug on 'er, or somethin'....wonder where she lives?"

"I'd say right about there." He said, looking at the dark house directly across from them. He shook out the match then.

"They heard th' shots, why don't they light a lamp or something?"

"If anybody's in there, they ain't gonna let us know it,...too scared....Put 'er on your horse, she needs to see a Doctor anyway, and he's probably still on th' square. Come on, I'll help ya." They managed to get the limp body of the girl across Dempsey's saddle and with Seth's help he managed to mount up behind her.

"Lead out, Rod, I'll be right behind ya." He mounted, and once the rope tightened around the Cultist's body, urged the animal in behind that of Dempsey.

Maynard, and two of his deputies had heard the shooting and were half running down one of the side streets when they met them.

"What was th' shooting about?" Queried Maynard loudly once Seth identified himself, and then Dempsey.

"Caught 'em takin' another woman, Alex." Returned Dempsey. "Seth had to kill him, too!...Another one got away!"

"Where's th' dead one?"

"At the end of my rope." Said Seth, and as Maynard and men walked along beside them to the square. "The other one might have had th' girl's baby in his arms, Sheriff,...too dark to see."

"I shot at 'im, Alex," Said Dempsey. "But I missed."

"Don't feel bad about it, Rod,...we been missin' for two months now."

They entered the square in time to see the Undertaker's wagon leaving the Courthouse and called him over. Doctor Welch was also crossing the square, and he hurried over to help Jeter take the girl from Dempsey's saddle,...and both carried her into the hotel. In the meantime, Dempsey and Seth dismounted and walked back to the dead Cultist with Maynard.

"Somethin' you ought a see, Sheriff." Said Seth as he squatted and struck a match to light up the killer's tattooed face.

"What th' hell is he, a nigger?" Asked Gibbs as he trotted up to look.

"Don't think so," Said Seth. "Creole Indian, maybe, or a Cajun,...and them tattoos could mean anything, or nothin' at all!"

"Don't see somethin' like that very often, that's for sure." Remarked Maynard as Seth dropped the spent match. "He carry one a them swords, too?"

"On my saddle there."

Maynard struck a match then and opened the robe. "Loincloth,...I see where you winged 'im first....Wouldn't have it that way, would he?"

"He could hardly stand, but he charged me anyway!...Left me no choice."

"You say a second man got away with a little girl?"

"All because I can't shoot worth a shit!" Said Dempsey with feeling.

"Not your fault, Rod, he was moving too fast, and it was dark as sin!... Now shake it off."

"Well," Sighed Maynard, dropping the match. "Still got a zero on our side a th' fence,...think they'll be back for another woman?"

"I'd say so." Returned Seth. "Maybe one with child, if it has to be that way,...and that gives cause to worry about this little girl!"

"They'd turn 'er loose, wouldn't they?" Queried Jeter.

"They're killers." Reminded Dempsey.

"Maybe it don't have to be th' woman's birth child?" Speculated Maynard.

"Let's hope not!" Breathed Dempsey.

"Yeah," Sighed Maynard. "Either way, we're losin'!" He turned toward the undertaker, who was calmly sitting atop the wagon's seat waiting. "Take th' Bastard away, Curt!" And then, as Curt climbed down. "Guess I better go check on our gal,...first black victim we had."

"Guess we had the intended in custody, Lieutenant." Said Jeter as he bent to remove Seth's rope from the body.

"You goin' to th' office, Marshal?" Queried Maynard as he started to leave.

"No reason to now, Alex." Sighed Dempsey. "I think they're gone for tonight."

"Okay then," He looked, as Jeter helped the Coroner load the body. "And you think he was a Cajun, huh, Seth?"

"Maybe, yeah,...ain't dark enough to be black, and I don't think Mexican or Indian. Them Tattoos look to me like some kind a writing,... could mean somethin', maybe not!" He coiled up his rope again and hung it on the saddle as he spoke.

"We'll never know!" Sighed Maynard. "See ya tomorrow." With slumped shoulders, he watched the wagon turn around and leave then shook his head and walked on toward the hotel, with Jeter at his side.

"He's takin' all this pretty hard, ain't he?" Said Dempsey as he watched him."

"His town's in trouble." Said Seth. "When a man's on a job as long as him, sooner or later, he becomes th' job!...Just like you, Rod,...you been a lawman most a your life. Badge or not, ya can tell it right off!"

"Come on, Seth,...how?"

"Oh, I don't know,...way a man walks, way he carries his self, ya just know!...I ain't no different,...most look at me, and know what I am."

"What are you?"

"I killed two men in one week, Rod,...that's what I am!"

"You wore a badge, they were legal!...Now, what's our next move, Seth, it's pretty plain these killers won't be taken alive?"

"I'm workin' for you, Rod, remember?"

"Then let's us put our horses to bed, and go get some sleep!"

*   *   *

Maynard and his deputies were in his office when they arrived, the deputies all sitting with elbows on their knees and staring at the floor. Alex Maynard was behind his desk, feet up and idly thumbing through all the wanted posters he had accumulated over the years. He dropped them on the desk as they walked in.

"This is a lively bunch, Alex!" Said Dempsey with a grin. "You get any sleep?"

"Couple a hours,...appears you did." He put his feet on the floor as they came to the desk.

"What's with th' posters, Alex, find our man there?"

"It's just somethin' to do,...helps me think sometimes."

Dempsey used his finger to sort through the top few then curious, picked up two of them for a closer look.

"Find somethin', Rod?" Queried Maynard.

"Yeah," He said, casting a sideways look at Seth as he was pouring his self some coffee. "You can trash these two,...Dancer cashed in a long time ago, before th' war, I think....And this, Reb,...he was killed in Paris, Texas in sixty eight!...Two of the most feared gunmen a their day, too!" He dropped them on the desk and grinned slightly at Seth before nodding at Maynard. "How's th' girl, Alex?"

"That, Rod," He leaned his elbows on the desk and sighed. "Is something I don't know!...She's alive, her vital signs appear normal, accordin' to Doc!...But she ain't there!...She just lays there starin' at th' ceiling....Doc says she's in a coma, and he can't figure out what they used on her....Can't bring 'er out of it neither."

"Maybe they're usin' a little voodoo along with their Devil Worshippin'." Said Seth, sipping at his coffee. "They put a hex on her."

"I don't believe in that shit!" Said Maynard angrily, but then frowned up at him. "What makes you think that?"

"Man I shot last night....I think he probably was Cajun,...and them tattoos likely had somethin' to do with their magic."

"Why not?" He said, gesturing wildly with his hands. "Nothing that says these Cults are all white neither....He was a young man, too, Doc says, not more than twenty years old."

"Insanity ain't just for old folks." Nodded Seth. "Younger they are, the more they can be influenced by somethin' like this....That, or they're on some kind a drug!" He looked at Dempsey then. "I think they'll try again tonight."

"What makes you so sure?" Queried Maynard.

"They'll have to, Alex." Replied Dempsey. "Th' moon'll be full in two days, and we got guards on th' women and children....They're still there, ain't they?"

"The Colonel sent replacements in this morning." He nodded.

"About two hours ago." Said Walt.

"You'd best go get some sleep, Walt." Said Maynard. "Got another long night tonight."

"Yes, sir, Boss." He said, getting to his feet. "Wake me before time to go, all right,...didn't take time for breakfast this mornin'?" He went into the cellblock then and closed the door behind him.

Nodding, Maynard looked back at Dempsey. "You gonna be on th' streets again tonight?"

"That's about all we can do, our clues all died last night!...Wouldn't a talked anyway, th' way it looks."

"Looks bad for us, don't it, Rod?"

Dempsey shrugged. "Like Seth said yesterday, we might not catch 'em at all!"

"We got a couple a days left." Reminded Seth.

"Yeah, I-..." Maynard quickly got to his feet as the banging on the door interrupted them and Jeter rushed to swing it open, but then stepped back in surprise as the black woman pushed her way in.

"You gots to help me, Mista Sheriff, please, Lord, you gots to help me!" She was almost hysterical as she yelled at them, prompting Seth to put his arm around her beefy shoulders.

"Calm down, mama, tell us what's wrong!"

She looked wildly up at him for a second, then back at Maynard. "My babies's gone!" She sobbed. "Somebody done took my babies, you gots to help me?"

"We will, we will,...just slow down!" Voiced Maynard. "Stop blubbering and tell me what's wrong!" And when she calmed down enough. "That's better,...now, how old is your baby?"

"She sixteen y'ars old,...ma, my Grandbaby's two, they's gone!"

"When, Mammy,...when did you miss 'em?"

"A while ago, they be in bed sleepin' two hours ago, they both gone now, dem heathens done took 'em, I knows they did!...They's gonna chops they heads off, I knows it!"

CHAPTER NINE

"Now, don't you fret too much, Mama," Said Maynard, gently patting the black woman's shoulder. "We'll find her….This man here is my Deputy, his name's Jeter….He's gonna walk you back home and figure out what happened, okay?...We'll find 'em, try not to worry!" He nodded at Jeter then, who turned her around and urged her back out onto the boardwalk to disappear from view.

"So much for thinkin' they only worked at night!" Said Maynard angrily. "Shit!" He closed the door and stood with hands on his hips. "Took 'em in broad daylight,…God damn it!"

"We don't know that, Alex." Said Dempsey. "It was still dark two hours ago,…we don't know what time it was, and she was hysterical….Besides, Jeter might find 'em."

"It don't make a damn now, anyway,…because we're th' ones with only two days left, and we all know Jeter won't find 'em!" He came back to the desk to sit on its corner and look at them. "They took 'em, we all know that!...But how in hell did they do it without bein' seen by somebody?"

"They didn't, Alex." Said Dempsey. "Somebody seen 'em, they always do. They're just too scared to say anything,…why?,…they don't want a be next!"

"That's why they left them bodies in th' square, Sheriff." Added Seth. "It was just to scare folks."

Nodding tiredly, Maynard got up and went around the desk to sit down then sighing, reached to open the bottom drawer and remove bottle and glasses before looking back at them. "I need this!" He said as he poured the liquor in his glass. "Feel free to join me." He drank the fiery liquid and shuddered as it went down. "What better way to celebrate a failure?"

"We got two days left, Sheriff." Voiced Seth. "We ain't done yet!"

"All right." He nodded. "You got any fresh ideas, I'll damn sure listen!"

"Just got one." Said Seth, getting all their attention. "It ain't a guarantee, but I think it's all we got."

"I'll try anything at this point, let's hear it."

"Now, hold it everybody," Said Dempsey. "We don't know if they took th' girl yet, let's wait on Jeter….."We'll know what to do then."

"We'll wait for Jeter, Rod." Nodded Maynard. "But I want a hear Seth's idea anyway….Go ahead, Seth."

"Reverend Peters said that if we wanted to find any place in th' county that was big enough to hide this bunch, and private enough to hold their rituals,…it was gonna be a place that nobody knows about!...Some place that was here long before Tyler was, one nobody remembers bein' there….He said Cults like these use fear and secrecy to do their work, and we've already seen that!...So,…I'm thinking they would need a place somewhere deep in th' woods, one that's overgrown and very hard to find,…in a swampy area, maybe….He also said we'd need to ask somebody who was here long before Tyler was, somebody who would know the area better than anybody else!"

"The Wichita Indian!" Blurted Dempsey. "I'd forgot about that."

"Joseph Peters." Nodded Seth and looked at Maynard. "Is there any place like what I just described around here?"

"Yeah, forty square miles of it between here and Bullard,…and it would take fifty men a week to go through it!"

"Might not need to." Shrugged Seth. "How far is this Flint Basin from here?"

"Flint Basin?...Twelve, fourteen miles, if you follow th' tracks. Train stops there to take on water and wood, when it runs. Nothin' else there, but a run down tradin' post."

"And Joseph Peters." Grinned Dempsey. "Reverend said he lived there, right along th' tracks."

Maynard stared at them both for a minute then sighed and shook his head. "It's a hell of a long-shot, gentlemen!...But if anybody would know of a place like that, it would be an Indian…. Only ones left around here are a few Wichita, and most a them won't talk to a white man….This one probably ain't no different."

"It's all I got." Shrugged Seth.

"Then, by God, do it,…we got nothin' else!" Maynard sighed then. "I was of a notion to take some of th' Colonel's men and search there myself, before you got here." He slapped the desktop then. "It'll take most of th' day to get there, even if you use th' tracks,…that's what you'll need to do anyway, ain't no roads in there….Army Corp of Engineers deemed it too swampy, and would cost too much."

"Then I'll take th' tracks." Nodded Seth and drained his cup.

"We'll take th' tracks." Corrected Dempsey. "With th' time we got left, there won't be time to come back here, if Joseph knows where they are? We'll have to find 'em in a hurry."

"Then how will we get th' word, you'll need help?"

"We can take Gibbs there with us." Suggested Dempsey. "Or better yet, one a them cowboys. If Joseph says he knows where they are, we'll send 'im back for ya."

"Guess you better point us at them tracks, Sheriff." Grinned Seth.

"Yeah, sure….Take Cedar street out there south, you'll cross th' tracks. Agent there'll point out th' tap rails….But if you find 'em, I can't see th' two of you stayin' alive long enough to do anything,…assumin' you're gonna go ahead and look for 'em?"

"We are." Nodded Seth. "And I don't plan on makin' my wife a widow."

"What if he don't know where they are,…or maybe there's several places they could be, what then?…I'm just bein' realistic here,…it is a gamble, ya know."

"First things first, Alex." Said Dempsey. "They ain't there, we'll be back tonight. If they are, we'll send word….It's the only hand we got, so let's play it."

"Gibbs," Nodded Maynard. "Go tell one a th' Colonel's men to saddle up, tell 'im to meet th' Marshals over here. Go now."

"Doin' it now!" He quickly left and closed the door behind him.

"You still gonna wait for Jeter?"

"No point in that now." Said Seth. "Whether it's them took th' girl or not, we don't know where they are!…And at midnight, day after tomorrow, they'll have their damn ritual and be gone for good!"

"Then I hope you have some luck out there!…Soon as we get word you found 'em, I'll have a posse on th' way."

"I'd still be on the alert tonight, Alex." Said Dempsey. Who knows what they might do,…might even try to avenge them we killed….And watch th' shadows, man, remember that!"

"We'll get our horses and meet back here." Nodded Seth.

*   *   *

"Do me a favor, Alex." Said Dempsey as they stopped their horses at the hitch rail. "Wire Judge Castle, fill 'im in on what's happened so far, and what we're doin'….Tell 'im I'll wire 'im again when this is over."

"I can do that, Rod." He turned to the Quinlan Wrangler then. "This is Jack Hawkins, he'll be goin' with ya."

"Pleasure's ours, Jack." He nodded. "Get mounted." He nodded at Maynard then reined his horse around and spurred it back to the square and then left on Cedar, with Seth and the cowboy bringing up the rear.

Several long city blocks later, they were getting directions from the ticket agent and once again urging their mounts the half mile or so to the seldom used tracks of the tap line, where they immediately settled the horses into a mile eating gallop along the overgrown rails.

Noontime found them still galloping their horses between the tracks, and the grass along both sides stood neck high to a tall man, with much of it beginning to poke through the thick layer of rock and gravel along the sides of the weathered crossties. Brush and briar thickets were never ending and behind those, thick, towering Pine Trees, dotted with Post Oak, Elm, Wild Pecan and dead timber,...and all of it so dense that to the eye, travel through the maze of undergrowth would be impossible.

It was steaming hot on the narrow railway, as any sort of a breeze other than what the galloping horses' forward progress provided, was something to wish for,...and it took its toll on the animals, forcing them to take frequent rest periods where they would walk the horses to cool them down. They had just slowed to a walk again when Dempsey coughed suddenly, causing Seth to peer at him.

"What's that God awful stink?...Smells like somethin' crawled out there and died!"

"It did!" Grinned Seth. "Swamp out there, rotting wood, stagnant water, rotting animals, everything's dead!" He turned in the saddle to look past Dempsey at Hawkins. "How ya holdin' up back there, Jack?"

"I been in worse places, Marshal."

"That's a fact!" He grinned at Dempsey then and once again spurred the gray to a gallop over the rotting crossties. They were silent then as the day wore on, their clothing wet from perspiration, and each thinking their own thoughts,...and it was that way until late afternoon when they slowed to a walk again, and was able to see the bulk of the distant water tank with its wired-up spout....It was also when they heard the gunfire echoing toward them and stopped the horses completely to listen.

"A hunter, maybe?" Said Dempsey when they didn't hear any more.

"Handgun." Said Seth.

"Think somebody beat us to Joseph?"

"Wouldn't nothin' surprise me anymore, Rod." He turned in the saddle to scan their almost impenetrable surroundings.

"There's a Trading Post by that water tank up there!" Said Hawkins from behind them. "That's where th shots came from."

"That's got a be it, Seth....Nobody knew about Joseph, but us."

"Stay alert!" Returned Seth and clucked his horse to a trot, quickly followed by Dempsey and Hawkins and long minutes later they were once again sitting their horses and watching the front of the sagging structure's open doorway,...and the drooping heads of the three saddled horses in front.

"This can't be good." Sighed Dempsey, removing the loop on his right hand gun.

"How do ya want a play it?" Asked Seth, doing the same with his pistol.

"Straight on." He urged his horse at a walk down the slight incline and onto the packed surface leading up to the store. Seth urged his horse in behind him, and once on hard ground pulled alongside and together, rode to within a dozen feet of the horses at the hitch rail before the two men came out,...each was carrying a side of salt-cured ham in one arm and a cloth sack of corn-meal in the other, and when they saw them sitting their horses there, stopped dead still to gape at them.

"Just keep on holdin' that meat, Gents." Ordered Dempsey as he pulled and cocked his pistol. "Now drop th' sacks and unbuckle them gun belts!" And once they fearfully complied. "Where's your other man?"

"He's right here, Gents!" Came a rough-sounding voice from inside the darkened doorway. "And he's got a rifle on ya!...Now, how about droppin' yours?"

"I don't think so, Mister." Replied Dempsey. "We are U.S. Marshals,... put th' gun down and come on out a there."

"Now, what's a United States Marshal doin' out here in th' middle a hell this way, can you answer me that?"

"Don't need to, now come on out!"

"Ya know what,...I do believe I will!" Responded the man. "After you holster yours!"

"Best do it, Rod." Said Seth in a low voice. "We don't know where he is."

"Okay, Mister, I will!" Said Dempsey then looked at the two men again. "But you two just hold on to that bacon, and move over next to th' horses.... Go on, move it!" When they did, he holstered the pistol. "My gun is put away now, come on out."

Another couple of minutes passed before the tall man appeared in the open doorway, and he was holding a Winchester Rifle in one hand, cocked and pointed in their direction, while with the other hand, he was hastily stuffing the tail of his sweat-stained shirt back into his pants.

Seth shifted his weight in the squeaking saddle as the man stepped down to the yard and walked toward them.

"We are U.S. Marshals, Mister. Put th' gun down and tell me your name."

"Yeah, I know, you told me already." He grinned then. "Oh,…that was meant to scare me, right?…I got a admit, it does a little!…But not enough to put this gun down! And ya know somethin' else?…Bein' a Marshal don't make you bulletproof neither!"

"What are you doin' here?" Asked Dempsey. "We heard shots."

The man snickered then and waved his hand at his cohorts. "Aint that a mite obvious, Marshal, we are buyin' supplies. They was loading them up, too,…till you stopped 'em!" He grabbed the rifle with his other hand then, and that gun's barrel never wavered from Dempsey's chest.

"I got a warn you, Mister." Said Dempsey. "You shoot a Federal Marshal, you'll have every lawman in the country lookin for ya."

"I guess that ought a worry me, too, huh?…Hell, they already are!"

"Then let me warn you, too!" Said Seth sincerely. "You even start to pull that trigger, and I'll kill ya!"

The man stared at him for a minute, and as he did, began nibbling at his lower lip while he thought about it "That's a mighty big threat comin' from an old fart like you,…now that really does scare me!…Okay boys, go ahead and load that stuff on th' horses and go get th' rest of it!"

"And I said, don't move!" Warned Dempsey again. "Now, look here, Mister,…we heard shootin' coming in,…what's that all about?"

"Aww, that weren't nothin' atoll, Marshal.…Old Fucker didn't want a give us credit, that's all." He grinned wider then. "His little girl did, though, hell, she begged me to make a woman of 'er!…Well, shit, man, bein' a man myself, I couldn't turn 'er down!…I like that young stuff, don't you?"

"You piece a shit!" Said Dempsey. "Drop that fuckin' gun!"

"Why don't you climb down from there and make me, Marshal?"

"Damn right, I will!" He quickly dismounted and walked in front of his horse to face the man. "You gonna put that rifle down?"

"Nope," He grinned. "I'm thinkin' I might shoot ya with it, ain't fully decided!…Problem is, I'm gonna have to shoot all three of ya, and I ain't decided which to shoot first!…You ever had to make a decision like that, Marshal?"

"You Bastard!" Said Dempsey, and started for his gun, but stopped.

"I wouldn't try that, Marshal, I really wouldn't." The warning caused Dempsey to relax some. "That's better." Grinned the man. "Smart, too, cause I'd a killed ya!"

"Why didn't ya then?" Queried Seth, his eyes watching those of the gunman. "Now you just relax old man.…I'm gonna give you a chance, too!"

"You're time is runnin' out, Mister," said Dempsy. "Now, who th' hell are you?

"You might ought a do what he says, Mister." Said Seth. "He ain't long on too much patience."

"Now old timer,…this is between th' Marshal there and me, you was doin' just fine sittin' up there with your mouth shut….Be smart, and keep doin' that!" He peered past Dempsey then. "Who's this other gent, you got with ya, he a Marshal, too?"

"He's a cowhand, just ridin' with us….Now who are you?"

"Why don't you all just get off them horses now, I don't like lookin' up at ya, makes my neck hurt!…And be careful, boys." He held the rifle ready while Seth and Hawkins dismounted, and once in front of their horses. "Guess you're wonderin' why I didn't insist on you all droppin' your guns, ain't ya?"

"Why didn't you?"

"Cause I ain't met a lawdog yet any good with one!…Then I seen them two pistolas tied to your legs there and started to wonder if I might a found me some competition?…Oh, th' name's Weylon Altman, by th' way."

"From Waco?"

"Hey!" He yelped. "You hear that, boys….Marshal's heard a me up here!…What have you heard about me, Marshal?"

"You are under arrest, Altman….Now put down that rifle and drop your pistol."

"You got some guts, Marshal, I like that!" He smiled then. "Means you must be pretty good with them guns,…are ya?"

"Put th' rifle down and find out!" Gritted Dempsey. "It's getting' late."

"Altman!" Said Seth then, getting his attention. "You ain't actually dumb enough to believe you can get all three of us with a Winchester, are ya?…Now, th' Marshal is givin' you a chance here, why don't you take it?"

"Old man,…my Mama, rest 'er soul, raised me to respect the elderly, but you are makin' it real difficult….Now, shut your face, I'll get to ya!"

"Your call, Rod!" He watched Altman's eyes as he said that, and by the tone of Dempsey's voice knew he was close to pulling on the man, rifle or not, and tensed himself….He knew also that his friend might die if he provoked the man too much,…and he knew that Altman was obviously a gunfighter, and good with a gun,…and like all gunfighters, would not pass on an opportunity to prove it! But with that rifle pointed at Dempsey's middle, anything he might try and do just could result in him being shot, and that made him reluctant. He continued to watch the man's eyes however, knowing the decision would come from there and if it did, he would have to try and take him down himself.

"What say, Altman?" Said Dempsey tightly. "Are you that dumb?… Huh?…You pull that trigger on me, he'll kill you dead, turn on him, I'll kill you dead!...Come on, man, way I see it, you got only two chances here,... drop th' guns and live, or drop th' rifle and draw on me."

"Tell ya what, Marshal." Nodded Altman. "You a bettin' man?...I'll bet you a whole five silver dollars, I can shoot you with this here rifle, and still have time to shoot that old fart with my pistola....What says ya,...that a bet?"

Seth drew and fired, and the explosion was sudden, and tremendously loud in the clearing as the bullet struck the Winchester's breach with such force, the stock splintered as the gun was sent flying from Altman's numbed fingers to fall at the feet of the two gunnies holding the meat.

Stunned, Altman's open-mouth expression was one of surprise and disbelief for a second, but turned to one of rage as his hand swooped toward the gun on his hip. Dempsey drew and fired as Altman's pistol was coming into line, the bullet taking him in the chest as the second ear-shattering explosion rocked the clearing, knocking the man from his feet to be thrown to his back on the hard ground.

Dempsey stared at the body, his eyes wide for a minute before letting out his breath in a relieved rush of air. He looked at the gun in his hand for a moment then at Seth. "I like this gun!" He nodded, and quickly holstered the weapon.

"That was good shooting, Rod." Nodded Seth with appreciation, and then glanced back at the wide-eyed Jack Hawkins. "Wouldn't you agree, Jack?"

"What, oh, yes, sir!...Best I seen in a long time."

Grinning, Dempsey walked to the two men, who were still holding the heavy hindquarters of meat on their shoulders, and staring at Altman's body in disbelief.

"All right you two,...Hey!" He shouted, getting their attention. "Take this stuff back inside and put it where you got it!"

"Sure thing, Marshal."

They all three followed the two men back inside the semi-dark interior of the trading post to watch as they re-hung the meat on the hooks and put the sacks down. Seth had walked on into the cluttered room, as did Hawkins, and were both staring down at the old proprietor's lifeless body as the two men came to stand in front of Dempsey.

"Is he dead, Seth?" He called out, and when Seth nodded. "Who killed that old man?" He asked, pulling and cocking his gun.

"A,a,a,...Altman, I mean Weylon did!" Said one of them. "He done all th' killin', we just watched."

"Who are ya?"

"B,b, Bo Jenkins, Marshal,...that's me, I'm Bo Jenkins." Said the man nervously.

"What about you?" He asked the other.

"Ben Webb."

Nodding, Dempsey looked across at Seth. "Best see about th' girl, Seth." He watched as Seth crossed the room and went through another doorway,… and in a second returned with a grim-faced expression.

"Dead?"

"Throat's cut!"

"Son of a Bitch!" Cursed Dempsey, looking back at the two men. "I ought a hang you two, right here!" He breathed deeply a few times, and then nodded. "Okay, Bo Jenkins,…you and brother Ben there grab you one a them shovels over there, you got three people to bury,…and I do not want that slime out there buried anywhere close to these people in here, you hear me?"

"Oh, hell yeah, Marshal, yes, sir, plain and clear!" They hastily went to grab a shovel from the room's overstocked corner and come back.

"Mister Hawkins?" He called loudly. "Would you please oversee these two out there,…and sir,…if they try to do anything other than bury these bodies, shoot 'em!"

"I believe I'd like that!" Nodded Hawkins and followed them out.

Dempsey walked over to stare down at the old man's body. "Th' world's goin' to hell around us, Seth."

"It ain't th' world, Rod, it's th' people in it." He said, coming to stand beside him. "We're all destined for hell, I think….We just do th' best we can till we get there….You got it worse than most though, your job's to protect folks from scum like Altman. Me,…I try to live and let live. Sometimes it works, sometimes it don't!"

"Man!" Blurted Dempsey. "I took you for a lot a things, Seth, but never a philosopher!" He held up the Colt Peacemaker and looked at it again. "I really like this gun, too,…handles real nice!" Seeing Seth grin, he ejected the spent shell and reloaded it, as did Seth before holstering the weapons again. "He could a killed me, Seth, he was way too fast for me!"

"I wouldn't say that, Rod, looked damn good to me!"

"I didn't realize I shot 'im for a minute out there, till I saw th' gun in my hand."

"Yeah, well, you got mad, Rod, and that ain't never good….Got many a man killed!"

"I can believe that!…Would a got me killed, he hadn't been in shock!… Okay, let's us find some blankets for these folks."

Once the bodies were wrapped in blankets and lying in front of the store, they both rolled and lit a smoke, and as they exhaled, Seth caught a glimpse of movement at the corner of the building and turned in time to see the white-haired old Indian, who in turn quickly turned to leave.

"Joseph?" He called out loudly. "Joseph Peters, wait,...Reverend Peters sent us."

The aging Wichita stopped and slowly turned back to face them as they both hurried forward to stop in front of him.

"Joseph," Said Dempsey. "We are United States Marshals, and Seth here is right, Reverend Peters said you're the only man in th' county that can help us,...and we do need your help!...Will you talk to us?"

"Yes," He nodded. "I will talk." He quickly sat down on the ground and crossed his legs in front of him, prompting them both to do the same. "You got tobacco?" He grunted approval when Seth gave him tobacco sack and papers then deftly rolled the smoke and pocketed the tobacco. "You got match?"

Grinning, Dempsey struck a match and held the flame for him to light it.

"Now we talk." Said Joseph as he smoked.

"Okay,...Do you know about th' murders in Tyler?"

He shook his head. "Don't like Tyler, too many people, all going no place."

"Okay, I agree....But let me tell you about the murders, so you'll understand why we're here....So far, there's been twelve people murdered there, their heads were cut off, and the bodies left in th' town square....We think a bunch of evil people are doing this, Joseph,...and we believe they're hiding right here in this wilderness somewhere."

"Reverend Peters said they would need a large building, or a house to do their rituals in,...and it would be a place nobody knows about, a place that was here before Tyler was....He said that you would know where such a place might be."

"Uhhh," He nodded. "I have hunted in swamp for many years, see many houses,...many things!"

"Is there some place big enough for such a thing?"

"One place,...a place for teaching children...it was built with stones, long before I was a boy."

"A schoolhouse!" Nodded Seth. "That might do it."

"Did you go to school there, Joseph?"

"As a boy, yes, but only for a short time....I have not been there in many years.

"Where is it, Joseph?" Asked Seth. "More people will die if we can't find 'em."

"In the swamp." He raised his arm and pointed, almost in the direction of Tyler. "That way."

"Will you take us there?"

He shook his head. "No,...evil spirits are there now, many serpents, scorpions, spiders!" He shuddered then. "I am old man now, soon I will join my family in sky....But I do not wish to die in swamp!"

"Joseph," Sighed Dempsey. "If we can't find these killers in two more days time, they will kill a young girl and her baby in a ritual."

"Why do they do this evil thing?"

"To bring Satan back to earth!...Th' Reverend taught you about th' Devil didn't he?"

Joseph made the sign of the cross on his chest and mumbled a prayer before looking tearfully at them. "Maybe they are not there."

"Do you know of any other place?...A place nobody remembers ever bein' there?...Because they have to be somewhere close, Joseph,...and most all th' county is populated with farms and such. Where else can they be?"

"Many old houses, all over," He sighed. "But none so big that sons of Lucifer can live there....I will take you to schoolhouse,...but only when the evil spirits sleep....Tomorrow, we go!" He got to his feet and turned to leave.

"Joseph, wait!" Said Dempsey, stopping him. "Can we take our horses in there?"

"Horse will die in swamp."

"Okay,...how do we find you?"

"I will come here when sun rises. We go then!" He turned and walked away toward the tracks and disappeared in the trees.

"I ain;t lookin; forward to this." Sighed Dempsey, looking back at Seth. "But it's all we got!...And they still might not be there."

"We do what we have to do, Rod, go where the clues lead us....This ain't much of a clue, I know, but like you said, it's all we got!...Now,...can I borrow th' makin's, it appears I'm out?"

Grinning, Dempsey gave him tobacco and papers then grunted to his feet, as did Seth. "No, sir,...I sure ain't up to this!"

"Guess we bed down here for th' night." Replied Seth as he licked the cigarette and lit it. "And I don't reckon we'd be stealin' by takin' a few supplies for supper tonight."

"I don't think we would....You know,...Joseph pointed almost straight back toward Tyler, you notice that?"

"I did." He gave the tobacco pouch and papers back. "I know what you're thinkin', too!...A direction don't tell us where this schoolhouse is, we send Hawkins back with just that, they still won't find us....If he goes with us to find it, he won't have th' time to go back, not without a horse."

"Exactly!" He rolled and lit his own smoke then. "It took us most a th' day to get here, at a gallop!...It'll take all day tomorrow to wade through that swamp out there....Even if we had th' horses, by th' time Alex got word, the ritual would be over before they could get to us."

"And what does that tell ya, Rod?"

"That being the case?...We'll have to stop these Bastards ourselves!... Yeah, right! Who are we kiddin',...two against thirty a th' most ruthless killers we've ever encountered?...That's th' most ridiculous thing I ever heard you say, Seth!"

"I didn't say it, Rod, you did!"

"I did?...I guess I did,...well it's still ridiculous. Two men can't pull that off!"

"Three men." Grinned Seth. "If Hawkins goes with us."

"Hey, you're right!...I'd call that even odds then, wouldn't you?

"Three against thirty,...yeah, I'd call that even!" They both laughed then and went back around the corner of the building to where Hawkins was watching the two men dig the graves.

"Best spot I could find, Marshal," He said as they walked up. "Land's pretty sorry out here."

"I understand." Nodded Dempsey.

"I see you found th' Indian, He tell you anything?"

"Yeah, he did, but he's gonna have to show us th' way, Jack. If we tried, we'd never find it on our own."

"These graves deep enough, Marshal?" Asked Bo Jenkins as he peeled the soaked shirt off and draped it across a pine branch before reaching down to pull Ben Webb out of the hole. "Can't go down no more'n that, it's too hard?"

"Where's Altman's grave, Jack?"

"Off yonder a ways, Marshal."

"Go ahead and bury 'em,...I'll say a few words when you're done."

"You heard th' man, you two, bring those bodies over here and lay 'em to rest. Move it!" They watched the make-do burials and once done, Dempsey said last rites, and after, had the two men gather an armload of branches and dry grass for a fire then they all walked back to the old trading post in the dark.

"Have 'em start a fire, Jack, in front a th' door there."

"You heard 'im." Said Hawkins hatefully, and they watched as the two men hastily built the small fire, and once the flames cast a flickering light on them, and the front of the store, Dempsey walked up to face the two men squarely.

"Okay, Mister Bo Jenkins, and Ben Webb!...If I was any other lawman, but who I am, I'd hang both of you assholes right here, and right now!... But I am, who I am,...and I ain't got th' time to fuck with ya....But I will remember your ugly faces, and your names!...And when I get back to Tyler, I will issue warrants for your arrests....You won't be safe in Texas any more, so I suggest that you not stop anywhere this side a Louisiana."

"Ya,...You lettin' us go?" Blurted Bo Jenkins.

"Get out a here, you assholes, and don't even think about takin' any guns with ya!...Walk over to them horses and pull them saddle-guns out a th' boots, Altman's, too! Give 'em to Mister Hawkins here before you mount up!...Mister Hawkins, go with 'em, please?" He looked back at the two men then. "My description of you will be real good on them posters, do you understand?"

"Yes, sir, Marshal. We ain't comin' back to Texas, that's for sure!"

"Then, git!" They watched them scamper to their horses, and after giving the rifles to Hawkins, swing aboard their mounts and spur them toward the tracks and out of sight.

"Sons of Bitches!" He watched as Hawkins placed the rifles and belted guns on the ground in front of them. "Jack, you notice a lantern in that store anywhere?"

"Sure did."

"Then lets go light it, see what we can find in there for supper. We'll need a fry-pan, salt, pepper,...you know, let's go. Be right back, Seth."

Once the horses had all been unsaddled and staked out to graze, they placed their saddles around the fire and spread the bedrolls,...and were soon frying thick slices of ham in a deep skillet, along with a large tin of canned of beans Dempsey had poured in with the meat and that, along with a crusty loaf of day old bread, they were prepared to eat their supper from tin plates Hawkins found in the store, then, as they all three settled around the fire to wait, Dempsey stirred the food in the skillet as it cooked.

"Who was this Weylon Altman, Rod?" Queried Seth suddenly. "How'd you know about 'im?"

"Didn't,...Texas Rangers sent fliers out on 'im some time back, said he was a killer, reputation backed it up!...You should remember Chuck Hammond, though, he'd a been about my age now....I saw him kill a man in Nacogdoches, too,...before you got there!"

"You chase him, too?"

"Would have,...Naw, if I recollect, I was all hot to trot to face 'im down though....The Sheriff ran 'im out a town ahead a me!...Pissed me off!...Probably saved my bad ass, too!....Anyway, Altman killed Hammond a couple years ago in Waco. Rumor was, it was almost a dead heat!...You ever meet 'im?"

"In passing once, in Austin, before th' war started. Would a tangled, I guess, hadn't been for th' Rangers. They was pretty new back then, only ten or twelve strong,...but th' sight a so much law in one place, sent 'im packin'....Never met 'im again."

"Good thing!" Replied Dempsey. "Ain't a doubt in my mind, you'd a killed 'im!"

"I'd a tried!" He sighed then. "I was quite a romper-stomper back then."

"You was a Gunfighter, Marshal?" Queried Hawkins, who until then had only listened. "Don't get me wrong, I actually thought so when I saw you shoot Altman's rifle, never seen anything that fast!"

"I'd never a beat 'im, if he hadn't, Jack." Said Dempsey.

"He was about to shoot you, Rod, I had no choice."

"I know that!...And I do appreciate it, Seth." He sat the skillet aside then and grabbed his plate. "Let's eat."

They all filled their plates and leaned back to eat while the coffee was boiling, and it was done as they finished the meal. Hawkins used his bandana to grab the pot and pour their tin cups full of the scalding brew and passed them around before sitting back again to roll himself a smoke.

"Thanks, Jack." Grinned Dempsey. "You're a good man to have around."

"I do what I can."

"How long, you been with Quinlan, Jack?" He asked as he rolled his own then passed the sack to Seth.

"Not too long, Couple a years, maybe. It's a hell of a big spread!...Got more cows than I ever seen in one place."

"How is he to work for?"

"He's a likeable man, real friendly when ya speak to 'im,...course we don't see that much of 'im, he talks mostly to Wade, he's th' foreman....I've sure been in worse places."

"Ain't we all....Alex said he came here after th' war,...did real well, that's for sure."

"Wade said he was a Carpetbagger."

"Does appear likely." Grinned Dempsey. "You met Ms. Quinlan?"

"No, sir,...real pretty lady though."

"If she's like her sister, she is." He saw Hawkins frown then. "Her Brother in law is my boss, Judge Castle over in Dallas."

"Seems Wade mentioned that, too. Never hurts to have a Judge in th' family."

"I agree."

Hawkins looked across at Seth's stone-like expression then. "If you don't mind me askin',…Seth, is it?…How did you learn to shoot so quick? No offense, Marshal,…but I saw Bill Longley shoot a man once in Indian Territory, real quick, too!…Th' man had a bad reputation."

"I don't like talkin' about what I was, Jack, but,…I've had a gun in my hand ever since my Papa let me fire his old flintlock pistol, I was around ten, or eleven years old. Killed my first man then, too,…drunken Caddo Indian. Shot 'im in back a th' head, right after he killed my father.…I love guns, always have, Knives too,…and I still do, I guess!…And to answer your question, it ain't all in the learning how!…I can't explain it, but I guess a man would have to have nothin' else in his life, but his gun, and he wouldn't let anything interfere with his using it. He'd practice day and night, sleep with it, eat with it, know where it was at all times, and how to get to it real quick.….Once ya learn all these things, they will eventually become part of who you are, and you won't have to practice any more."

"And, Mister Bill Longley was after my time, I was a rancher by then. Never met th' man!" He sighed then. "Had me a Reputation once, felt good at th' time,…made me feel important!…I don't have one anymore, and don't want one!"

"Sorry I asked, Marshal."

"That's okay, Jack." He grinned. "I don't mind folks knowin what I was back then, long as they know what I am now.….Let's leave it at that, now, okay?"

"You bet.…Okay,…do I start back to town now, or what are we doing?"

"We have a problem there, Jack," Sighed Dempsey. "And it just won't work the way we planned it!…So let me run it by ya,…because the decision is gonna be yours to make."

"What is it?"

"First, if you left right now, you wouldn't get back much before daybreak, and you wouldn't have anything to report to Alex, anyway,… because we don't know where we're going!…We have a direction, that's all. Alex would not find us in time to help us!"

"So, what are you sayin', Marshal?"

"Joseph is going to guide us in tomorrow at daybreak, It's an all day walk through that shit out there, just to get there, and you'd have to go with us to know where it was.…Then you'd have to walk all th' way back here to get your horse and go for help,…and that help is fifteen miles away!"

"I get it now." Nodded Hawkins soberly. "I'd have to walk back to Tyler from there, to know how to get back!"

"What it comes down to, is this.…You can leave now and go home, this is our job, not yours!…Or you can go with us, your choice all th' way."

Hawkins reached up to scratch his head, then studied their faces in the fire's light for a minute before looking down at the ground and laughing. "Can the three of us take 'em down, Marshal?" He asked as he looked up.

"It would depend on a couple a things." Replied Seth. "How many of 'em, bein' th' first!...How well we do our job is th' second....These people are Devil Worshippers, very well trained assassins!...They use the dark to hunt their victims. What I'm sayin' is this, Jack....If you look at a shadow and don't see 'em in time, you'll lose your head! They can kill without warning, and without a sound being made."

"And none a this scares you?"

"Damn right it scares us!" Said Dempsey. "We're scared right now!...But so is that little black girl and her baby, and so was the twelve grown people they beheaded!...That girl and baby will both be killed in a fuckin' ritual come Thursday night at midnight,...and somebody has to stop 'em!...It's our job, Jack, not yours. We're gonna try and stop 'em, because if we don't, who will?...They'll just move on and murder thirteen more people if we don't!... That's what I meant by, your decision!"

"Oh, shit, Man!...That's layin' it bare all right!" He sighed then. "No choices, no options!"

"You got a choice!" Reminded Seth. "You might be smart to go."

"Then I'd have to live with it!...I think that would be worse than dying,...looks like I'm in!"

"Good man!" Said Dempsey. "Now listen real good!...Ain't no man anywhere with a better nose for trouble than Seth here. He feels it, senses it, and then acts on it....We find these Bastards, you do what he says, when he says it....I intend to, because if we do, we might come out a this alive!... That's th' bare facts of it!"

"You any good with a Winchester?" Asked Seth, looking at the rifle in Hawkins' saddle-boot.

"Yes, sir,...I was a sniper for General Lee. I'm an exceptional shot....Not so much with a hand-gun."

"That's what we need!...We have to get ready now, so, what I'd like you to do right now, is light that lantern again,...we'll need all the cartridges we can carry, both rifle and sidearm. Mine's a forty-four, same as my Winchester. I see you carry a forty-five, same as Rod there, so keep that in mind. Wouldn't hurt to grab one and them old boys' pistols for a spare, I'm goin' to....Somethin' else, too. We'll need some heavy leather strings."

"What's that for, Seth?"

"Won't be able to carry your rifle in all that brush, so we'll hang 'em across our backs with a strap a strap....Other than that, we'll be ready to go!"

"Except for grub." Said Dempsey. "Best see what we can find there, too,…each man carries his own rations."

"There's beef jerky, …maybe it's pork,…anyway, it's hanging in strips over th' counter in there." Said Hawkins.

"That'll work just fine!" Nodded Dempsey. "Jerky's easy to carry…. Guess we can put the spare guns and saddles inside, if we can lock the door?"

"Except for one Winchester." Said Seth. "That's for Joseph, put a strap on it for 'im….Altman's horse is his, too!" He grunted to his feet then and stretched his aching muscles. "Let's get to it!...Jack, you and me'll get th' Jerky and Cartridges. Rod, make sure th' horses are staked in a good place to graze, then bring in th' guns and all th' saddles, but Altman's….We best fill th' canteens, too, none fit to drink in that swamp."

                    *   *   *

They were ready at daybreak and waiting for Joseph to arrive, and after double-checking everything, were all standing around the fire's remnants when Hawkins picked up the long-bladed knives and passed them to them.

"What's this?" Queried Dempsey as he hefted the blade. "Machete!… Good thinkin', Jack, might have to make our own trail out there!"

"I'm thinkin' more about snakes, and gators." Returned Hawkins. "Nothin' I hate worse."

"Here he comes." Said Seth as Joseph walked toward them.

"Looks prepared." Commented Dempsey as he appraised the thick, leather leggings strapped snugly around the old Indian's legs.

Joseph stopped to briefly look them over and that's when Seth gave him the rifle. A look of surprise, and admiration showed on his wrinkled face as he accepted it then inspected it before nodding his thanks at Seth, and slinging it onto his back. He spied the Machete in Dempsey's hand then and took it from him, thanking him with a grin. "We go now!" He said curtly, and then looked at each of them.

"Walk in straight line behind me, step where I step!...This place is alive, and hungry, it will swallow a man." He led off around the side of the store and into the darkest, the worst, the hottest, most insect-infested wilderness any of them had ever imagined. The Swarming mosquitoes were as large as horseflies and with the clouds of accompanying gnats, swarmed over them from the onset in the bog's steamy-heat,…and they were constantly slapping at unprotected necks and faces.

For the next hour or more, they were in an almost impregnable barrier of trees, twisting vines, thick growths of pricking briars, with thorns that gouged at skin and clothing and leaving shirts and trousers stained with blood, which only made the insects more aggressive. Except for an occasional grunt, or curse, they continued to follow the wiry old Wichita as he hacked their way through the maze of thick foliage and dead undergrowth,…and coupled with dead, rotting timber, that constantly stabbed at them, it was another couple of hours before this torture ended, and another began.

Because now, they found themselves surrounded by murky, foul-smelling, very stagnant water of which was almost totally covered with rotting debris. Gaseous clouds, emitting from the thick, multi-layers of rotting mulch and debris covered the dark, dead water like a dense fog, making it hard to find any oxygen in the stifling heat to even breathe. Dead, waterlogged stumps of trees protruded from the water everywhere, and all around the fringe was nothing but dead timber, some being held upright by a thick forest of Pines, while most just littered the rotting surface of soggy earth.

The wily Joseph Peters never faltered, or slowed his steady pace through the poisoned water and almost immediately began hacking at several large Moccasins that slithered at them through the cover of debris, never slowing his forward progress until finally leading them out onto more solid, yet very mushy ground and there stopped to wait until they were all there beside him. Nodding, he bent, and using the Machete's wide blade, began scraping away the clinging leaches from Seth's pant-legs.

"Shit, man!" He stammered then began checking the rest of his body. That outburst caused Dempsey and Hawkins to begin checking themselves, and using their knives to dislodge the bloodsuckers.

"Thanks, Joseph." Breathed Seth. "I hate them damn things!"

Without a word, Joseph turned and once again began hacking at the undergrowth and leading the way into the swampy wilderness..

*   *   *

Alex Maynard poured his coffee then replaced the pot on the stove before taking the bandana from his neck and wiping sweat from his face and brow, and at that moment thought how stupid he was to have a fire in the stove in the middle of August and cursing mildly, raised his foot to open the grate, grabbed the half empty pot and doused the fire. Almost immediately, the room seemed to fill with smoke and cursing again, quickly went to open the door.

"Fuckin' dummy!" He said aloud, just as Jeter and Gibbs suddenly appeared in front of him. "God damn it, Jeter!…Don't do that!"

"Sorry, Lieutenant, we saw th' smoke and hurried to see what was wrong?"

"Nothin's wrong!" He opened the grate again and dumped the cup's contents in on the smoldering wood. "It's just dumb to have a fire in that damn stove in middle of summer!...Already sweated so much, my ass is chafed!"

"What's eatin' you, Lieutenant?" Queried Gibbs. "We make coffee on that stove two, three times a day, always have."

He nodded and sat down, and then coughed from the smoke before nodding again. "You're right, Mister Gibbs!...Hawkins should a been back sometime last night!...We got one day left to end this nightmare." He sighed then and reached to roll a smoke. "Somethin' went wrong out there, I think, else Hawkins would a been back!" He lit his smoke and exhaled it into that already drifting out of the office. "We ain't gonna make it, Gentlemen!"

"We still got time, Lieutenant." Insisted Jeter. "He could be on his way back right now, it's a long ride to that water tank."

"I know it is,...and we might not be able to find 'em in there if he does make it!...Won't know North from South, we get in that shit!...And they won't have a chance tryin' to take on that bunch alone."

"Might not be as many as we thought they was, Lieutenant." Said Gibbs. "Might not be but ten or twelve a th' bastards, they'll handle 'em okay."

"Get real, Gibbs,...we all know better than that!

"What do we do then?" Blurted Jeter. "We have to help 'em!"

"Jeter," Sighed Maynard. "You tell me how, I'll lead th' posse!"

"Sorry, Lieutenant, I'm just mad is all."

"Makes five of us, I'm sure,...or it would, where is Walt and Cliff?"

"That's what we came to tell ya, Lieutenant!,...what with th' smoke and all,...anyway, Walt's helpin' that nigger gal back home, we found her kid this morning,...she was dead! Cliff's over at Docs while he looks th' body over."

"Murderin' Sons a Bitches!" He cursed. "Where was she?"

"Back yard a th' house across th' street, guess they didn't want her without th' mama."

"She all there,...her head?"

"Throat cut is all, in a hurry, I guess."

"Guess we can send the other women home then."

"Already did." Said Gibbs. "Knew you'd want to. The Colonel's men are at Norma's, told 'em we might need 'em."

"Got Norma's food bill, too, Lieutenant." Said Jeter, taking the bill from his shirt and giving it to him. "Pretty good tab."

He looked at it and dropped it on the desk before looking up at Jeter. "I want you to take them wranglers a mile or so out Bullard road and pitch camp, get supplies for a couple a days....If Rod finds these Bastards, there's a chance you'll hear the shooting. Might be able to find 'em that way?...Better take some lanterns, be blind tonight without some light."

"We'll use torches, Lieutenant, gives off more light....Want us to go now?"

"No, it'll take 'em all day to find 'em,...if they do?...Be in place before dark."

"I'll go tell 'em right now." He left and then Maynard sighed before retrieving bottle and glass from the desk and pouring them both a drink.

"What do we do while they're out there?" Queried Gibbs as he drank the liquor. "We ought a be doin' somethin' right now, Lieutenant!"

"Tell me what, Mister Gibbs,...and we'll do it!...No, I want you three along th' fringe a that swamp tonight, there's five miles of it in front a that depot....There's a way in and out a that wilderness, Mister Gibbs!...It's there somewhere, and if there's any stragglers get's away, they'll use it!"

CHAPTER TEN

"Well," Smiled Emmit Castle as he looked up. "Jake Tulane, come in, Marshal." He got up to shake his hand. "How are ya, Jake?"

"I'm fine, Judge,…just wondered if you'd heard anything yet?"

"As a matter of fact, I have." He went to his desk for the paper. "Got this from Sheriff Maynard, yesterday, here, you can read it for yourself." He sat down as Tulane read the rather lengthy wire and when he was done, studied the expression on the Marshal's troubled face.

"Devil Worshippers, Judge,…ain't that th' same as voodoo?"

"Don't know that much about either, Jake….I do know that voodoo originated in Africa, and was introduced here by slaves. Devil worshipping goes as far back as the Middle-ages….But it's not the same, somehow,… talking about this one….This one uses people for a sacrifice, instead of animals! This one may be a starting trend in Satanism, I don't know, and I don't know when, or if the transition might have occurred, if it did?…The book I have on the subject leaves a lot to be desired, so to speak."

"You got this yesterday, that makes tomorrow the twentieth….Means they got till then to find this Cult and stop 'em!…Judge, th' way this reads, the whole thing is ridin' on th' memory of one old Indian!"

"That's what it amounts to, Jake!…They may not find them at all, and if they can't, it will be a shame." He leaned back in his chair then reached to close the book he had open on the desk. "You were right the other day, though, there has been only one other recorded case like this one. Five years ago in the New Orleans area. No doubt it's the same bunch!…They have to be stopped, Jake, before this transition becomes the norm."

"Rod and Seth ain't never been up against somethin' like this, Judge,… I'm worried they might not make it!"

"I have been worried since the untimely death of Henry Jones,…he was one of my best, fifty tough cases under his belt, always got his man!…They

124

are up against something quite unknown, all right,…and dangerous!…But do not give up on Roderick, or Seth Mabry, they are capable men."

"I know that, Judge….At least they got your brother in law's cowboys to help 'em."

"I'm sure they do,…if they can find the Cult!…You're not the only one chomping at the bit about this, Jake,…Alec Hayward has wanted this case from the start, almost told him yes, too."

"Why didn't ya?"

"At first, it was a bit personal, Gwendolyn's sister and all….And at the time, I thought it was just some deranged killer on the loose, nothing a U.S. Marshal couldn't handle!…I was wrong!…By the time Henry Jones was murdered, Hayward and his Rangers were fighting rustlers on The Rio Grande….I had no choice, but to send Roderick!…He's with Seth Mabry, Jake,…and that don't stop us from worrying, you understand,…but Seth Mabry is like a hound dog when he get's the scent, he won't quit!…And he just happens to be the best gun that I have ever seen!"

Tulane nodded with a grin. "Yeah, me, too, Judge!"

"It's okay to worry, Jake, and don't feel so helpless, your job is right here!"

"Yeah,": He said, getting to his feet. "See ya, Judge,…and thanks." Nodding, he went to the door before turning around, "If you hear anything?"

"I'll let you know, Jake."

*   *   *

It was mid afternoon when Joseph led the trio of tired, mud-caked and sweat-soaked man hunters onto solid ground by hacking through several large vines and clinging briars out of their path,…and seeing the bent foliage and deep impressions in the debris, told them to stop while he followed the wide tracks for a ways and then came back. "A wagon makes these ruts." He said flatly, and pointed down at them before waving his arm upward. "Men have been here, trees have been cut, limbs cut from them to make a road."

They looked closer as Joseph pointed out things about the makeshift road, and they could see the obvious path of bent brush and severed limbs. They were also able to see the path the road was taking through the wilderness until it disappeared,…and the even cuts on limbs where the debris had been hacked off with sharp knives to open the way for a wagon.

"This is the way they came in, Seth." Said Dempsey tiredly then looked along the path the other way. "And that's where they went!"

"Appears to be." He breathed and nodding, looked at Joseph. "Is the wagon going that way?" He asked, nodding his head northward.

"Yes,…wagon comes from there." He said, and waved his arm behind them. "It goes there, see how grass is bent?"

"I can see that." He grinned. "But right now, I don't really know East from West in here….Okay," He said, looking at Dempsey and Hawkins, who were watching him and still busy slapping at insects. "Looks like we turn right."

"Hallelujah!" Gasped Dempsey. "We got half that fuckin' swamp in our boots right now,…and we finally find a road!"

"Where's th' school from here, Joseph,…how far?"

"One mile, maybe two, maybe three,…but wagon goes there."

"Are you sure?"

"No roads in here for many years now, nearest road is many miles to the West. No trails this wide in here!...Men make this road for the wagon, see cuts on trees?...No new growth."

"How long ago?"

"Hard to say, two, maybe three month ago."

"Okay,…You'd best go back now, we'll take it from here."

"I wish you much luck!" He nodded and then took the rifle from his back.

"No, no,…th' rifle is yours, you keep it….I want a thank you, Joseph." He reached and took the Wichita's hand in a firm shake. "By th' way, back at the store, there's a sorrel horse with two white feet and blaze face, that's yours, too, saddle and all."

"No one take these things from me?"

"If they try, shoot 'em!"

Thanks be to you as well." He grinned. "And I accept this reward!" He nodded at them all and quickly shook their hands before moving back into the swamp.

"That's one tough old bird!" Sighed Dempsey, watching him until he disappeared. "Don't know about you, Seth." He said as he adjusted his gun belt so he could relieve himself. "But I need a small breather, man, and a smoke!"

"Amen." Replied Hawkins as he followed suit. "Don't that old man ever get tired?...I can barely stand up!...And my God, my boots are full a water, rubbed my feet raw!"

"They're ridin' boots." Said Dempsey as he rolled his smoke and gave Seth the makings. "Ain't made for much walkin' in a lake."

"Best not take 'em off to dump th' water neither." Said Seth. "Might not get 'em on again." He rolled and lit his smoke as he talked, and at the same time hoped the smell of smoke didn't give them away. "We find that School, we'll find us a place to hunker down and watch it….We can dry out our feet then."

"You sayin' you want a wait before takin' 'em down?" Queried Dempsey. "Why?"

"All of 'em might not be there tonight, and I want all these Bastards in my sights!...We hit 'em tonight, and they all ain't there, we'll be open for attack our self. Uh-uh,…I want 'em all at that ritual when th' shootin' starts!"

"Put that way, it makes sense!" Agreed Dempsey with a sigh.

"And we best be on our toes from here on." Continued Seth. "It's naturally dark in here as it is, good cover for 'em,…so watch th' shadows, both of ya."

"You understand what he means, Jack?" Asked Dempsey.

"I think so, yeah."

"If we have to open fire before we get to that school, we already failed!" Reminded Seth. "Be damn sure before you shoot at somethin'!...If we're lucky, we won't be spotted by comin' in this way, and let's hope they feel safe enough not to put any guards out!...One thing's for sure, I think,…they won't be expecting us!" He looked at them then, and nodded. "Let's go,…I want a be in a good place before dark." He took the rifle from his back and levered in a cartridge before leading off down the hastily made wagon trail. Dempsey and Hawkins, rifles in hand, walked gingerly in their waterlogged boots and raw feet as they trailed after him. They were quiet, and with nerves already on edge, peered intently into the dark underbrush on both sides, each half expecting to see a sword wielding, cloaked assassin at any tense moment.

Although the cultists had hacked out a crude road in a tangled wilderness, walking on the fallen branches and overlaying vines and briars was not an easy thing as they were forced to carefully choose each step they made, all knowing what a turned or twisted ankle would do to hinder their chances,…and none dared to chance a conversation because the closer they came to the schoolhouse, even the slightest sounds could be enough to detract from the norm, and be heard by those same cultists.

It was late, and almost totally dark along the widened trail when they heard what sounded like wood being chopped from somewhere just ahead of them. Seth had already stopped, and as Dempsey and Hawkins moved in beside him, he pointed through the maze of trees where three cloaked cultists were silently hacking away the limbs of several felled, smaller sized Pine logs,…and as they edged in closer they could see the large vine covered stone structure of the one-time school. The building was large, and oblong, a one-storied structure with small windows along the one side,…and all of them appeared to be covered with something from the inside.

Two more of the Cult members came out of the building then to lift two of the prepared logs to their shoulder and carry them inside, just as two more emerged to do the same. Two of the three doing the chopping put their swords away and began carrying the new logs toward the building to drop them in front of the door and then start back again.

Seth knew they must be building their altar with the timbers in preparation for the ritual and at that moment, felt a hatred he had not experienced in twenty years. At the time, he had called it being in a killing frame of mind. But this, he knew was only rage toward a group of murderous, moral-less, evil killers,…and they deserved to die!…He thought of Laura then, and of Greg, both waiting for him at home and wondered what they would do if he failed to come home?…They might never know what happened to him!

Shaking his head, he forced the thoughts from his mind and watched as the last of the logs were carried inside the building, and then slowly moved in behind the trunk of a large Pine to intently scan the open area around the school,…and not seeing any movement in the fast approaching darkness, moved out even further to squat beside one of the many stumps to search the area of the building. There was a pale, orange light emanating through the school's door-less opening, lighting up an area in front of it for several yards out.

Satisfied they were all inside, he lifted himself enough to sit down on the unevenly hacked stump, placed the rifle on the debris underfoot and proceeded to force the swollen, waterlogged boots off and dump the water from them.. Dempsey and Hawkins quickly did the same, and after wringing out their cotton socks, spread them across their shoulders and used their bandanas to clean and dry their sore feet, and then to wipe out the boots.

"It's gonna be a chore getting' in there across all this open space!" Whispered Dempsey. "We'll be seen for sure, if there's a guard."

"We won't use th' front door." Returned Seth. "Roof on that place has got a be rotten and fallin' in, I can see light from th' fire shining through it, see it?…And there's plenty a smoke coming through."

"I see it,…but how do we get up there?"

"We climb up th' rocks."

"You're jokin', right?"

"I never joke when it comes to killin'!…See how uneven them rocks are, they weren't cut to fit!…Ought a be easy to climb." He glanced at Hawkins then. "How ya feelin', Jack?"

"I got a tell ya, Marshal,…I never seen anything like this, scares the shit out a me!"

"You as good as you claim with that gun?"

"If I can see it, I can shoot it, yes, sir!"

"That's good, cause when it starts, you'll be in th trees, somewhere in front a th' door yonder….They'll be comin' out a there fast, and they'll be outlined by that altar fire….Don't let 'em get away!"

"I'll do my best!" Breathed the wrangler. "How far you think it is from that door to them lone trees yonder, forty, fifty yards?"

"About,…Course, we'll be shooting down from th' roof there in front,… we'll get th' bastards!"

"Okay." Whispered Dempsey. "I'm so tired, I'm trembling, where we gonna hold up for th' night?"

"Somewhere across th' road back there, they'll be out and about early."

"Well, th' snakes'll be out tonight, Seth,…I don't cotton to bein' snakebit."

"Find you a good stout limb to sit on, climb a tree, Rod." He reached for one of his boots and tugged it on, and then the other one. "Put your boots on, and let's move."

*   *   *

"Jeter and the cowboys gone?" Asked Maynard as Gibbs and Walt came in.

"Left out about four o'clock, Lieutenant." Said Gibbs with a frown. "You think it's gonna do any good, them bein' there, that's forty-odd miles a twistin' road out there?"

"They ain't that far away, they come and go too quick….They're within one or two miles a that depot, I'd bet on it!…If Rod can flush 'em, there's a good chance some of you will see 'em comin' out a there somewhere….If any of 'em get's away?" He sighed then. "Where's Cliff?"

"Waitin' on us at th' depot. We just came to tell ya we're on our way, everything's in place."

"Good!…Just keep movin' along that stretch a wilderness there, you'll hear 'em if they come out."

"Ride and wait," Sighed Walt. "Guess it's better'n doin' nothin' a'tall…. But I sure do wish I knew where them Marshals was right now."

"Yeah," Nodded Maynard. "But I know there's a road in that swampy shit-hole,…they might a built it themselves, but by God it's there!" He reached to angrily roll and light a smoke as he got up to go to the window.

"There's something about that Marshal Mabry, too,…I can't figure 'im out, but he's different than most men I've seen."

"How do ya mean?" Queried Gibbs. "All I see is a long in th' tooth, old has-been!"

"Then you ain't lookin', Mister Gibbs." He said, turning to grin at him. "He don't talk much, he listens, he deciphers things that he sees and hears.…. And when he talks, it makes sense.…And don't forget what Rod said about how he can shoot!"

"Come on, Lieutenant,…I didn't believe that shit!…He was just makin' excuses for 'im bein' here."

"Believe what ya want, old son,…but he's a man knows what he's doin. He's in charge here, too, not Rod!…Don't tell you ain't noticed how Rod asks his opinion before doin' something?"

"Yes, sir, I did notice that." Returned Walt "We'd a never thought about that clock tower if he hadn't, neither!"

"Exactly,…This Marshal Mabry is everything Rod says he is, and maybe a lot more!"

"Like maybe an outlaw, or a wanted gunfighter?" Queried Walt.

"Good question,…but I can't find any posters on 'im, old, or new!… Anyway, that's why I think they'll find these sons a Bitches!"

"Well, I sure hope you're right, Lieutenant,…but I never knowed but a couple a men you ever showed that much respect for!"

"Never been but a couple, Gibbs, still ain't!…I respect what Mabry is, and what I believe he's capable of, that's all."

"Well, if you don't mind me sayin' so, it's confusin'!…What do you think he's capable of?"

"If you don't beat all, gibbs!…I think he's a gunfighter who was lucky enough to escape the wanted posters,…and good enough to become that long in the tooth, old man!…I can't recall any, of any fame, that was able to live past forty,…but he has."

"I ain't never gonna argue with you again, Lieutenant." He laughed then. "But they's got a be plenty a gunhands give it up and go to ranchin' or somethin'!…Besides,…I ain't seen anybody any better'n you are, hell, I bet you could take wes Hardin down!"

"I wouldn't try, Mister Gibbs, thanks anyway!… Now, before ya go. How'd that nigger girl seem when Jeter took her home, she awake and walkin',…she know what happened that night?"

"All she remembered was th' window being opened, next thing, her eyes was burnin and she passed out.…Must a blowed some kind a powder in her face or somethin'."

"Opium, Maybe. Seems I heard a some Indians using dried snake venom....I don't know." He bent to grab a chunk of firewood, opened the grate on the stove and shoved it in, and then went for the torn page of a newspaper and started a fire under the coffee pot.

"Thought it was too hot for coffee?" Grinned Gibbs.

"It's not right now!" He came back to the desk and sat down. "You had your supper yet?"

"Yes, sir....Lieutenant,...you think Marshal Dempsey's any good with a gun?" He went to a chair along the wall and sat down. "I mean, you'd expect a man who wears two guns would be."

"Maybe so,...but I don't think he's always worn two guns."

"How can ya tell?"

"Way he walks, I guess, ain't used to 'em....What's all this talk about gun-fighting anyway?"

"I always wanted to be fast on th' draw, Lieutenant, I practice when I can."

"I didn't know that, Mister Gibbs...But ya know, bein' fast is only part of it, you got a be accurate, too!...Most times a man that's accurate will kill a man that's faster."

"Yes, sir,...if he's got th' nerve to stand there and aim."

"That's what it boils down to, Gibbs,...no man wants to die, and very few have that kind a nerve! Ain't a man alive who ain't afraid a dyin' when he faces a man that wants to kill 'im."

"That's what we thought, too, Boss," Said Walt, going to sit down with Gibbs. "If you'd seen that fucker in th' clock tower, you might not say that!... He weren't afraid a'tall, believe me!"

"Any sane man would be, Walt, that one had th' Devil in 'im....There's somethin' wrong with them freaks, they're lunatics, and dangerous as hell!"

"Yes, sir!" Said Walt, nodding his head. "He acted like he wanted to die."

"Okay," Sighed Maynard. "Better get on down to th' depot now, Cliff's alone down there."

"Yes, sir." Said Gibbs, and they both got up. "Lieutenant, some a them Bastards is bound to get away, ain't no way, three men are gonna take 'em down, got a be twenty or thirty of 'em!"

"What's your point, Gibbs?"

"No point, Lieutenant....But don't ya think them that gets away might come on into Tyler, you know,...for revenge, or somethin'?"

"That's why you'll be there, Mister Gibbs, to stop 'em!" He sighed heavily then. "It all boils down to this, fellas,...if we want a keep our jobs, this nightmare has to be over by tomorrow night. If there's any more murders like these, I'll never be re-elected!...We are paid very well here, all of us!...I like my job, too! Way I see it, them three men out there is my only hope a keepin' it!...So stay alert, Gibbs, all of ya."

"Shouldn't we ask th' Colonel for more men, Boss?" Asked Walt.

"No,...Th' Colonel's done enough!...We're th' law here, not th' Colonel."

"Yes, sir!...See ya tomorrow, Lieutenant."

Maynard watched them leave then sighing again, rolled and lit another smoke before getting up to check the coffee pot. It was hot so he used his bandana to carry the pot to the desk and pour his coffee, which only amounted to a few drops and cursing, carried the pot into the cellblock, and the bucket of water there and dipped water into it, and then fresh grounds before taking it back to the stove. His mind was on Dempsey and Seth as he went back to sit down,...and of what they were trying to do in the swamp,... and he immediately found himself wishing he knew where they were also. He knew there was more than an even chance the Cult would not be where they thought it was, and if they were not, all was lost, even his job, not even the Colonel could save it this time,...his Government clout was lost at the end of Reconstruction.

He hated the thought of someone else doing the job he should have already done, hated that he had not the expertise he needed to be the lawman he should be! But most of all, he hated that damn Cult, he thought angrily. To now, his job had been one of luxury, so why now?...Why hadn't those crazies gone elsewhere to commit their mayhem? He used the bandana in his hand then to wipe sweat from his face and neck while staring through the window at the occasional pedestrian that passed. It could be a lot worse than what it is, he thought then. One thing was for damn sure, when this was over, if he still had a job,...he would damn sure take that job a bit more seriously!...All he could do now, however, is wait,...and hope for the best!

*   *   *

Dawn introduced its self late in the morning to the dank interior of the swamp's rotting floor, as it took time for the light of day to filter through the heavy foliage of deep woods,...everywhere, Seth noted, but the clearing where the schoolhouse was. It was quite bright there compared to where they were hiding, and the Cultists were out early, their heads covered and once again cutting and de-branching more of the immature trees and saplings, while others carried the finished product back inside the school. The work had been going on for an hour before the morning sun showed its self and bathed the clearing with sunlight.

"Must be some altar they're building in there." Whispered Dempsey as he swatted at the biting insects.

"I guess Lucifer demands perfection." Returned Seth. "Wish we knew they were all in there, ain't seen more than eight or nine since we got here."

"Maybe they are, takes a few to build th' thing….We don't how many there are anyway, could be all of 'em!"

"Be easier, if it is!…But I doubt it….Got a be fifteen or twenty of 'em, anyway!" He turned to Hawkins then. "Picked your point of attack, yet, Mister Hawkins?"

"I'm thinkin' them two lone Pines we talked about,…looks to be about forty yards away from that doorway, gives me room to fight!"

"Good thinkin'."

"When do we start this shindig?"

"Sometime around midnight." Replied Seth, still in a whisper. "We'll all be in place right after dark though. Once you get in position out there, me and Rod will work our way down and scale that wall to th' roof….They should all be in there when that ritual starts!"

"I'd say, they're all in there right now." Said Dempsey. "I can see the wagon and team a horses back in th' trees, behind th' school yonder."

"I saw 'em, Rod,…but it don't mean anything….There could still be more of 'em out and about….We have to kill 'em all,…only way to be sure this won't happen again!"

"Too bad that place ain't made a wood!" Said Hawkins. "Serve 'em right."

"Yes it would!" Returned Seth.

"You do know we'll be shootin' down unarmed men tonight?" Whispered Dempsey. "Might be considered murder in a court a law."

"You want a go ask 'em to give up?…Maybe loan 'em a gun?"

"Hell, no!" Returned Dempsey with feeling.

"Then don't think about it that way, Rod, they'll damn sure kill you without warning!"

"That's easy said." Replied Dempsey. "Guess they got that poor girl and her baby in there somewhere, too, be nice to hear some kind a sound from 'er, be sure she's still alive.'

"She's alive." Whispered Seth. "They won't kill her before it's time….You won't hear anything till then."

"They don't even talk to each other," Breathed Hawkins. "It ain't natural."

"We best keep it down some." Said Seth. "Sound carries….If you can sleep any more, do it!…We gat a busy night ahead of us." He resigned himself then to watching the cultists work on the saplings at the edge of the cleared ground.

*   *   *

"I'll put th' horses away, Greg." Grunted Trey as they rode up to the corral and dismounted.

"Thanks, Trey." He could see his mother on the front porch of the house. "Grain 'em good, okay?" He gave the reins to him and walked on down the grade toward the house, leaving Trey watching him and shaking his head worriedly.

"What are you doing, Mama?" He asked as he walked up to the steps, jerking an uncontrollable gasp of surprise from her.

"What?...Oh, honey,...nothing. Just thinking of your father." She smiled at him then looked back up the road. "Guess I was hoping to see him ride out of those trees there."

Nodding, he climbed the steps and put his arm around her. "Daddy's okay, Mama, there ain't nobody can beat him, you know that."

"I know, honey,...but he's not dealing with ordinary folks now, it's voodoo!...They have powers unheard of,...magical powers."

"Mama, come on now." Urged Greg. "You don't really believe in magic!...Voodoo or not, they are people, and daddy knows that!...It'll be the sorriest day they ever had if they fight him."

"I hope so, Sweetheart....But I have heard such terrible stories about voodoo Cults, some from my own father, and I have never known him to lie!"

"Daddy's only been gone a week, Mama, he's okay. Besides, if anything happens, Marshal Tulane will get word to us, he's daddy's friend, too."

"You're right, of course." She sighed. "Well, I'd better start supper now, didn't know it was so late."

"Okay, Mama." He kissed her cheek then watched her go into the house before looking back up the road. He was worried, too, and it was getting harder to not show it in front of her. He had not thought much about it, because it upset him too much, but just what would they do if something did happen to him?...Shuddering, he took another long, longing look up the road and went into the house.

*   *   *

Alex Maynard poured his coffee then watched as Quinlan stepped out of his Surrey and tied up at the hitch rail,...and with a look up and down the street, removed his hat and came into the office.

"Afternoon, Colonel." He grinned, shaking his benefactor's hand. "What brings you in today?"

"Not knowing what's going on." He sighed. "These murders are keeping me on edge, Alex,…how about an update?…I was at the hotel, as well and didn't see any of the hands, or the women that was there."

"We sent th' women back home, Colonel,…they got their thirteenth victim, the other night, no need to hold 'em any longer."

"They took another victim, right under your nose?"

"Yes, sir,…Marshal Mabry caught 'em takin' a girl earlier that night, and killed one of 'em, another one got away. They saved the girl's life, but the baby was found dead yesterday.…Anyway, they must a sent another two men in, because they took another black girl and baby sometime before daylight yesterday."

"My God!"

"Yes, Sir!"

"And my men?"

"They're camped out on Bullard Road, Colonel, Jeter's with 'em.…Our two Marshals are in th' swamp out there, they think they know where these killers are hold up at in there!…They been gone th' better part a two days now."

"And why th' roadblock?"

"I figure them Bastards have to be somewhere close, Colonel, not more than a milw away.…If Dempsey finds 'em, there's no way three men are gonna get 'em all, some are gonna run. That's why the roadblock!"

"You said three men,…I thought you said the Marshals were there?"

"Jack Hawkins is with 'em."

"Jack's a good man, served under Lee.…How do you know where they'll come out?"

"We don't!" He sighed then and sipped at his coffee. "But I figure there's got a be a hidden road there somewhere close, they come and go too quick!… And they use a wagon when they bring in th' bodies, so there has to be a road."

"That does make sense, Alex, thank you.…There been any more murders?"

"Not since we found Garner, and if we can find 'em today, there won't be,…they have their final victim. And if our men can't stop 'em, they'll murder her tonight.…We found our spy, too, by the way,…he's dead as well."

"Billy Gaye?"

No, sir,…he was an Elder at th' Methodist Church."

"My God, Alex, that's Lucy's Church!…Was Reverend Peters involved?"

"Marshal checked it all out, he wasn't involved."

"Thank God for that!"

"They knew our every move, Colonel,...used th' tower lights to send messages."

"Yeah, I knew about the tower....But an Elder?...That's unbelieveable.... How about the first girl, was she okay?"

"She is, Jeter walked her home yesterday mornin'...I don't know about now."

"Good Lord, Alex." He sighed heavily then. "You need any more hands out there, I can have another thirty guns here by sundown?"

"Jeter has eleven men with 'im, Colonel, and I have my four patrolling this end of that swamp, down by th' depot,...we'll have enough, I think. There won't be more than three or four of th' Bastards escape, if any.... Besides, Colonel, it shouldn't be up to you to supply men for this, th' fuckin' Army ought a be helpin', would, too, if that yellow-bellied Captain Lamar would do what's right!"

"Lamar's up for retirement soon, Alex, he won't muddy th' waters any,... we'll handle it ourselves."

"If we don't, I think I'll be out of a job, Colonel. Folks are a little upset with me over this, and I don't blame 'em!"

"We can worry about that later, Alex....Me and Lucy will stay in town tonight, if you need me."

"The Windsor?"

"You can join us for dinner tonight if you like?"

"No, thanks, Colonel,...I want a stay on top a this thing."

"Keep me informed, Alex, We are in this together." He donned his hat and left, leaving Maynard to reconstruct their conversation and to wonder if he might be construed as crying on Quinlan's shoulder about losing his job?

"Shit!" He blurted aloud, and wondered why he had even brought it up?" He went to the doorway to watch Quinlan turn the buggy around in the street and leave then went to pour himself another cup of coffee. It was a hell of a thing to have to rely on another man's success to preserve your own future, he thought drearily,...but that was exactly what he felt like he was doing. There had not been a time in the war when he did not know what to do, none he could remember!...So why hadn't he thought of that clock tower as a possible place for the spy to hide?...And not only that,...why hadn't he gone with Gibbs to question Reverend Peters, he might have gotten the same information Peters gave Rod and Seth? Instead, Gibbs was turned down completely, and it was left at that!

He had believed the Church had nothing to offer in the case, that's why? Who would have suspected a Church Elder of such a thing, or that he was the very spy they were looking for?...Only an inferior law man, that's who!

He had had it too soft since Quinlan brought him here, that was the answer, Quinlan had done the thinking for him during the war, and had done so ever since!...That was his problem, he thought, and that had to change!...And by God, it would, too! Once this was over, and he still had a job, he would not ask Spencer Quinlan for anything ever again. He would be his own man, and that man would be a lawman!

*   *   *

The three of them had watched the cultists cut and trim their logs for most of the day, and no one had left, or returned to the compound at all,...and this made Seth pretty confident that they were all in the school. However, he had been watching the workmen assembling something with the saplings on the ground, in front of the schoolhouse door for the most of two hours now, and the activity had all three of them stymied.

It was steaming-hot, and had been for the two days they had been in the swamp, and sweating profusely was only an invitation for the swarming, large mosquitoes and pestering gnats,...and they were kept busy slapping at their necks and faces. The stench of a rotting wetland only tended to make each of them irritable as they waited for nightfall, which they did until just before darkness settled in,...and they watched the four Cult members dig a hole and then raise the sapling .structure.

"What is that?" Whispered Dempsey. "Looks like that drawing we saw at th' Church."

"It's exactly what it is!" Returned Seth. "Reverend called it a Pentagram,...a symbol for th' Devil!"

"Bastards go all th' way, don't they?"

"Gonna burn it, too." Said Hawkins. "They're piling wood under it."

"Part a th' ritual." Sighed Seth. "You're right, Rod,...they're all here!... Ain't been nobody come or go since we been here."

"I'd still like to hear that gal scream or somethin'!" Whispered Dempsey.

"Well, I can't believe they ain't sent nobody out to look around." Said Hawkins. "Do they feel that safe?"

"I think they do," Returned Seth. "Would be, too, if not for Joseph.... And Rod, th' girl's alive, she'll be lettin' us know before long."

"Yeah, while they're raping 'er, th' Sons a Bitches!"

"Don't worry about that neither!" Whispered Seth. "It'll be the most expensive piece of ass they ever had,...we'll see to that!"

"Amen, Seth."

"They're all inside now." Whispered Hawkins. "Want me to go?"

"Wait till they light that thing." Replied Dempsey.

"Might not do that till midnight." Said Seth. "We'll wait till it's good and dark! Now when you go, Jack, go slow, stay close to the ground and watch that door!...You see somebody coming out, hit th' ground fast, be enough trash there to hide you as dark as it is."

"And when you get there, hide yourself good." Added Dempsey. "Don't start shootin' too soon, the first ones out will be lighting that thing."

"Be plenty a light to shoot by!" Whispered Hawkins.

*   *   *

"What brings you out in this heat, Lieutenant?" Queried Cliff as Maynard stopped his horse to peer at the entanglement of wilderness.

"Longer I sat in that office, edgier I got!...That Mister Gibbs yonder?"

"That's him,...Walt's farther on down th' way....Gibbs sees ya, he's on his way." They waited as Gibbs slid his horse to a stop in front of them.

"Decide to join' us?" He grinned. "Don't guess ya heard anything?"

"Nope," Sighed Maynard, still looking with distaste at the thick forest of Pines. "Ain't likely to now....But I think they probably found 'em out there."

"I don't know, we ain't heard no shootin' if they did?"

"Likely won't till around midnight....Get 'em all together at that ritual." He looked back toward the depot then up at the sky. "Gettin' dark pretty quick now. How you doing your patrols?"

"Quarter mile apart, Walt's at the other end....He rides this way while I ride his, we meet and turn back, Cliff here rides my way, we meet, he turns back. Only way we can do it."

"Whatever works." Nodded Maynard, as he looked at the thick mass of timber again. "Why in hell can't we see that road, Mister Gibbs,...we know it's there?"

"Beats hell out a me, Lieutenant! " Said Gibbs, also looking at the trees. "We walked ever foot a this frontage all th' way to th' Tap Line."

"Yeah, I know ya did. But it's here, I think,...somewhere!"

"Could be on Bullard road, too!"

"Could be anywhere,...but if any a those Bastards get away, I'm sure they'll use it." He fished the watch from his vest and checked the time before putting it away again. "It's seven-thirty now, four and a half hours!...You'll hear th' fireworks, I think...If they find that bunch, gonna be hell to pay about midnight!"

"You really believe that shit about th' full moon, Lieutenant,...What make ya think they'll wait till midnight?"

"You're asking th' wrong man about that, Gibbs. All I know is what Rod said come from that book th' Reverend had,...but it makes sense, they would!...Moon'll be directly overhead about that time....Besides,... everybody knows that's when th' ghosts and goblins come out!"

"Devil, too!" Added Cliff.

"You're both full of it!" Said Gibbs with a chuckle. "You stayin' with us tonight, Lieutenant?"

"No,...I'll be at th' depot, likely on th' platform....I can watch th' road from there....It's almost dark now, you men get on with it, and keep your ears open, moon ought a give off plenty a light to see by tonight." He reined the horse back toward the depot then and left.

*   *   *

"Okay, Jack." Whispered Seth. "Remember what we told you, go ahead. When you get there you can cover us, we'll be goin' to th' rear a th' building." They watched the dark figure of Hawkins leave the tree-cover and disappear until he reappeared in the lighter area of the clearing a few seconds later, and from there, saw him crouch and slowly move the several hundred feet between them and the two lone pine trees and once there, could no longer see him.

Waiting another minute, and with rifles ready, Seth and Dempsey left the deep dark of cover and crossed the road. The old school building was eerie-looking in the pre-moonlit clearing as they left the road, and bending low, were in a half crouch as they weaved their way slowly around the many pine stumps and debris until finally arriving at the rear of the ancient structure.

Dempsey continued on to the opposite corner and peered around it, and satisfied no one was there, quickly came back. Seth ran his hands over the unevenly laid stones, most of which protruded outward enough for hand and footholds and then placed his foot on one, and his right hand on the one above his head and began to climb the thirty foot wall to the roof of the building, where he slowly got to his feet and moved aside to squat and wait for Dempsey.

"You okay, Rod?" He asked in a whisper.

"Am now," He panted. "Almost slipped a time or two, but I'm here!" He peered down through the rotten saplings covering the very old roof, at the torch-lighted interior of the school. "You seein' this, Seth?"

The building's interior was large, more than fifty feet across, and more than double in length, with burning torches midway up the inner walls and about ten feet apart, all around the inside. Below them, midway of the rear wall was the large, crudely-built oblong altar of hewn logs, the top of which was of logs split into planks and laid tightly together then lashed in place with what appeared to be rawhide bindings. The top had been sanded smooth and also lashed to the undercarriage of logs.

They could see what appeared to be an excavated trench circling the entire altar, except for where it began and ended, at the head of the altar. Enough room had been left between the trench and altar for people to move around the Devil's shrine.

The trench had hollowed out logs placed end-to-end and cemented together with dried mud and swamp grass. Behind the altar, against the wall stood another large Pentagram made of saplings.

They studied the altar's area for a few minutes then leaned down enough to see through the deteriorated thatch-work at the rest of the large room. The Cultists were all sitting in a circle at the front of the building, and not twenty feet from the open doorway. Their hands were together, and legs crossed beneath them, and all had dark robes and hoods over their heads, the robes hanging loosely on their bodies. One man sat in the center of the circle as if in a trance, and it was then that they heard the mumbled chanting.

"What th' hell are they doing?" Whispered Dempsey.

"Praying, I guess." Returned Seth. "That one must be th' head honcho."

"I don't see the girl and baby, do you?"

Seth held onto Dempsey's arm for support and leaned out a little farther. He could see the naked girl and child then. Both were nude and lashed snugly to a rack of saplings, of which were propped at a forty degree angle against the wall. "I see 'em, Rod." He said regaining his balance. "In front there, against th' wall."

Dempsey used Seth's arm then and leaned out. "I see 'em now!...Can't tell from here, but it don't look to me like they're movin'." He regained his place then. They was naked,...spread out like some side a beef on a spit!"

"Got no hair on 'em neither, Rod, nowhere."

"I seen that, Seth, them Sons a Bitches!"

"Don't get careless, Rod." Warned Seth, shifting the rifle on his back. "This wall's about two feet thick, feels like....If we are lucky, and move real slow, we can make it to the front a this thing while they're in a trance."

"I'm right behind ya, Seth,...can I crawl?"

"Don't dislodge any a this mess, won't take much to warn 'em we're here!...They still got them swords on their backs, remember that."

"I'm behind ya." He said again.

Nodding, Seth began the slow, nerve-wracking, half-crawl, half-walk along the uneven top of the wall, careful not to step on any part of the disintegrating thatching,...and at the same time trying to keep an eye on the chanting group of Cultists on the floor below them. The arduous journey along the wall took a good quarter hour, but at last, they were breathing sighs of relief and sitting cross-legged atop the building's tall front as they continued to watch the silent killers.

Seth pulled his watch, and in the pale light filtering up through the mesh could tell it was a good three hours yet until midnight, then showed it to Dempsey, who shook his head and shifted his sore backside atop the gouging rocks. He put the watch away and leaned forward enough to see the teenaged black girl and her baby. Both her and the child had been completely shaved of any body hair. They were lashed tightly to the long travois-type rack of saplings,...they were both breathing, but their heads had not moved at all, nor were their eyes open,...and he figured they were both still under the influence of whatever they used to drug them.

The girl's long, slender legs were spread wide and straight out, and were lashed there. Her arms were straight out from her body on either side and lashed,...and the baby was lashed there beside her. He knew what was in store for both of them and for that reason alone, was tempted to open fire. But he knew that, as close to the building's open doorway as they were, it would be possible that half of them would make it outside, and as good as Hawkins might be, he couldn't get them all, some would escape! Calming himself, He counted thirty assassins seated around the High Priest.

If they had any chance to get them all, they would need to be around that altar at the rear of the building....That was a plain, but simple truth!

"What are you thinkin'?" Whispered Dempsey.

"Just weighing our chances."

"Of what, takin' 'em now?"

"I was tempted."

"We could, ya know, they're sittin' ducks!"

"Too close to th' door, Rod!...I want 'em all at that altar,...we got a get 'em all!...Farther they have to run to get outside, better chance we got."

"They'll rape that little girl if we wait!"

"They might, but she won't be dead, she'll get over it!...If even one a them gets away, this same thing is gonna happen again somewhere else. It has to end here, tonight!"

"You're right, Seth. I just don't cotton to seein' a girl raped!"

"Me neither, but I want a save these kid's lives, not chance 'em bein' killed by shootin' too quick."

"I agree, Seth. We wait!"

Nodding, they continued to watch them, and the drone of their chanting went on for the better part of another hour before the High Priest suddenly rose to his feet. The chanting stopped, and when he pointed at the unconscious girl, two of the cultists got to their feet, each taking a bowl from the ground in front of them and going to the girl where they began dipping their hand into the bowl's contends and anointing her body with what appeared to be an oil of some kind, their hands working the substance onto her body and most intimate places, the misintrations causing her to moan and unconsciously move her body to meet the probing invasion.

When they were done, yet another cultist got to his feet and went to her side, and from a small vial, reached with one hand to open her mouth and with the other dripped a few drops of the vial's content into her throat causing her to swallow the liquid and as she did, she opened her eyes and began whimpering,...and then crying as she saw her surroundings and realized that she couldn't move.

Seth and Dempsey watched all this, and didn't understand until the High Priest suddenly threw off his robe and as his followers regained their seats and began chanting again, he stepped between them and approached the girl's exposed, spread-eagled body, his rigid manhood evident as he moved in between her splayed legs,

She screamed loudly as he entered her, but then only cried, then to moan and whimper as he raped her, only to eventually cry out in pleasure as it was culminated.....Then to leave her sobbing quietly as he stepped away and went back inside the circle, donned his robe again and sat down.

Seth had to quickly grab Dempsey's arm when the lawman raised his rifle, stopping him from shooting the Priest, and then squeezed his arm in reassurance to settle him down before once again watching the strange gathering below them.

The chanting continued for another hour, with Seth checking his watch every few long minutes, and then watching the moon's arcing advance above the trees,...and when the clearing was finally flooded with the bright lunar light, the Priest got to his feet again, as did all of them and as he stepped between them and walked toward the rear of the building, four of the cultists went to the girl and quickly released her by untying the leather straps, pulled her screaming from the travois and half carried her as they forced her to walk the length of the building, only to lift her to her back on the altar's flat, narrow, wood surface where she was bound again, her legs spread wide and dangling from the side of the altar. Her arms were stretched out to either side and bound there, leaving her head to partially hang over the altar's opposite side.

The child was then carried in and placed beside the girl, its head resting on her outstretched arm. The baby was bound tightly before the cultist with the vial came and dropped the liquid into its mouth. They were both conscious and crying loudly now as they were left alone and completely ignored by the cultists.

Dempsey and Seth both gritted their teeth and watched the unnatural proceedings, each gripping their rifles tightly. They saw the two cultists as they carried a wooden bowl to the altar and placed it on the ground beside the open trench, and sight of the dark, reflecting liquid told them both what it was,…the blood of twelve beheaded, brutally murdered victims! The cultists then returned to the front of the large room and regained their circle of seats to begin chanting again.

Seth checked his watch in the light from a full moon, which had fully cleared the trees and was slowly arcing its way almost directly overhead. It was eleven-thirty, and they were now quite visible to anyone who might happen to look up at the rising moon,…and if they did, they would have no choice but to start the killing. He put the watch away again and turned his head for a look at Hawkins' place of concealment, seeing him raise his hatless head for a look at the door-less building,…and seeing them on the roof, he lifted the rifle slightly to acknowledge his readiness. It was then that two of the cultists got to their feet and went to either side of the room, removed a burning torch and went outside to drop them at the base of the Pentagram, and as the flames began to burn the debris, they turned and went back inside as Seth checked his watch again. It was eleven forty-five.

He put it away and then watched as the two cultists continued down the length of the building where they took two more torches from either wall and placed them at the foot of the Pentagram behind the altar. At that time, the other Cultists slowly walked the buildings length and gathered around the altar, all chanting their unrecognizable words, and using the same syllables over and over again. Several Cultists along the side where the girl's splayed legs were dangling, and her womanhood displayed, discarded their robes and were standing naked and waiting,…and seeing them there caused the girl to begin screaming again and to struggle against her bindings.

It was almost midnight when the High Priest made his appearance at the head of the altar and raised his arms above his head. As if on signal, the cultist beside him removed the long, curved cutlass from the scabbard on his back and held it across his chest. The Priest then raised his voice and began calling to Satan in some unknown tongue, and as if on cue, one of the naked Cultists proceeded to rape the helpless woman.

Dempsey raised the rifle and fired, a loud, vibrating explosion as the rapist was knocked away from the girl, instantly dying as he was pitched into, and upending the bowl of blood as he fell. Seth had almost pulled the trigger on the High Priest when Dempsey fired, but then saw the cultist as he raised the cutlass to murder the girl and shot him first. He quickly brought the rifle back to the Priest, but he had ducked from sight. And then they both began firing as fast as they could lever a cartridge and take aim at the scurrying cultists, that by then were all running toward them and the only exit in the long building.

The Devil Worshippers were falling as they were hit, and the bodies literally covered the packed dirt floor of the ancient schoolhouse, yet they continued firing and reloading, and almost immediately heard Hawkins begin firing at those that escaped through the door and then suddenly, it was over. All that was left for the next few moments was the reverberating echoes of dissipating gunfire in the swampy wilderness, and smoke from the many shots that were fired.

After surveying the kill-zone, and seeing no movement from the bodies, Seth shouldered the rifle and immediately began his hand and foot descent down the front of the old rock building, half climbing and half slipping as he went to finally jump the last few feet to the rotting debris of ground cover. He saw Hawkins as he was turning over the bodies to check them then quickly entered the building, and with pistol in hand worked his way around the dead, kicking and toeing the bodies with short nudges to see if they were faking as he made his way to the altar.

As he neared the hysterical girl, he scooped up one of the discarded robes then pulled his knife and freed her legs, of which she quickly closed.

"It's okay, little girl." He soothed as he leaned over her to cut the child's bindings. "You're safe now, it's over." He covered her nakedness with the less than clean robe. "I'm gonna free your hands now." He leaned over her again and cut her arms free, and she quickly pulled the screaming baby into her arms and cried.

"Come on, little girl." He urged her to a sitting position, then took the robe from her and helped her wrap it around herself. "Sit still now." He soothed, and quickly bent to remove the sandals from a dead Cultist's feet to slip them on her own and tie them in place. He helped her to the ground, holding her up to regain her balance before steering her around the bodies toward the exit.

"We count thirty bodies in here and outside!" Said Dempsey as both him and Hawkins came to help him with the girl, taking her arms on either side and relieving Seth of the burden. "We got 'em all, Seth, we did it, man!"

"I counted thirty one, Rod." He said tiredly. "I think th' Honcho got away!"

"You what?" Gasped Dempsey. "No way, Seth, there was thirty men in that circle, I must a counted 'em a dozen times."

"Th' Honcho made thirty-one, Rod,...I counted 'em, too....If he ain't outside somewhere, he got away!"

Dempsey frowned as he peered over the girl's shoulder at him. "Are you sure, Seth, cause I know I counted thirty?"

"You counted th' men in th' circle, I think, cause I counted thirty there, as well."

"Christ all-mighty, Seth!" He blurted, looking up at the deteriorated remnants of rotting roof, and then stopped, forcing Hawkins and the girl to stop to let Seth walk around them. "And you think it was th' head man?"

"Don't know, never saw his face….I was about to shoot 'im when you fired, but then that Bastard raised his sword to mu-…" He looked at the girl then. "I shot him instead. When I brought back to bear on th' Honcho, he was gone." He turned to scan the body-littered floor. "He might be any one of 'em, Rod, and maybe none of 'em,…can't tell 'em apart."

"Yeah," Breathed Dempsey. "All I saw was his God damn bald head, when he ra-…" He looked down at the wide-eyed, and still sniffling black girl. "They're all bald headed." He saw the girl suddenly reach up to touch her own hairless head then. "I'm sorry, maam, didn't mean to upset you." He put his arm around her again.

Seth moved in closer to her. "You okay, Little girl,…we're not making fun of your head at all. You know that, don't ya?"

"Yeah, suh, I's scared is all, Mama gonna kill me, I has anotha baby!" She sobbed then. "Tell me, I ain't?"

"Course not, none a this was your fault….We'll fix it with Mama, don't worry. Your hair will grow back, too, so come on, you and your baby are safe."

"Yeah, suh, I knows 'at….Can we go home now, Mama be worried?"

Seth looked at Hawkins then. "Let's move some a these bodies out a th' doorway, Jack, little girl needs to rest a bit." Together, they dragged a half-dozen of the bodies to one side of the room, clearing a space large enough for them all to sit before coming back to help Dempsey sit the girl down on the ground.

"Okay," He said tiredly, looking at them both. "That head man was wearin' something around his neck,…I think!…I was pretty upset at what he was about to do, but I'm almost sure he had a medallion, or somethin'…You see anything, Rod?"

"All I seen was his bald head, and his large pec-…Sorry Seth, that's all I saw!"

"Yeah, well, we got a be sure he's not one a these here, Mister Hawkins, you check them on the outside, we'll look in here,…and gather up all them swords."

"Yes, sir." He turned and left while they began opening the robes on the bodies of the Cultists inside and as they did, took the sharp swords and tossed them to the center of the room. For the next half hour, they disrobed and searched the loincloths of the dead for any kind of concealment that might tell them they had found the High Priest's body, but there was none.

"Seth, it don't make sense that he could get away like that!...There's thirty bodies here, and outside there. If he got away, how did he do it?"

"Black Magic, maybe?"

"Yeah, right!...Okay, what now,...search th' woods?"

"Knowin' what he's capable of, do you want to?"

"No way, let's get out a here!"

"My kind a language." He grinned and followed the lawman back to where the girl was sitting, and squatting beside her, placed a hand on her shoulder. "You okay, little girl?"

"Yeah, suh,...is we goin' home now, Mama be worried?" She whined.

"In just a few minutes, okay?" He looked up as Hawkins came back with his armload of weapons, saw those on the ground and went on to drop his. "Mister Hawkins," He said as the wrangler came back. "Don't guess you found anything?"

"None of 'em had a necklace on, no, sir!"

"Think you can hook up that wagon and team out there, Jack, we'll need transportation out a here?"

"I think I can manage that!" He nodded and left.

"As soon as he gets here with that wagon, we'll go home, okay?"

"Yeah, suh,...but we's hungry, too, ain't had no suppa!"

"We can fix that, too, little Miss." Said Dempsey. "Got plenty a salted down beef hangin' in th' front there,...you like beef?" When she nodded, he looked at Seth. "Want a take th' time, I'm a little tired a jerky?...Got plenty a fire to cook on?"

"You're th' Marshal, Rod,...it appears we got th' time."

"Then we eat first!"

"Is that a stack a hides, I see over there?" Asked Seth as he peered at them.

"I think it is, guess murder ain't all they was doin'."

CHAPTER ELEVEN

Jeter's eyes popped open at the first faint sounds of gunfire and quickly got to his feet to find all the cowhands standing in the road listening as the rumbling sounds echoed toward them.

"Where's it comin' from?' He asked as he stared eastward over the trees. "There's a fire out there, too!" He yelled. "See th' glow….Must be northeast of us!"

"If it ain't a fire, th' sky sure is bright over there." Commented a wrangler. "What ya want us to do, there's a hell of a lot a shootin' goin' on out there?"

"Give 'em hell, Marshal!" Yelled another man.

"Okay," Yelled Jeter. "It appears they found th' fuckers!...I figure if any got away, it'll take 'em an hour to get here."

"More like two, Deputy." Said yet another of the cowboys. "That's a tangled bunch a shit out there, and they'll be runnin' in th' dark!"

"We got a be ready!...Couple of you stoke up this fire!...Three of you light them torches and ride up th' road a ways, rest of ya, grab your torch and string out between here and town, and keep your eyes on that swamp, we don't know where they'll be comin' out….And Gents, we don't need any prisoners!"

*   *   *

Alex Maynard had been smoking and pacing the depot's long platform for the better part of four hours when the sounds of gunfire echoed toward him and to him, sounded more like a small war had broken out in the swamp. Straining his eyes at the swamp, he could see the faint glow above the treetops.

"By God, they found 'em!" He voiced excitedly then quickly hurried across the platform to step into the saddle of his waiting horse. The shooting sounded as if it were coming from the same area as the glow and with that in mind, spurred the horse across the half dozen train tracks and on toward the swampy outer fringe of the wilderness where he knew his deputies would be.

He knew the area to be flat, packed ground and so urged the horse to a gallop in the brilliant yellowish light of the full moon overhead, and it was another five minutes before he saw the pitch black shapes of trees and slowed the animal to a walk along the swamp's outer fringe, his eyes on the dark foliage of green, and patches of lighter greens from being touched by moonlight. He knew it would be an hour of more before anything could be seen exiting the forest, if anything at all and so, urged the horse to a trot again while he looked for Cliff.

The moon was already beginning to cross the sky toward the West by the time he spotted the pale rider coming toward him and called out, and seeing Cliff wave stopped to wait on him.

"It's me, Cliff!" He called to identify himself.

"Didn't know it was you, Lieutenant." Returned the Deputy. "You hear th' shooting, it just stopped a minute ago?"

"I heard 'em,…keep your eyes open, moon'll be down behind th' trees before long."

"Don't worry, Lieutenant,…if any of 'em got away, it's gonna take 'em a while to get out this way. It's a hell of a lot darker in there than out here!"

"Yeah, but they got a road in there somewhere, remember?…Besides, I ain't worried too much about them getting' away, as I am about th' Marshals!…Be a mess if they're killed, too."

"I heard more than two dozen, maybe even three dozen shots, Lieutenant, they're still alive!…If you're that worried, we can go in after 'em?"

"You'd be lost in half an hour, Cliff, and dead in two!…I do wish I'd told ya to bring lanterns though. Damn it, I hate feelin' helpless like this!… Okay,…keep up th' patrol along here, I'm goin' out to find Jeter."

"Don't worry about us, Lieutenant."

*   *   *

Dempsey had a small fire going on the school's hard, dirt floor by the time Hawkins stopped the wagon in front and came inside, and at sight of the fire, and Seth slicing meat from a hind-quarter of beef, went back out and returned with a strong, pointed stick, retrieved the meat from Seth and skewered it onto the make-shift spit, along with a couple more strips then squatted to hold them over the licking flames.

Dempsey got to his feet as Seth finished and put his knife away, and as he sat down to roll a smoke, turned and went back to the stack of hides.

"You did okay tonight, Jack." Said Seth as he took a burning twig and lit his cigarette. "Wouldn't a made it without ya."

"Scared hell out a me, Seth!" He grinned. "When I started shooting, half of 'em charged me, one almost got me!...I managed to get th' rest before they made th' trees....I am glad it's over....Cause if you was askin' me to come with ya right now, I wouldn't!" They both laughed then.

"Little different than snipin', huh?"

"By quite a bit,...might a turned out different, too, if they'd had guns.... This was pretty much a massacre!"

"Yeah," Breathed Seth as he exhaled. "I don't cotton to somethin' like that myself, but they had to be stopped, Jack,...remenber that."

"Oh, I agree, yes, sir!...I still don't know how we did it without them knowin' we was here?...Don't make sense them not postin' a guard somewhere."

"They didn't have any sense, Jack, none at all!...Figured folks were scared enough that nobody would look for 'em in here....They was safe here, and still would be, if not for Joseph."

"That reminds me, Marshal, my best cow-horse is still at that store back there."

"Mine, too." Nodded Seth. "But I ain't walking back th' way we come to get 'im." They were laughing again when Dempsey returned carrying three holstered pistols, complete with sheathed hunting knives and dropped all but one of them by the fire.

"This was Marshal Henry Jones' gun!" He said, taking it from the holster to check the loads. "Never got off a shot!" He holstered it and looked down at the other two. "Guess those belonged to Alex's deputies."

"I'm sorry about your friend, Rod."

"Yeah, me, too!" Dropping the gun belt, he sighed as he surveyed the dead cultists again. "Think we ought a search th' woods for that Priest?... Bastard could be watchin' us right now."

"No doubt about that!" Sighed Seth. "But that ain't a chance I want a take, not in a swamp, and not with an angry assassin!...Man's in his element here, we ain't."

"I guess you're right,...but he sure needs to be found!"

"He'll show up somewhere."

"That's what worries me." He looked at the bodies again.. "Something's still wrong here though."

"Like what?"

"Ain't no poles with heads on 'em, Reverend Peters said there would be."

"Go figure!...Maybe this Cult was different."

"Then where are th' heads?"

"Let it go, Rod!...Nothin' about any a this shit makes sense!...Must a thrown 'em away in th' swamp somewhere,...we'd never find 'em."

"If it means anything, Marshal," Said Hawkins. "Them people gave their lives to help us catch this bunch, that Marshal Jones, and both them Deputies died in the line of duty....They hadn't, you wouldn't be here, Seth neither!...And we wouldn't a found 'em."

"Mister Hawkins," Grinned Seth. "That was very well said."

"And very true." Added Dempsey. "Thanks, Jack."

"You're both welcome," He grinned. "Now I got a better one for ya." He held up the stick for Seth to remove the cooked meat for himself and the girl. "You are about to eat some a Mister Quinlan's prize beef!"

"Prized beef?" Queried Dempsey curiously.

"Yep,...pure blooded white faced beef cows. Breed originated in England....These Bastards took a dozen of 'em right out a th' holding pen at th' ranch, not thirty yards from th' house and nobody seen 'em. Never knew it till th' next day, couldn't even track 'em!" He skewered the last two strips of meat and held them to the flames. "Mister Quinlan lost a couple a dozen th' last two months,...lost one of his hands too, must have caught 'em at it."

"Who?" Asked Dempsey.

"Miles, somebody, I didn't know 'im except to speak, he stayed in another bunkhouse....But, speakin' of th' man that got away tonight,...I thought I might a seen somebody in th' trees while I was hitchin' up th' team, course it was dark and I couldn't be sure....But it sure felt like somebody was watchin' me work."

"Well," Said Dempsey. "You here telling us about it, says it all!"

"Meaning nothing was there!" He nodded. "I'll be glad to leave this place!"

"We all will." Replied Seth. "And Jack, you better drive th' team when we leave, me and Rod'll keep watch. If our man's still here somewhere?...He's still dangerous."

"I understand, Marshal. My problem will be keeping 'em on th' road in the dark."

"Just keep 'em moving, Jack" Replied Dempsey. "They'll follow the road, they've been over it a few times."

"Meat's done, Marshal." Said Hawkins, raising the stick.

While the two men ate, Seth decided to do a walk around of the school's interior. Even though Dempsey's count was one short of his own, he was fairly certain that not more than half of the cultists made it to the outside, and Hawkins said none of those made it to freedom.....If his count was the right one, there had to be another way out of the building, and that would mean, in all likelihood, the Priest was the missing man....If it was him, it was not over yet, he would prove to be a danger,...if not in Tyler, then somewhere else!

They could not have found a better place to hide, he thought, wet as hell when it rained, but otherwise okay. He walked along the wall to avoid the corpses, and then across to the altar thinking that he'd had a shot at the man a split second before the other one raised the cutlass to behead the girl, but when he levered to shoot again, he was gone!...He could not have moved that fast, he thought. He had to have ducked behind something, the altar, maybe, he thought as he neared the burning Pentagram. He stopped to look up at the large, sapling symbol, which had already burned to the point of near collapse...but as he stared at the rear of the altar, he could see the narrow hole in the ground.

Well, he thought, if that Priest was suicidal, he did not show it! He expected to be found and planned for it! Shaking his head, he turned and started to leave when he saw the skulls, and squatting for a closer look, counted thirteen in all and wondered about the extra one. He sighed heavily and stood up again, deciding not to say anything about any of it, at least for now. It would upset Dempsey a lot to learn that the head of his friend and the rest had been burned, likely to keep down the smell. They were likely all beheaded while they were alive, too, he thought sadly, so that the heart could help pump out the blood! Becoming nauseated, he walked slowly back toward the others, thinking that Lucifer might not have appeared in the flesh tonight, but the son of a bitch was certainly in control!

"He whirled then, his hand streaking for the gun on his hip at the sound of the falling Pentagram, but then straightened to watch the embers float upward into the rotten thatch of the roof.

"We about done here?" He asked hoarsely on arrival. "I have had about enough a this."

"We're done!" Said Dempsey, getting to his feet. "We just gonna leave these bastards here to rot?"

"Bugs got a eat!" Said Seth as he bent to help the black girl to her feet. "Come on, little girl, we're goin' home now."

"I's ready, Mama be worried."

"She'll be too glad to see you to be worried, now come on." He helped her out to the wagon and lifted her to the groaning bed. "Move on up front there, behind th' seat, and watch th' splinters." He turned as Hawkins came out. "Stay with 'er, Jack, we're gonna burn that altar." He intercepted Dempsey as he came out with the holstered guns, and after placing them in the wagon, they went back inside to remove the wall torches and toss them on the already burning altar before coming back to climb into the wagon.

"What about this one, Seth?" Asked Dempsey, looking up at the blazing symbol.

Let it burn, maybe it'll burn it all down….Okay, Jack," He said, taking the rifle from his back and reloading. "Head back to the road and go north."

"Would that be left, or right?"

"Go left," Said Dempsey. "We came in the other way."

*   *   *

Light from the moon was still quite bright on the road to Bullard, and Maynard's anxiety was working overtime as he kept the horse at a full gallop along the wide lane,…and it wasn't long before he met one of the wranglers and questioned him before moving on again. Twenty minutes later, after questioning seven other of the wranglers, he spotted the fire in the road a quarter of a mile ahead of him.

Jeter was in the road watching him as he rode up and dismounted.

"What brings you out, Lieutenant?"

"Th' gunfire!...Everything quiet?"

"Yes, sir, hell of a racket out yonder for a while, a big-ass fire, too!" He said, looking back over the trees. "Ya can still see th' glow off yonder."

"I could see it from town….Had any activity?"

"Mail Coach through about dark, nothin' since!...I got three men with torches up th' road a ways, eight back th' way you came. If anything comes out a there, chances are, we'll see 'em!"

"They won't come out at all if they see them torches." Sighed Maynard. "And we won't see 'em without any light, moon'll be down in another hour."

"So what'll we do, Lieutenant,…want a douse th' torches?"

"I wish I knew, Jeter!...Where do you think that fire is from here?"

"East, and a little North from here, could be a lot North, it's hard to tell."

"How far in?"

"No more than a mile, Lieutenant, if that far,…why?"

"If there's a road in there, it ain't gonna run backwards. I think you need to pull them three back from th' road ahead there, and take three more a them I just passed. Send all six to th' depot side a this swamp. I got th' other three men there, but that's a five mile stretch of wilderness."

"I'll go get 'em." He mounted his horse and galloped away, leaving Maynard there to stare in worried panic at the faint glow above the wilderness of trees.

Did they get them all, he wondered? He rolled a cigarette and lit it as he paced up and down a short span of the road, thinking that if they were a mile or so in, and any did escape, they would have to use the road. Running blind in a place like that would be impossible. Even if they used a road, they would likely be on foot and that being the case it would take a man two hours or more. He took out his watch and checked the time by the moon's fading light. It was after one o'clock, and he believed that it would be three o'clock before anything happened. He was standing in the road when the three torch-bearing cowboys rode by, followed by Jeter, who stopped and dismounted again to join him.

"They'll pick up three men on th' way, Lieutenant....How long we gonna keep this up,...must a been a hundred rounds fired out there, lasted a spell, too!...I don't think any of 'em got away, you ask me."

"We stay till somethin' happens, Jeter,...if none got away, then Rod and th' others will use that road to come out....Somebody's gonna come out a that swamp tonight, Jeter,...and we're gonna be there!"

"Yes, sir,...and I think you're right about them torches. If I just escaped with my life, and I seen riders with a torch out here, I ain't comin' out a'tall!"

"Then put 'em out, moon'll give off a little light for a couple hours yet!...But I don't want even a cottonmouth crawlin' out a there without somebody seein' it!"

"We're doin' all we can, Lieutenant, this is a big place!"

"Yeah, I know. We got a lot ridin' on this, Jeter, that's all. It has got to be over with tonight!...If it ain't, we'll all be movin' on come election day!"

"I ain't thought much on that!...Don't get me wrong, I like my job a lot, but we ain't done nothin' wrong!...This ain't no ordinary bunch a killers we're dealin' with,...it was, you'd a solved it already!...Ain't no lawman could a done better than you on this, there weren't a clue to work with!"

Maynard chuckled and placed a hand on the deputy's shoulder. "You done?"

"I'm done, Lieutenant." He sighed heavily then. "You ain't done nothin' wrong, that's all I'm sayin', none of us have!" He stared back at the swamp then. "If they come out a that swamp tonight, we'll catch 'em, too."

"Ain't a doubt in my mind, Jeter!...And thanks, you're a good soldier, and deputy!...And now, I'm gonna leave it with ya." He went to his horse as he spoke. "I'll be at the depot....You might want a put out that fire and go join your men, that road won't be this far south."

"Yes, sir." He went to kick the fire apart then on to his own horse and mounted. "I'll ride with you a ways, got a put out them torches."

*   *   *

"Jesus Christ, it's dark out here!" Complained Dempsey in a low voice. "And that damn squealing wheel's enough to tell everybody in this swamp we're comin'!"

Seth grinned in the darkness. "Maybe that's what drove these creeps loco."

"Well, it's doin' the same for me….I'm seein' things movin out there that ain't even there!"

"Dark does that to a man,…false images….Old sayin', it's th' Devil's imps playin' their tricks!…Just remember what I told you about that, you'll know the real thing when you see it. Besides,…that Priest is alone now, and he's got nobody to do his dirty work….He won't be comin' after us!… Probably the only sane one a th' bunch,…he had an escape route."

"He knew this would happen, that what you're sayin'?"

'Oh, yeah,…he didn't get his own hands dirty at all, had his lap-dogs do it for 'im!…And in the end, which he knew would come someday, he knew he'd be the only one to get away with it!…He might a been crazy, but he was crazy smart, too."

"Son of a Bitch!…You still on th' trail, Jack?" He queried. "You're beatin' us to death back here!"

"None a my doin', Marshal, I can't see a thing!"

"That always helps!"

"This thing just now getting to you, Rod? Asked Seth, still peering into the deep, dark surrounding trees.

"Don't know, Seth,…somethin' is, guess it's knowin' one got away….It ain't us hunting them anymore!"

"They're all dead, Rod….I wouldn't worry too much about that Priest, either, he knows we're ready for 'im! If he wants revenge, it'll be on all of us, not just one."

"What's that mean?"

"If he attacks this wagon, he's gonna die doin' it, he knows that!…He also knows he might, at best, get only one of us before he does….He would want us all dead!"

"Using that logic, I feel some better, I think!…But these bastards weren't logical, they were crazy, and that includes that fuckin' Priest!"

"That's a good point as well!" Said Seth. "Just watch the shadows, you'll see 'im!"

"How far you figure we've come,…can't be that far from Tyler now?"

"Without knowing where we was, I couldn't even guess. I'd say it depends on where this road comes out, couple hours away, maybe."

"Wish we had a lantern, better yet, one a them torches, smoke would keep these damn bugs away!"

"Guess they ain't heard about th' feast we left back there."

"Don't you ever get scared, Seth?"

"I'm some scared right now, Rod. Always am when I don't who I'm fightin'."

"You don't show it!"

*   *   *

Maynard rode in beside the tall depot platform, and standing up on the saddle, stepped off onto the planking and walked to the ticket office.

"Hey, ya, Sheriff, back already?...Must be somethin' important going on, you hangin' around here all night!"

"It is, Harvey,...when's th' next train due in?"

"Five o'clock in th' A.M.,...but it's us'ly late, why, got folks comin' in, have ya?"

"Don't want anybody leavin'. Listen, Harvey,...there might, or might not be some shooting going on around that swamp out there in a couple hours. If it is, I want you to lock up when you hear it!...And blow th' lamps out!"

"Wh,...who's gonna be shootin' this time a morning?...Hey, that why your deputies been off there all night?"

"You just do what I told ya, Harvey, and don't let anybody in!"

"I'll lock 'er down, Sheriff, don't worry about that!"

Nodding, he left and crossed the wide platform to ease his tired frame into the saddle before spurring the horse back across the tracks.

Gibbs and Walt stopped their horses for a minute to look up the Bullard road, and were about to turn around for another tour along the swamp's outer fringe when they heard the approaching horse and stopped to draw their pistols and watch the rider.

"That's th' Lieutenant's horse." Said Gibbs, and they holstered their guns to wait on him.

"Cliff said you was out with Jeter, Boss?" Said Walt as he stopped the hard-breathing horse.

"They got it well covered,...th' six cowboys on th' job here?"

"Down th' way there with Cliff, Lieutenant." Said Gibbs. "It's bee a couple hours sine we heard them shots, what ya think's goin' on?"

"I wish I knew,...but somebody's gonna come out a that swamp tonight, Mister Gibbs,...might be our killers, might be Rod and Seth,...but they'll be usin' that road we can't find. So be ready!"

"You think it'll be along here somewhere?"

"Pretty much, yeah….As quick as them killers came and went, it's got a be along here somewhere,…and I think more-so here, than up th' road there. So keep your eyes open, your ears, too! You'll likely hear 'em before ya see 'em." He stared at the wilderness again and shook his head. "This waiting's got me nervous as a whore in Church!" He chuckled then. "I should a went with 'em to talk with that old Indian, be with 'em when they hit them Sons a Bitches!"

"They was just followin' a clue, Lieutenant, you didn't know they'd go on in after 'em!"

"That's right, Boss." Said Walt. "You weren't here, we wouldn't be here waitin' on 'em,…they might get away."

"You men are th' best a man could have!" He said laughingly. "And I thank you all…..Well, guess I'll join ya for a while, can't stand th' waitin'."

"Company's always welcome, Lieutenant." "said Gibbs. "Maybe they got 'em all, was a hell of a lot a lead flyin' around out there!"

"Then they'll be th' ones comin' out!…Either way, we'll be here."

*   *   *

"We got a be gettin' close to town, Seth." Said Dempsey, looking up through the thick maze of branches. "Woods are thinnin' out some, I just got me a good glimpse of the moon, off to the side there."

"I'd say we're pretty close to somewhere!" Said Hawkins. "I can see parts of the sky ahead of us. Think I saw a light or two off yonder, could be th' depot."

"None too soon for me." Breathed Seth.

The team of mules continued slowly along the soft road's debris for another half hour before they suddenly balked, and confused, Hawkins swatted their backs with the lines, yelling; "Get on there mules, gid'yup there!" But they wouldn't budge.

"What's wrong with 'em, Jack?" Queried Seth as he turned around in the wagon's bed.

"Damn if I know, Marshal, they just stopped!…Too dark to see anything."

"Better take a look then." He removed his damp bandana and wrapped it around the rifle's barrel, then struck a match and finally got it to burn enough to throw the wagon's bed into light. "Here I go." He said, and holding the rifle high, climbed out of the wagon and made his way along the side and then beside the team to finally walk out in front of them.

"We got some brush and limbs to move up here, Rod, come on down and help me."

Maynard, Gibbs and Walt had already stopped their horses when they heard what sounded like a dry wagon wheel squeaking, but for several minutes couldn't place its direction, or be sure that it was actually what they heard. So they drew their pistols and waited as they watched the dark foliage intently….They heard the distinct sound of someone's voice then.

"It's them, Lieutenant!" Said Gibbs. "But where th' hell are they?"

"Them six cowboys still got torches?"

"All six of 'em."

"Go get 'em, and hurry!" Gibbs turned his horse and left, leaving them still trying to pinpoint where the voice had come from. "Where the hell is that road?"

"It's right over yonder, Boss." Said Walt. "Somebody just lit a torch, see it?"

"I do now." He breathed, and both of them urged their horses the twenty-odd feet back the way they had come. "This'll do, Walt, be ready!" They heard the sounds of brush being moved then, and could faintly see the movement as the heavy limbs were being shoved aside in the shoulder-length grass and brush, not thirty feet in front of them.

"Just stop right there, Gents!" Ordered Maynard. "Make yourselves known." He said in a threatening voice. "And be advised we have guns on ya."

"That you, Alex?" Yelled Dempsey. "Cause if it is, we're comin' out a here!"

"It's me, Rod, come on out!" He yelled excitedly. "Hold on, we got some light comin'"

A few seconds passed before Gibbs, Cliff and the six cowboys arrived, the firebrands lighting up the entire area as Hawkins drove the team out of the bog and up the embankment to dry ground.

"Good Lord, it's good to see you men!" Exclaimed Maynard as the light flooded the wagon. "Don't think I ever seen anybody that filthy before." He chuckled. "Or anybody I was happier to see, welcome back!...Did ya get 'em all?"

"All but one, Alex!" Replied Dempsey tiredly. "Don't know where he went, or how he got away. We brought th' girl back, though, baby, too!"

"Hallelujah!" He said, looking in the bed at her. "You okay, Girl?"

"Yeah, suh,…ain't gots no hair, though." She uncovered her head then.

"They do that to you?"

"Yeah, suh,…can we's go home now?"

"Soon's we get to town, you sure can!" He looked at Seth then. And shook his hand. "You look beat, Marshal, you okay?"

"I've been better, Sheriff, feelin' a little long in th' tooth about now, but okay."

"Can we get on with it, Alex," Asked Dempsey. "We don't get a bath, and some decent sleep, we'll keel over?"

"Damn right we can!" He turned to the others then. "Walt, you go on ahead, bring Doc Welch to th' hotel, rest a you men with torches, lead out, right up Cedar street,…light th' way for these heroes." Once the wranglers were in position. "Okay, Mister Hawkins." He said happily. "We're goin' to th' Windsor Hotel,…let's go, people!"

Hawkins slapped the animals' backs with the lines and the old wagon lurched forward toward the distant rails and a well-lighted depot.

CHAPTER TWELVE

The day dawned clear, hot and humid, nothing unusual for August, except that the steeple-bells in all three Churches were tolling loudly. The entire city of Tyler, Texas was astir with activity as more and more people received word of the Cultist's demise, and by noon-time, there was a crowd congesting the boardwalks and immediate square in front of the Windsor Hotel,...as well as that portion of wide street in front of the Sheriff's office.

Insistent pounding on the office door brought a half-dressed and bleary-eyed Alex Maynard out of his sleeping quarters to open the door.

"David Clopton!" He sighed. "I might a known....What's all this about, what's this crowd doin' here?"

"Come now, Sheriff," Grinned Clopton." A story of this magnitude, and you pass it off as just another day?...Look out here, Sheriff, the people of Tyler have not experienced this sort of relief since the end of Reconstruction!" He was drowned out then by cheers from the street.

"I need an interview, Sheriff." Yelled Clopton. "I intend to write the biggest story since the end of the war,...can we do that right now?"

"No, no, no!" He said flatly and shaking his head vigorously. "I ain't awake yet, Clopton,...give me an hour, okay?"

"Sheriff, There's even more people in the square there by the Windsor, and they all want to hear from you and the Marshal about how you caught these killers!"

"Okay, okay!" He yelled. "I'll come to th' Windsor,...let me get dressed, okay?"

"All right, Sheriff." Nodded Clopton, and turned to the crowd. "Let's go to the Windsor, folks, he'll be there in an hour!" There was more cheering then as Maynard closed the door.

As he heard them leaving, a grin appeared on his face. This could be just what he needed, he thought as he quickly pushed away from the door and hurried back to finish dressing.

Seth was fully dressed as he left his room, and stopped a man in the hallway to ask what the noise was all about in the street.

"Hell, man, ain't you heard?" Returned the man excitedly. "They caught the Ritual Killers, killed 'em all!" He hurried on down the stairs.

"News spreads fast." He said softly, then continued on to Dempsey's room and knocked several times, but then stepped back as the door was opened.

"I thought I told yo-..., oh, mornin', Seth!...I thought you was that newspaper man again, woke me up two hours ago, and again a few minutes ago!...I'm up, let me get my hat."

"Appears we're heroes, don't it? Grinned Dempsey as he closed the door and looked at him. "Jesus, your face looks as bad as mine does,...bugs had a field day!"

"Yeah, they did!...And you're th' hero here, nobody woke me up!"

"Oh, no, my friend!" He said as they started down the stairs. "Weren't for you, this would not have happened, and I'm gonna let 'em know it!"

"I wish ya wouldn't, Rod, I ain't th' hero type. I'm just ready to go home."

"All right, Seth, I understand, and I won't push th' fact....But I won't take all th' credit, neither!"

"Why take any of it,...give it to Maynard!...Way I see it, you just done your job. Besides, bein' famous ain't what it's made out to be."

They were mobbed as they entered the lobby, and along with the handshakes, arm squeezes, pats on the back, loud laughing and cheers, coupled with a hundred questions, all being asked at the top of their lungs, Dempsey had begun yelling back to try and quiet them when the pistol shot rang out, doing the job for him.

"Okay, folks!" Said Maynard loudly as he came through the front doors. "Give th' Marshals some room here!" The crowd moved aside to make a lane for him and David Clopton to come across the lobby and stand beside them. "Good people, I'm just as excited as you all are that this God awful crime has been finally solved!" He turned then and took Dempsey's hand and shook it just as Clopton's photographer touched off the flash-pot, sending sulfuric smoke and fumes toward the ceiling

"These two Marshals right here, Rod Dempsey, and Seth Mabry, received a tip from the good Reverend Peters at the Methodist Church. That tip lead them to speak to one of our local, Indian residents, Mister Joseph Peters!...As you may, or may not know, Joseph Peters lives out at th' Flint

Basin. Joseph Peters knew of a place they might be hiding, and sure enough, they were."

These two men right here, with the very appreciated help from one of Colonel Quinlan's cowboys, who, by the way is not among us this mornin'..."

"Yes he is, Alex!" Came the voice of Spencer Quinlan in the doorway, and that caused everyone to loudly clap amid several yeas and loud whistles as Quinlan ushered Hawkins in ahead of him to shake Dempsey's, and Seth's hand.

"Folks." Said Maynard, also shaking Hawkins' hand. "This is Jack Hawkins, he was quite instrumental in this operation, his marksmanship with a rifle kept any of these killers from escaping their due justice." He nodded at Hawkins then. "Thanks, Jack." There was a series of sulphur flashes then as more pictures were taken by the photographer, and the acrid smoke in the large room was prompting bystanders to exit the hotel for fresh air.

"Folks." Yelled Maynard. "I have been told by Colonel Quinlan here that hot coffee and sandwiches are available in the Council Room back there. So, if you will go on back, Federal Marshal Rod Dempsey here will give you the details of what occurred in the swamp last night."

"What?" Gasped Dempsey as Maynard took his arm, and he cast a glance at Seth as he was ushered through the crowd.

"Go ahead, Rod." He grinned. "I'm goin' to breakfast!"

"But Seth, you-..."

"Come on, Rod." Urged Maynard before he could resist. This is the biggest day ever in Tyler, come on!" He led Dempsey away through the cheering crowd.

Once the room was partially cleared, Seth grinned as he rolled then lit his morning smoke, and with a last look at the crowded meeting room left the hotel to shoulder his way across the boardwalk, and then stepped down into the square to make his way across the wide expanse toward the café.

People were still coming into the square, he noticed as he saw the many wagons and teams of horses with drooping heads and swatting tails. Even cowboys on horseback, he thought, and marveled at the city's gratefulness. He turned and continued on toward the crowded boardwalk in front of Norma's and as he stepped up to the walkway, turned for a last look at the square in time to notice one of the horsemen stop a woman, take off his hat and lean from the saddle to talk with her.

"Must be catching on." He grinned when he saw the man's perfectly bald-head and still grinning, walked inside and seated himself at the window.

"I do declare, Marshal." Chimed Norma as she came to the table. "What's one of our heroes doin; in here, get tired of the back-slapping?"

"Something like that." He nodded. "And I ain't no hero, Norma, remember that!"

"Well, to me, you are, sweetness, and you remember that!...You got the job done when old shit for brains couldn't! Asshole will likely be re-elected now!.....Anyway, what'll it be, lunch or breakfast?...I got steak, potatoes and beans for lunch, steak and eggs for breakfast,...beans and taters with that, too, if ya like?"

"Must be a couple hundred people in th' square today, Norma,...don't seem right, me bein' customer number seven. What's wrong?"

"Hell, I don't know,...too excited to eat, I guess, and I can't blame them! Scared me to death to open every day....You are my hero, Marshal."

"Thanks, Norma....I'll have scrambled eggs, potatoes and sausage, Norma, and coffee!"

"You got it, sweetness!" She grinned and left, leaving him to sit and watch the passing people on the boardwalk. He couldn't see the bald headed cowboy any more, but grinned again anyway. Might not be such a rarity at that, he thought, he just never noticed people's heads all that much, could be a lot of bald men around! It was hard to see the square anyway, for the people outside, so he relaxed to finish his smoke.

"Here's your coffee, dearest." Said Norma, placing the cup in front of him, and the pot on the table. "You can help yourself when ya want....Food's comin' up!"

His mind turned to Laura and Greg then as she brought his breakfast, and as he ate, wondered if they were okay? He thought he knew where Laura would be right now,...on the porch peering up the road. He sighed then as he swallowed the last of the eggs and cut the sausage with his fork, and then found himself looking back out at the square, and at the same time wondering why the bald headed cowboy held any interest to him?...Shaking the thought from his mind, he finished his breakfast, and was resting over coffee and a smoke when Dempsey finally came in and sat down.

"Enjoy your breakfast, Seth?" He asked tiredly.

"I ain't no hero, Rod, you're th' Honcho here!...You get 'em satisfied?"

He nodded. "Took your advice, laid all th' glory on Alex. He's still there with his chest stuck out answerin' questions!...Must be election time."

"Well, hey, Marshal number two hero." Boomed Norma. "What'll it be, dearest, lunch or breakfast?"

"Steak, eggs and coffee, Norma, thanks."

"Brought your cup with me, pour your own....Breakfast comin' up!"

"How many bald headed cowboys you ever seen, Rod?"

"What?...Totally bald? Don't think I ever did,...well, maybe an old man a time or two. A few younger ones with a bald middle now and then,...why?"

"I seen one out there in th' square today, tipped his hat to a woman. Weren't a hair one on his head or face."

"And that's strange, how?"

"He ain't no cowboy, number one....And whatever it was he asked that woman, she pointed at th' hotel. I lost sight of 'im then."

"Your gut talkin' to ya again, Seth?"

"I don't know, maybe....Whoever he is, he's got a be a drifter not to know what th' commotion in town was about."

"Why don't you think he's a cowboy?"

"Don't know that either, just somethin' a cow-man knows. Hell, I still don't sit a saddle like a cow man,...you neither, according to Trey!"

"Well just ho-..."

"Don't even ask, Rod, I can't explain it anyway."

"Well, whoever th' man out there was, drifter, outlaw, gunman, whatever,...let Alex handle it!...I'm tired....I don't think he's our missing man anyway....Now, that's what was on your mind, Seth, don't look so bewildered!...I'm learning how you're mind works."

"You're beginning to worry me some, too.... What are you now, a mind reader, or just getting' smarter?"

"Smarter, I guess....Naw, nothin' like that!...When you said bald cowboy, I thought a them bastards myself, weren't hard to figure."

"Our man could be anybody, Rod, remember that...And he does have an axe to grind."

"Here's your breakfast, doll-face!" Beamed Norma as she placed the heaping plate in front of him. "Eat hearty." She picked up the empty pot and headed for the kitchen.

"Doll-face?" He grinned, and began eating.

*   *   *

"And that, "Finished Maynard. "Is the whole story as I know it!...And now, unless I start repeating myself,...thank you."

"I would like to say something!" Said Spencer Quinlan, stepping up beside him. "Alex Maynard has been our Sheriff here for quite a few years. He is not liked very well by some of you,...but it's not a Sheriff's job to be liked by everyone, his job is to keep the peace!...This murder case was one for the books, there were no clues to work with, but he did not quit! Instead, he called in the United States Marshals for help....He even lost two of his deputies to these Cult Murderers, but ladies and gentlemen, he came through for us!"

"Now, there's an election coming up soon and I, for one, want to keep Alex Maynard on the job!...Don't you?"

There was an uproar then, a din of whistles and applause, and a lot of handshakes as they left the podium and pushed their way through the crowd.

"Thanks, Colonel." He said as they reached the outside boardwalk. "I was catching a lot of flack over this, had it coming, too! Didn't know what the hell to do about it!'"

"Sure you did, Alex, you just ran out of ideas, the Marshal just brought in some new ones. Don't sell yourself short!...Well, I'm off to send that long-awaited wire to my brother in law, giving him the good news." He shook Maynard's hand and walked away.

Smiling happily, he started to turn down the boardwalk and almost ran into a man standing in his way. "Whoa," He grinned. "Sorry, man, didn't see you."

"No need to apologize, Sheriff." Smiled the tall, slender man as he reached to push his hat up slightly. "That was some speech in there, Sir, very,...uplifting!"

"Yeah, thanks." He nodded.

"No, no, don't thank me, you earned it!...But tell me, were you one of the men that raided that Church?"

"My friend,...That was no Church!" Said Maynard. "It was a Cult of Murderers!...And no, I was not one of the men to bring it down, I just sent them to do it!...Now, if you'll pardon me, I have to go." He pushed past the man and stepped off into the square to disappear in the crowd....Leaving a hard-eyed slender gunman staring after him.

Maynard thought about the man as he walked across the square, thinking it strange that he would ask a question like that, and turned for a quick look back at him,...but he was gone and so, thought no more about him as he stepped up to the boardwalk in front of Norma's. He started along the boardwalk with his office in mind, but spotted Seth and Dempsey through the window and went in to pull up a chair.

"Have a seat, Alex." Grinned Dempsey. "Things go all right?"

"Thanks to you." He nodded. "And, Rod, thanks for what you did in there, I owe ya for that!"

"A Marshal's job is best done without publicity, Alex."

"Unfortunately, mine ain't!" He sighed. "Seems I have to kiss babies and dance around on tippy-toes to keep mine!"

"That's politics for ya." Nodded Dempsey. "Too much conflict for me."

"Me, too,…first time I was ever in front of a crowd like that! Everybody in the county must be in town today, and half of 'em heard my dumb speech!…To top it off, a cowboy stopped me on the boardwalk to ask if I was one of the men to take that bunch down?"

"What did you tell 'im?"

"The truth!…I wish I had been with ya, sure would a helped my sleepin' at night.…I am damn glad it's over, Rod, thank you, much,…you, too, Seth, it has been a pleasure."

"Sheriff?" Queried Seth then. "This cowboy that stopped you,…was he bald headed?"

"Why,…I couldn't tell, had his hat on,…why, you know 'im?"

"Nope, just wondered.…Did you know 'im?"

"Never seen 'im before.…But I thought it strange he would ask me a question like that?" He shrugged then. "Guess he got to the activities late."

"He armed?" Asked Seth.

"I didn't notice." Returned Maynard. "Why, Seth,…there somethin' I might ought a know?"

"He saw a bald headed cowboy in th' square out there, Alex." Said Dempsey with a grin. "The Cultists were all bald headed,…and one did get away."

"I see what you mean." Nodded Maynard seriously. "Damn, I wish I had paid more attention to 'im!"

"What did he look like?"

"I don't know, Rod,…he was taller than me by an inch or two, no beard, smooth-skinned, and come to think about it, hard-eyed!…I noticed that when he smiled, his eyes didn't."

"Probably just a drifter." Shrugged Dempsey. "But after today, you still need to watch for that Cultist, Alex. He likely left for parts unknown, but ya never know!"

"I'll keep that in mind, Rod, thanks. And I'm with you, I think he's gone, too."

"We need to get our horses, Sheriff." Said Seth. "Any suggestions how?"

"Sure I do!…I'll have the ticket agent tell one a th' engineers to fire up that old tap engine and move it onto the tracks. They can put a flat-car behind it and go get th' horses, how's that?"

"Today?" Asked Seth. "We need to to get home."

"Today, it is!…Gibbs and th' boys'll be up about now. Soon as they check in, I'll put 'em on it.…You'll have 'em by tonight."

"I do thank ya."

"Well, if it ain't th' Sheriff?' Voiced Norma from behind him. "What'll it be?"

"Coffee and apple pie, Norma, thanks."

"Coming up!"

"Ya know," Said Maynard as he stared thoughtfully through the window. "I think I saw that same cowboy on my way to the Windsor today....Yeah, I did!...Me and David Clopton was crossing th' square out there, and he was sittin' his horse at th' hitch rail by th' barbershop. I'm sure it was him." He sighed then. "I didn't pay much attention to 'im then, either!...And that's one a th' things I got a work on. I've had it too easy here for two many years."

"I wouldn't worry about it, Alex. You weren't a good law man, you wouldn't a been here this long,...and I don't know of a good law man anywhere that's liked by everybody....Besides, you did notice him enough to remember 'im."

"Guess I did, Didn't I?...And he was armed, come to think about it again. He was sort a neat-lookin', black shirt, black pants, black hat and, oh, yeah,...he looked part Mexican."

"Like th' man I killed th' other night?" Queried Seth.

"Yeah, maybe....You think he was one of 'em?"

"Nope," Said Seth. "But I think he's a gunfighter."

"We get gunslingers in town, sometimes." Nodded Maynard. "Ain't had no trouble yet!...I see 'im again, I'll ask his business."

"Here's your pie, Sheriff, and a cup, pour your own." She said then looked up as several men with women came in and sat down. "Guess the excitement's dying down!...Thank th' Lord for good things." She walked away to greet them.

"That is some old gal there." Chuckled Dempsey.

"More like a pain in the ass!" Said Maynard, cutting his pie.

"Mister Quinlan leave town already?" Queried Dempsey.

"Went to wire your Judge Castle, probably leave after that.....Ya know, I wish you two would stay a couple more days, th' Colonel's got a lake on his place that's chock-full a catfish, big ones!...You deserve some time off."

"Sounds good." Grinned Seth. "But I need to get home."

"Me, too, Alex." Nodded Dempsey. "Judge probably has a dozen jobs lined up for me, and th' bad guys never rest."

"You're right about that." He nodded then looked through the window again. "Maybe th' Colonel can change your minds, here he comes now." Maynard got up to pull another chair in beside his and go to the door.

"Guess we're right popular today, Rod." Said Seth as they both got up to shake hands with Quinlan.

"Glad you could join us, Colonel Quinlan," Said Dempsey. "Have a seat."

"Don't mind if I do." He smiled and sat down. "You two didn't give me a chance to thank you properly."

"We weren't quite in our element over there!" Replied Dempsey.

"I was tellin' 'em about th' fish in that lake a yours, Colonel, told 'em they ought a stay a day or two."

"By all means, Gentlemen. It would be my pleasure."

"Sorry, Sir." Sighed Dempsey. "We have to get back, but thanks anyway."

"The invite is always open," Smiled Quinlan. "Bring your families, we'll have a party right out at that lake."

"We'll keep that in mind."

"You send your wire, Colonel?" Asked Maynard.

"Yes, I did, got a reply, too!" He unfolded the paper and gave it to Dempsey.

"My congratulations to Marshals Dempsey and Mabry, awaiting their quickest possible return. Our love and best wishes to you and Lucy, signed Judge Emmit Castle"

"Direct and to th' point, as always." Grinned Dempsey as he returned the paper.

"Yes, it is!" Said Quinlan. "I want to sincerely thank you two men, we were all at the end of our rope here. If there is ever anything you need from us, just name it!" He shook their hands again and pushed his chair back. "I must get back to the ranch, Lucy will be a nervous wreck, I've been gone since yesterday noon....I'm surprised she has not gotten the foreman to bring her in already!...Gentlemen." He nodded and abruptly left.

"Nice fella." Grinned Seth.

"The best!" Said Maynard, sitting back down. "He was my C.O. in the war, ya know....Town won't admit it, but they owe 'im a lot!...I know I do." He pushed his own chair back then. "Well, I've got paperwork to bring up to date, see you two in the morning. What time you pullin out?"

"Daybreak." Nodded Seth. "See ya, Sheriff." They watched him leave then looked at each other.

"What do ya think, Seth, it's over?"

"I don't feel good about sayin' so, Rod....But I think it's more his problem now, than ours!"

"You're right, of course....But I just don't feel like th' job is finished!... We should a looked for that High Priest!...I know, it was too dangerous out there, Seth. We did the right thing by leavin',...But it ain't over!"

"You might make a good lawman yet, Rod!...I don't think it is either. But I still think he can handle it,...and I still need to go home!"

"Amen." He nodded.

*   *   *

Dempsey was waiting in the hall as Seth opened his door. "Morning, Rod." He nodded and shouldered the bedroll to close the door before grabbing his rifle.

"You ready to leave all this luxury?"

"Seth, I have been ready!" They walked across the hallway and down the stairs to the lobby to stop at the registration counter.

"That, we are," Said Dempsey as they gave him the keys. "What are we in to ya for?"

"Not a thing!" Smiled the Clerk. "All taken care of, compliments of Colonel Spencer Quinlan."

"In that case, please give him our thanks."

"No need, he told me to tell you he would meet you at Norma's for breakfast." The Clerk pulled his watch. "I believe he said six o'clock, you have five minutes to get there....Come back to see us now, ya hear?"

Dempsey looked up at Seth and shrugged. "Guess we eat first."

"Seems we do." They shouldered their belongings again, walked across the lobby and out onto the boardwalk where they stopped.

"Seems somebody came to town last night." Said Dempsey as they stepped off the walkway into the square. "Been a while since I seen a covered wagon, and now suddenly there's two of 'em!" They continued to look the wagons over as they crossed the square's wide expanse toward the café. "Strange, them bein' there without a team, don't ya think?"

"Everything's been strange about this place, Rod." He replied as they passed the dark wagons, and it was then that Seth stopped.

"What's wrong now?" Queried Dempsey, turning to peer at him in the pale predawn light. "What are you lookin' at?" He followed Seth's direction of sight then and was just able to make out the horse across the square opposite from them, and then saw the tall gunman leaning against the hitch-rail. "Is that th' man you saw?"

"Can't tell,...but he's a gunfighter." Said Seth evenly. "I can feel the challenge from here."

Challenge?...What do you mean?"

"A challenge, Rod,...It's somethin' that passes between two gunfighters, and I can't explain it!...You'd know if you ever lived that life. Come on, I'm hungry, he ain't botherin' anybody."

"Yet!" Breathed Dempsey as they continued on to the café and went inside.

"Here they are now!" Said Maynard, getting up to come forward. "Put your things down and take a seat, Rod, you, too, Seth....I'd like you to meet

Ms. Spencer Quinlan, Judge Castle's sister in law." After they greeted her. "Sit down here,…You know everyone else." And as Maynard regained his seat, Norma brought the large pot of coffee and poured their cups full before leaving.

"I hope steak and eggs are in order." Smiled Quinlan. "I took the liberty of ordering for everyone."

"Oh, Marshal," Said Lucy Quinlan, reaching in her bag and bringing out a letter. "Would you mind seeing that my sister gets this, the mail is so slow?"

"Be a pleasure, Ma'am." He put it away and noticed Seth looking back toward the front window. "You worried about him?"

"Worried about who?" Queried Maynard, also looking at the window.

"That gun-slick you mentioned yesterday." Replied Dempsey. "He was at th' barbershop hitch rail as we came in."

"He weren't there a while ago." Said Maynard, pushing his chair back. "Be right back!" He got up and went out onto the boardwalk before coming back to sit down. "Nobody there now." He grunted. "Man sure moves around fast, whoever he is." He looked at Gibbs then as he sat down. "After we eat, I want you to find out who drove them wagons in and left 'em unattended."

"I wouldn't worry none about the man out there, Gentlemen." Said Quinlan. "No need to ruin a good breakfast." He looked at Seth then. "Alex tells me you're not a full time Marshal, Mister Mabry. What do you do, Sir?"

"I own a small spread south a Dallas, along with a wife and son."

"I know you enjoy that, too!...Nothing in the world like ranch life. So tell me,…How'd you become an honorary Marshal, I have never heard of such a thing?...Don't get me wrong, sir, I think it's remarkable, I'm just a bit nosy."

"That's quite okay." Said Dempsey. "He doesn't think he deserves it!... Truth is, he helped Judge Castle and me out on a case two years ago. The Judge gave 'im th' status of U.S. Marshal."

"Thanks, Rod." Replied Seth with a forced grin. "I'm not a Marshal, Mister Quinlan, plain and simple."

"From what I've seen, you ought a be!" Laughed Maynard. "You, Seth, have a knack for seein' things most men miss. I wish I had it!"

"Both of you have our gratitude, gentlemen," Said Lucy Quinlan. "You have Tyler's gratitude!"

"Ma'am," Said Seth shaking his head. "Before you put all this praise and glory on us, I think it best to remind everyone that one a these killers got away the other night!...So don't get so excited about all this that you put your guard down."

"What do you mean, you didn't get them all? No one said anyth-... Spencer, did you know about this?"

"Yes, honey, I did." He said apologetically. "But there's really nothing to fear from one man, everyone assures me that he is probably long gone from here by now!"

"I'm sorry, Mister Quinlan," Said Seth. "I sure don't mean to spoil th' good feelings here, but if he is here, he can be just as dangerous as all thirty of them were. I think he left, too,...but we just don't know."

"Oh. My Lord!" Sighed Lucy. "Then it isn't over."

"Where would he be, Seth?" Asked Maynard. "In your estimation, of course."

"Sheriff,...it's hard to figure what an insane killer would do!"

"They were all quite insane, Alex." Said Dempsey. "That's what he's saying....And that's what makes this one very dangerous, he's also very smart,...and suicidal."

"What exactly does that mean, Marshal?" Asked Quinlan.

"It means he's willing to die, to be with his God!"

"His God?" Gasped Lucy. "The God all mighty, you can't mean that?"

"The Devil is his God, Honey." Said Quinlan. "That's what he means."

"It isn't over!" She sniffed and looked across at Dempsey. "Well, you can't leave until he's found, Mister Dempsey!...Please,...the good people of Tyler just can't go through this all over again, they just can't!"

"She's right, Seth." Sighed Dempsey. "We have to at least make sure he's gone! Why don't you go on home, I'll stay here a day or so, see if I can find 'im?"

"Can't do it, Rod." Sighed Seth. "We'll se it through together."

"It's settled then." Nodded Quinlan. "Your rooms are paid for already, or will be....I'll wire Judge Castle to that effect, I'm sure he'll agree."

"Breakfast is served!" Boomed Norma and began placing their food on the table from a rolling cart she was pulling behind her.

"I've lost my appetite, now." Sighed Lucy Quinlan.

"No need for that, Ma'am." Said Seth. "And I do apologize for bringing all this up when I did,...I figured it would be more disappointing to find out after we left, don't ya think?"

"Why sure, Ms Quinlan." Assured Maynard. "Between the five of us, and help from Rod and Seth there, we'll find 'im,...you'll see! Come on now, it's a great day."

"I agree." Said Quinlan, and began eating. "Come on, people, Lucy, I'm talking steak and eggs here!" Lucy giggled then and began eating also, as did the rest,...and once they were finished and pushed their plates away, and after the men had all lit up after-meal smokes, she stood up.

"Mister Maynard, you are the Sheriff in Tyler, my husband appointed all of you!...I propose to know what you are going to do to rid us of this menace?"

"Exactly what we've always done, Ms. Quinlan, keep searching the town till we find 'im....And I might add, that's all we can do!"

"It's all we can do, Ma'am," Exclaimed Gibbs, speaking for the first time. "We don't know who he is?"

"They only done their killin' at night, too!" Added Jeter. "No disrespect intended, Ms. Quinlan."

"Okay then." Said Quinlan. "I'll bring in more of my wranglers to assist in patrolling the city. The Marshal will stay a couple more days to help also. What more can we ask?" He leaned toward Lucy then. "Right, honey?"

She let her breath out slowly then finally nodded. "Yes, I suppose so, please forgive me, Mister Maynard, for my callousness."

"My wife has been afraid for more than two months, gentlemen." Said Quinlan. "Today,...well, I have not seen her happier.

"I guess that's my fault." Said Seth. "Again, Ma'am, my apologies!.... Now, if you'll excuse me?" He got up from the table. "Th' Hostler saddled up our horses for us this mornin', guess I'll go unsaddle 'em, tell 'im we're not leavin'."

"I'll go with ya, Seth."

"I can handle it, Rod, you stay. Maybe you and th' Sheriff can work out a plan of action....I won't be long." He nodded at Lucy, donned his hat and left the table, picking up bedroll and rifle as he left the café to stop momentarily on the boardwalk.

He visually searched the faces of a few early risers, and then the empty square for the gunman, but saw nothing except the two covered wagons, alone and team-less in the middle of the large expanse, and that's what he studied for a half-minute before stepping off the boardwalk.

It was strange someone driving two covered wagons to the square like that and taking the team away, and he continued to look them over as he walked, and seeing the bulk of something beneath one of them. Somebody was sleeping under his wagon, was his thinking as he stopped to momentarily look it over again. No law against it, he thought, and looked back at the café's large window before continuing on toward the Windsor to put his things back in the room. Maybe Rod was right, he decided. He could be associating the gunman's baldhead with that of the Cultist's. Sighing, he went on to step up to the boardwalk and go inside to register.

*   *   *

"I don't believe I have ever seen a man so serious minded." Said Quinlan as he watched Seth step into the street. "He tells it like it is,...I like that."

"He's th' best man I've ever known!" Said Dempsey also turning to watch. "And the most dangerous!"

"Dangerous?...How do you mean?" Queried Quinlan.

"Let's just leave it at that, Mister Quinlan. "He's also a very private man, and my friend!"

"The other day, you said he was fast with a gun." Reminded Walt. "How fast would you say he is, Marshal?"

"Hey, Rod." Chuckled Maynard. "Walt has dreams of bein' a gunfighter, Jeter, too, I think!"

"Awww, Boss, I never said that!...I just want a be fast on th' draw, never know when I'll need to be."

"That's okay, Alex," Grinned Dempsey. "I used to practice a lot myself,...Till I figured out it was a waste of time!...Anyway, that old man there is the fastest I ever saw, gun or knife, he's th' best!...He's also the best crime investigator I've ever seen."

"That's hard to see by looking at him." Smiled Quinlan.

"Well, if my Brother in law likes him," Said Lucy with a smile. "So do I."

"Amen!" Said Maynard. "He don't say much, that's for sure. But when he does, it makes sense....Anyway, what's all this about gunfightin',...what we need right now is a plan of action!...Any ideas, Rod?"

"You know I don't, Alex." He sighed heavily. "One thing's for sure, as big as that swamp is, we'd never find 'im in there, and he's likely not there at all!...No, he's either long gone from here, or he's right here in Tyler. And I believe Seth thinks he's somehow tied in with that gunslinger we saw out there."

"Then let's go find 'im!" Blurted Gibbs. "Get to th' bottom a this."

"Where do we look?" Reminded Maynard. "Man's there one minute, gone th' next?...He;ll show up again, then we'll find out!"

Quinlan pulled his watch from a vest pocket. "It is seven o'clock, gentlemen, and we must be getting back to the ranch fairly soon. So, how many men do you think you'll need to thoroughly search the town, Alex?"

"Colonel,...I hate for you to have to do this, but a dozen men will do. If he's here, we'll find 'im in a day or two."

"When we do." Said Jeter angrily. "I'd say we hang 'im right there in the middle a th' square, too!"

"There's a lady present, Mister Jeter!" Said Maynard.

"Sorry, Ma'am."

"No need." She said. "I think I feel the same way."

"Well," Laughed Quinlan. "That's a side of you, I've never seen?"

"I'm just thinking of all those unfortunate victims, Spencer."

"I know you are, we all feel that way. Now listen, Alex....If at all possible, I do not want the people of Tyler to know about this, do it quietly....Now with that, gentlemen,...we must be going." He stood and helped Lucy to her feet, and every one stood as they walked toward the door, but once there, Quinlan stopped, and after a second he looked back.

"Alex," He said, looking back at the square. "Is this your man?"

Curious, Maynard got up and went to the doorway, as did the rest. "I do believe it is!" He said tightly, and all six of then tried to push past Quinlan, only to be stopped by Maynard.

"This is my town, boys,...Rod!" He said angrily. "I'll tend to this." He went across the boardwalk and stepped off into the square, and when he started across, the gunman pushed away from the hitch rail to wait for him....There was twenty feet between them when the gunman raised his left hand to stop him.

"That will be close enough!" He said in a thick French accent, and then he smiled and dropped his right hand beside the gun he wore. "What is on your mind?"

Maynard stopped when told and peered at the gunman's olive-colored complexion, and then at the gun on his hip before looking back at his face. "Well, right now, you are." He replied. "Mind if I ask your business in Tyler?"

"It is my own." He said Calmly, the half smile still on his face.

"No, sir, it is not!...You bein' here makes it mine, and I'm afraid I do need to know your name, and why you're here?"

"And you are?"

"Sheriff Alex Maynard!...Now please, sir, your name and business here?"

"You are Sher-iff Alex May-nard." He repeated slowly, his voice thick with the accent. "And this is meant to frighten me?"

"I don't aim to scare anybody, Mister. All I asked was who you are, if that scares you, it's your problem!...If you're here to do business with that gun, I'll have to ask you to leave, too."

"Very well, Sheriff,...my name is Jules Regard." He smiled wider then. "You have heard of me, I can tell."

"That's right, I have!...You're a killer from New Orleans. And now, I'm tellin' you to leave town,...gunfighters are not welcome here."

"But a gunfighter is already here, I saw him only this morning!... And I have grown to like it here these past few weeks....So now I ask you, Sheriff,...have I made trouble?...No, I have not!...So I ask you," He nodded at the café's boardwalk where Dempsey and the other Deputies waited. "Do

I frighten you so, that you need all these body guards? They do look very dangerous over there?"

"They don't concern you, Regard,…now get on your horse and leave Tyler!…You don't, I'll arrest ya."

"Do you actually believe you can do that?" He asked curiously.

"I do, and I will!"

Regard shrugged then. "Then, by all means, do so!"

"You're under ar-…." He had hardly wrapped his hand around the pistol's butt when Regard drew and fired,…and he yelled in surprise and pain as the bullet tore through his right shoulder, knocking him to the ground. The explosion was unexpectedly loud in the square's wide expanse and caused every pedestrian around the square to stop and stare at them, and then to scurry into the surrounding shops and stores to watch the happenings from cover.

Dempsey and the four Deputies had been watching from the boardwalk, while Quinlan and Lucy watched from the large window. When Maynard went down, Dempsey and the four deputies all yelled at once and with drawn guns, left the boardwalk at a run toward the gunman, who by now had walked to stand over Maynard with his own gun relaxed at his side.

Dempsey held out his arm to stop Gibbs and the others as they came to within a dozen yards of the killer, who had raised his left arm again to stop them.

"You will stop there!" He said savagely. "And you will lower your weapons."

"In your dreams!" Said Dempsey, and with all five of their guns cocked and leveled at the gunman, he used his arm to hold them back then moved forward a step or two. "Mister, you might kill that man at your feet there, but if you do, we'll send your black ass to hell where ya belong!"

Regard smiled then. "You have me at a disadvantage, it seems,…I have no wish to kill this man!…But it is plain to see, you do not want your Sheriff May-nard to die!…Of which, he surely will if you shoot me!…Now, please lower your weapons?"

"Not till we get some answers!" Said Dempsey. "It's your choice, man,… shoot him now, and die, or tell me what this is all about?…Come on, man, you're right,…we don't want that man to die, none of us want a die. Now what's goin' on here?"

*   *   *

Seth had found it strange that the old Hostler was nowhere to be found when he arrived at the stables, but did not think too much about it because their two saddled horses were waiting in the open doorway,…and not able to roust him by calling out to him, shrugged and unsaddled the animals himself and turned them back into the feedlot. He had come back through the barn and was standing in the opened double doors when he heard the sudden crack from a pistol shot, the echoes of which were quick to dissipate. Knowing in his mind what had happened, he quickly moved to peer around the double doors and could see the distant figure of the gunman as he moved from behind the covered wagons to stand over the fallen man.

His first breathtaking thought was that it was Dempsey that had been shot, and he knew he had to find out. He also knew, that a running man would be noticed by the gunman! He continued to watch, and then he saw the five men as they moved in to face the man with drawn guns,…and knew who the fallen man was. He recognized Dempsey as one of those facing the gunman. He also saw the dozen or so curious pedestrians as they ran toward the square.

That being the case, he thought, he just might have a chance to get there unnoticed, there were already onlookers along the boardwalks, and more moving toward the square all the time. Making the decision to move out, he was about to go when he heard the whisper of sound from somewhere behind him and froze, his mind searching for memory of such a sound. It was not a common one, more of a whisper than actual sound, but never the less was like the one he had heard the night he had stopped the kidnapping….His missing Cult leader was somewhere in the stable's dark interior behind him! The sound he had heard was one the cutlass made as it was pulled from its scabbard.

If he used his gun now, he knew it could start the shooting in the square all over again and with that in mind, slowly twisted his body enough to pull the hunting knife from his belt without the Priest seeing it, and worked the blade into the palm of his hand. He was still turned to the side, but was able to see the darker shapes of stalls, tack-room and stacked hay from the corner of his eye,…and he waited. But as prepared as he thought himself to be, he almost missed seeing the cloaked, shadowy figure leave a rear stall and rush him, but he had seen it and choosing that split-second to whirl, he threw the knife, the blade of which buried itself to the hilt in the cultist's chest. He stepped aside as the killer's momentum caused him to stumble and fall at Seth's feet, the raised cutlass sliding into the dirt of the street.

Breathing a sigh of relief, he quickly turned and half ran to mingle with the crowd of onlookers.

*   *   *

"I am not usually this patient." Smiled Regard, with a shrug. "I usually know who I must kill,…however, that is not the case today, because I do not know the men I want….But I also must tell you that if I choose,…I can easily kill you all!"

"You'll die doin' it!" Grated Dempsey. "Now drop your gun before anybody else gets hurt."

"Oh, I think not" He said with a smile, and ignoring Dempsey's request. "Because that would not save your friend….But that is of no matter here! Why?,…Because I want something from you!...So, I will tell you, as you said,…what is going on!....My name, of course, is Jules Regard."

"He's a gunfighter," Said Gibbs. "A killer from New Orleans, got a poster on 'im!"

"Just stay back, Gibbs,…and don't do anything, too many people here….I'm listenin', Regard!" He said loudly, not taking his eyes off those of the gunman. "Start with why you didn't kill th' Sheriff?"

"Who, Mister Alex May-nard?" He responded mockingly then smiled down at the pain-wracked Sheriff. "Because he is not one of the men I hunt, I shot him because he drew on me,…and because I wanted the entire town's full attention!"

"Well, it seems you got it!...Who did you come to kill?...And I'm warning you, make one move with that gun and we'll kill you!"

"Many men have tried to kill Jules Regard, Mister,…what are you, a Marshal?...Well, that many men have failed….But I require information, so I will tell you why I am here,…and it will not be because you threaten me!"

"I'm still listening."

"Very good….Three nights ago, three men attacked my brother's Church!...His entire congregation was murdered without warning! They had no guns with which to defend themselves, why?...Because their religion did not allow it!...My mission here is to find these same three men and kill them,…and to avenge those that were so brutally murdered."

"Then you didn't know your brother, Sir!" Snapped Dempsey. "That place was no Church, it was where they worshipped the Devil, and those people, that congregation brutally murdered and beheaded twelve citizens of this town, and then taunted them by leaving the bodies here in this square for children to see~…So watch who you call a murderer!....Now drop that gun!"

Regard silently appraised him for a moment, and appeared completely undaunted by the demands. "I see you wear two pistols, am I to assume you use them well?...Does your knowledge of my brother's congregation mean that you are one of the men I came to kill?...Because if you are, it will also mean that the man I saw with you this morning is also one,...where might he be, this,...gunfighter?"

"He's a United States Marshal, Regard, and he's not here right now."

"No matter, I'll wait! But now, I will give you a fair chance to kill me, and you may use both guns....Are you this man?"

"What I am is a Federal United States Marshal, and these four men are sworn deputies....I am asking you to drop your weapon before any of these bystanders get hurt?...I will never give you the men you hunt, so give it up!... Your brother was an insane killer. He worshipped the Devil, not God all-mighty, and so did the rest of them!"

"You do not seem to understand, Marshal....I do not care who my brother worshipped, what god, what anything, nor who you think you are. He is my brother,...and I do not care about the safety of your puny, prying bystanders. I am here to find and to kill three men, three cowardly men!... These men murdered thirty of my brother's congregation, and you will give them to me!...Do you know why?...No?...Then have one of those sworn deputies give you his pistol, and then go pull the tarp from the wagons."

Curious, Dempsey took Jeter's gun and nodded at the wagons. Jeter ran to the first wagon and pulled the tarp from it, and as it fell to the ground, the crowd of bystanders gasped loudly at sight of the fifteen bound and silent people in the wagon's large bed. Jeter pulled the tarp from the second wagon to find fifteen more people, all staring at nothing, and sitting bound and docile.

"You Bastard!" Shouted Dempsey. "What are you doing?"

"I am avenging my brother's congregation, an eye for an eye, thirty for thirty! And to keep you from doing anything rash, have him remove the tarp from beneath the wagon."

Jeter went to pull the tarp away, revealing the two kegs of gunpowder, and beside that, a jar filled with a clear liquid. The sight caused Jeter to quickly rejoin them. "That's nitro, Marshal!" He gasped.

"You will tell me who these men are, Marshal, because if I shoot that small bottle, not only will these thirty innocent people die, many will die along the boardwalks as well....And now that we understand each other,... are you one of the men I seek?"

"No!" Shouted Seth, as he stepped away from the far wagon and stopped almost twenty feet from them. "He ain't one of 'em!...Put your guns away, Rod,...Gibbs, you three, put 'em away!"

"This is my job, Seth, stay back!" Said Dempsey. "He's the brother to that slime that got away."

"You mean th' slime that was hidin' in th' stables?...I wouldn't worry about him, I just killed 'im!....Your brother is dead, gunfighter,...so put your gun away and go to jail,...or try me!...Either way is okay, because that man in front a you is th' law, and he won't wait!" Seth could see the insane hate in the gunman's eyes as he watched him, thinking he had only a split second should the gunman try and shoot the explosives instead of fighting him. But then Regard slowly lifted the gun and dropped it into his holster as he backed away from the injured Maynard a few feet.

"Now you're talking, Gunfighter." Grinned Seth, and the grin was meant to intimidate Regard, because he was suddenly becoming very tense. Before him stood one of the most dangerous gunmen he had likely ever met, and that thought scared him. "You want the man who killed your brother, I'm right here, Gunfighter,...I was one of th' men at that so-called Church, too, so what's it gonna be?"

"I will kill you first." Said Regard tightly. "And then the others, and then I will destroy this town and all these sniveling nothings....You may draw first, if you like?"

"I wouldn't want it said I took advantage of a crazy man, I'll wait on ya." He watched Regard's eyes for several long seconds before the signal came. He drew and fired at almost the same instant as Regard, feeling the tug at his armpit as the gunman's bulled passed beneath his arm,...and in that same fleeting instant, he fired again, seeing Regard being lifted and thrown to his back on the hard-packed dirt of the square.

Releasing the breath in his lungs, he holstered the gun as the thunderous explosions echoed away, and rushed in to squat beside the wounded Maynard. "You hurt bad, Sheriff,...hold still while I take a look." By then, Dempsey and the deputies were all on their knees beside him. "No, no, one of you keep folks away from that wagon, nobody yells, nobody talks, no nothin', that stuff can explode over nothing!"

You got it, Said Jeter and Cliff in unison, and both scampered off to move the crowd of on-lookers back, while they attended to Maynard.

"Better get th' Doctor, Gibbs, Said Dempsey.

"Never mind that!" Grunted Maynard. "Help me up, I can walk!" They helped him to his feet and waited while he peered at the gunman's body for a minute and then, with a respectful, appreciative nod at Seth, allowed Gibbs and Walt to help him across the square amid cheering and yells from the crowd.

"Jesus," Said Dempsey still eying the bottle of Nitroglycerin. "How do we handle that, we need to get help for those people there?"

"Very carefully." He said, and then motioned for Jeter to come over.

"Yeah, Marshal."

"There an empty lot, a city dump, anything close?...We got a blow up that bottle a nitro."

"Nearest lot is a block away there on Houston."

"Okay, Jeter, you make me a lane through that crowd there, tell 'em to run away. Rod, I need your bandana." While Dempsey removed his, Seth removed his own, and taking Dempsey's quickly approached the explosives. "Rod, when I leave with this thing, get some help and get these folks out a th' wagons....Here I go!" Using the bandanas together, he used both hands to lift the small bottle of Nitroglycerin and carefully walk away with it toward Houston Street, and then down toward the stables where Jeter was standing in front of the large vacant lot. Once there he told the deputy to leave while he carefully walked through the tall weeds and debris to finally place the bottle on the ground and back away from it.

On the street again, he looked around to make sure no one was within range of the explosion, drew his gun and fired. The force of the blast sent debris in all directions and literally obliterated the plot of ground by leaving a hole in the earth some twenty feet in diameter and four feet in depth. Windows in the structure adjoining the lot was blown inward, and a few were broken across the wide street. Seth had thrown himself on the ground as he fired at the bottle, and was now picking himself up to brush off his clothing and holster the pistol.

Good God, all-mighty!" Yelled Jeter as he rushed up to slap Seth on the back. "Loudest thing I ever heard, louder than a cannon!...You okay, Marshal?"

"Yeah," He nodded. "Lets go check on them people."

*   *   *

Both Doctor Welch, and Doctor Harrison were at the wagons as the thirty medicated people were lifted down and loaded into other wagons to be transported to the local hospital at Camp Ford. A man, from the Commissary at Camp Ford was there along with two noncoms, and they were removing the kegs of black powder from beneath the wagon.

"Fuckers get here in a hurry when ya don't need 'em!" Said Jeter in disgust.

"Who, th' army?"

"Hell, yeah, ain't got th' time to help solve a crime, th' Bastards!"

"Looks like they got it covered now, let's check on th' Sheriff." They went on across the square and could see the wounded Maynard, his arm in a makeshift sling, sitting on the boardwalk in front of Norma's. Quinlan and his wife were sitting next to him, while a crowd of people stood behind them on the walkway, and every so often one would reach down and pat Maynard on the back.

"Don't you think you ought a be in bed with that wound, Lieutenant?" Asked Jeter when they walked up.

"We've been trying to get him to do just that!" Said Quinlan, getting up to shake Seth's hand. "He insisted on waiting for you to get back."

"Did I hear you say out there, you killed that man that got away?" Asked Maynard painfully. "Tell me you said that?"

"He jumped me at th' Stables, Sheriff!...I got lucky."

"Lucky's ass!...From what I seen out there today, luck's somethin' you don't need!...Thanks for savin' our lives, man....It's over now, right?"

"It's over, Sheriff."

Maynard looked up at him and shook his head. "I never even saw his hand move when he shot me, Seth. It's hard to believe you beat 'im."

Almost didn't, Sheriff....You done your best out there, too, nobody can expect any more than that!"

"That's right, Alex." Said Dempsey as he walked up to join them. "Nobody can ask for more than that!"

"I thank ya both for a job well done." He looked up at Jeter then. "Bring that body in from th' stables, Jeter."

"See if you can find th' Hostler, Too." Said Seth. "He weren't anywhere to be found when I got there, hope he ain't hurt....And get th' undertaker!"

"You got it." He turned and trotted back across the square.

"Rod," Said Maynard with a grin. "Did you see Seth here shoot that Bastard?"

"I saw it, Alex."

"Damnedest thing I ever saw!...I'll never doubt you again, man."

"How is he, Marshal?" Asked Doctor Welch as he walked in beside them to sit down next to Maynard and check the wound. "Went clean through, Alex,...You was lucky this time."

"Luck is not getting' beat to th draw, Doc....I ought a be dead, to tell ya th' truth!...Don't know why I ain't!"

"Well, you could be, if I don't tend to this wound pretty quick."

"And don't question it, Alex, it wasn't your time!" Said Quinlan as him and Lucy stood up. "But it was a damn brave thing you did out there."

"It was a stupid thing, Colonel, I ain't no gunfighter!...I thought I was better than that, though."

"You're as good as we expect you to be, Alex." Quinlan grinned at Dempsey and Seth then and became serious. "That man at the stables, he was the last of them, right?"

""Yes sir, he was." Said Seth with a nod.

"And this gunfighter?"

"He was the brother." Said Dempsey. "Here to avenge our attack on the cult....It's over!"

"Unbelievable." Gasped Lucy Quinlan.

"Yes, Ma'am, it is." He said with a grin. "He made a big mistake!"

"Mistake?" She asked curiously. "I don't understand."

"He tried to draw on Seth." Replied Dempsey with a wide smile.

"I know....Thank you Seth." She smiled. "Thank you so much."

"Don't mention it, Ma'am."

"Okay!" Said Maynard and pushed Welch's hand away. "You're killin' me, Doc,...ain't you got somethin' for th' pain?"

"Sure I do, at the office, but you was all determined to stay here!"

"Well, I ain't now, let's go." He reached out for Seth to help him get up, and between him and Dempsey got him on his feet and walked him toward the steps up to the boardwalk.

"No, no, not yet!" Shouted David Clopton as him and his photographer pushed through the crowd. "Hold up a minute, Sheriff!" He moved aside then, and the photographer quickly ignited the flash powder to snap the picture then to quickly grab his equipment and leave, because they all wiped at their eyes and coughed.

"Gentlemen." Said Clopton. "Thank you one and all, this story will put Tyler, Texas on every map in the country. Make the Telegraph a household word in every newspaper, too. You will all be heroes by the end of the month."

"Mister Clopton." Said Quinlan with forced Patience. "Would you mind moving, we have a wounded man here?"

"What, Oh, I'm sorry gentlemen, I was so excited." He moved as he spoke. "I'll need statements from all of you this afternoon, Sheriff,...okay?"

He turned away then as he spotted Jeter, Walt, and several civilians carrying the body of the dead Cultist, as well as that of the old Hostler across the square toward them, and called for his photographer again.

*   *   *

They were all at the large table, Norma had set up for the occasion, when Seth and Dempsey stopped their horses at the hitch rail and dismounted. All were standing as they walked in, and after the handshakes were done with, all but Spencer Quinlan sat down again.

"Marshal Dempsey, Mister Mabry." Smiled Quinlan. "Here we are again. Let's hope this farewell breakfast doesn't end like the one yesterday."

"I'm for that one!" Replied Dempsey, and they all laughed.

"You have our gratitude." Smiled Quinlan as he sat down. "Now, maybe this time, we can enjoy our steak and eggs." He turned to nod at Norma then and she brought the large pot of coffee and began filling their cups.

"How are you feeling, Alex?" Grinned Dempsey as he reached to pat his shoulder. "Bullet packs a wallop, don't it?"

"And then some." Nodded Maynard. "But that's what Laudanum is all about, I was not going to miss breakfast with you men."

"Thanks, Alex….That was somethin', you facin' that killer like you did,…what made you do that?"

"What made you let me?" This brought more laughter all around.

"I don't know, Alex," He said seriously. "I've had to face down a few gunmen in my time, but I don't think I ever had one willin' to pull on th' law,…let alone shoot me!…I didn't figure he would neither, in fact,…I didn't think he was part of this thing at all!"

"I didn't think so, neither." Nodded Maynard.

"You drew on him first, Lieutenant, remember?" Laughed Jeter.

"No,…I tried to draw on 'im, Mister Jeter, and that's enough out a you!"…He looked at Seth then and nodded. "I didn't think any living man could handle a gun the way you do, sir!….Till I saw you,,…I didn't think I'd ever see anybody as fast as Regard was!…But you sure are!"

Seth reached and pulled the underarm portion of his shirt out to reveal the ragged hole. "Not by a hell of a lot, Sheriff!"

"My Lord!" Gasped Lucy Quinlan.

"I'll say." Said Walt. "I'd swear only one shot was fired that first time, that's how close it was. Matter a fact, all three shots was damn close!"

"By the way," Said Maynard, pulling the wide-bladed hunting knife from his belt and passing it to Seth. "Coroner pulled this from that Cultist's chest, I assume it's yours!"

"It is!" He grinned. "Thank 'im for me."

"Yeah!" Said Gibbs. "How far did you throw that thing?"

"No time to think about that, Gibbs. Almost didn't see 'im at all." He grinned and put the knife away.

"Well, it's over and done with." Said Dempsey. "And best forgotten!…We had a lot a luck on this case, and I think a special thank you is due Reverend Peters, he's feelin' pretty low and disappointed right now!…As for everyone else, a job well done."

"BREAKFAST IS SERVED!" Boomed Norma.

*   *   *

"Ahhh!" Blurted Emmit Castle as Jake Tulane entered without knocking. "Come in, Jake, come in."

"What's wrong, Judge?" He asked, quickly coming to the desk.. "Has something happened?"

"As a matter of fact, Jake, it has." He smiled then. "And by the looks of it, my jailor led you to believe I had bad news."

"That was the impression, I got, yeah….You sayin' it's good news?"

Still smiling, Emmit gave him the two-page wire from Spencer Quinlan, and as Tulane read it, nodded at the slow smile that spread across his face.

"Jules Regard!" He said, looking up at Emmit. "I got a poster on him at th' office,…he was a gun for hire."

"I have one as well." Nodded Emmit. "He was a bad one."

"Good old Seth, came through for us again."

"They both did, Jake,…and I'm so proud of them, I could burst…. But It's remarkable, a man of Seth Mabry's age using a gun that well!...So much so, that I began to think about it….That's why I did some digging this morning in Marshal Riggs' old files." He picked up the poster from his desk and gave it to him.

"I believe this is our Mister Seth Mabry, Jake."

"Dancer?...Judge this was issued back in fifty-eight, that would make this fella-…"

"Somewhere around sixty years old." Nodded Emmit. "Seth Mabry's age."

"It can't be Judge,…most gunfighters don't live that long….Are you sure?"

Emmit looked at him for a few seconds before shaking his head. "No, I'm not sure,…but it's the oldest flier I could find on anyone fitting the description it gives."

"He's a good man, Judge,…what are you gonna do, if it is him?"

"Oh, I'm not going to do anything about it, Jake. I happen to agree with you, he's a very good man!...And,…it probably isn't him anyway!...That's why I think you'll agree that it's best we not even mention it to anyone else."

"Yes, Sir, Judge, I agree a hundred percent!...Somethin' like this could really upset, Rod, if he knew."

"Roderick already knows, I think." Smiled Emmit. "He fretted for the longest time, because he thought he knew him….And he has not even mentioned it in the last two years!...I don't think you and I should, either."

"What about this?" He held up the poster.

"Oh that!" Said Emmit. "Tear it up, Jake, it's old news anyway. Besides, I believe this fellow, Dancer, died more than twenty years ago."

END